"Elisha, I don't understand why you feel you have to go back."

"Maria, they're saying I was wrong, that I made a mistake, that I didn't know what I was doing. How can I just sit back and let them say those things about me?"

She must have known from the strain in his voice that his mind was set. When his mind was set it was like flint, and whether wrong or right he could not be derailed from his course. But that did not help her see around the many dangers that rose up in her imagination.

"Elisha, what is a sixty-four year old professor doing preparing to climb up such a mountain? I don't love you any less for it, but I can see the wrinkles around your eyes and your gray hair. You think you're immortal, but you're not. You don't realize how risky . . ."

"Maria, I have been up that mountain several times already." His temper was rising now. "I've been there. I know what it's like. And I don't think it's risky."

"You have always underestimated the danger in situations. You believe God will get you out of any situation you put yourself in. But how do you know it isn't tempting God to go back there? What purpose does it serve to go back?"

"Maria, when my life is done how will they remember me? As the man who almost found the highest mountain? The man who tried but failed to measure the Black Mountain? That's not the way I want history to remember me. That cannot be the measure of my life."

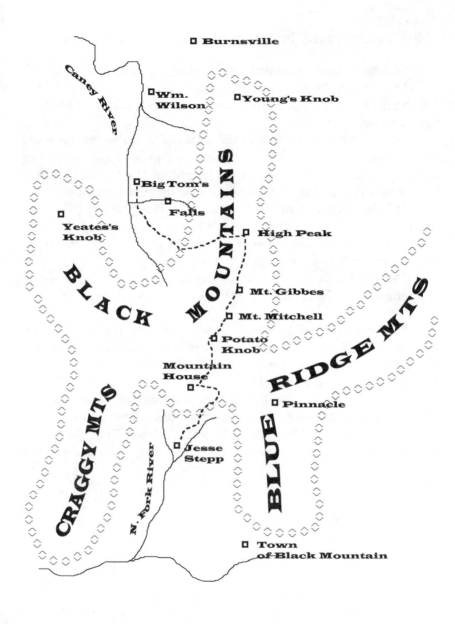

Mitchell's Peak

by

Robert Dellinger

Sometimes we all need someone to show us the way

Robert Dellinger

Caleb's Press
High Point, NC

ISBN 0-9729568-3-2

LCCN 2003091615

Cover photo of the Black Mountains: Paul Holcomb.

My thanks to Pastor Alan Cox for standing in as Elisha Mitchell on the cover photo.

ATTENTION CORPORATIONS, UNIVERSITIES, COLLEGES, AND PROFESSIONAL ORGANIZATIONS: Quantity discounts are available on bulk purchases of this book for educational, gift purposes, or as premiums. For information, please contact Caleb's Press, 421 Seminole Ct., High Point, NC 27265.

Acknowledgements

My grandfather loved the mountains and passed that love on to my father. As a boy I made many trips to the Blue Ridge, Great Smokies, and Black Mountains with both these men. I'm thankful to them for carrying on the tradition of summer visits to the highest point in eastern America.

More recently my good friend, John Lind, accompanied me on a research trip to the Black Mountains. John and I hiked through some steep rhododendron hells and lived to tell about it. He also provided creative inspiration in the early stages of the book.

My wife and children endured my obsession with the subject of this book for many months. Thank you, Wanda, Brian, and Erin.

Several authors provided facts that helped ground this story. Kent Schwarzkopf introduced me to the true story of Elisha Mitchell in *A History of Mt. Mitchell and the Black Mountains.* Thomas E. Jeffrey detailed the Mitchell-Clingman controversy in articles for *The North Carolina Historical Review.* John Parris documented the mountain culture of North Carolina in his newspaper articles for *The Asheville Citizen-Times.* The Elisha Mitchell Manuscript Collection at the Wilson Library, University of North Carolina at Chapel Hill, gave me a first-hand look at the events of Mitchell's life. Behind all these people stands the Lord who made them and who made the mountains. To God be the Glory!

Preface

Several hundred thousand people visit Mt. Mitchell State Park in North Carolina each year. They come, as many have come before them, to walk to the top of eastern America's highest mountain. Yet how many of them leave understanding the human drama that unfolded on the mountain between 1835 and 1857? How many of them learn of the character of Elisha Mitchell, the man for whom the mountain and the park are named, or why he was on the mountain on that fateful day in 1857? A new museum in the park provides an excellent introduction to the story, but in my many trips to the park as a boy the life of Dr. Mitchell remained an unknown, little more than an old portrait of a man on a wall.

As an adult I was intrigued to learn that Mitchell was a preacher as well as a professor. The more I read about him the more I saw him as a Renaissance man and an example of how Christians can integrate their faith into life and achieve excellence.

The facts of Mitchell's life are woven faithfully into *Mitchell's Peak*. The conversations, thoughts and motivations of the characters are my own interpretation. The story deviates from what I know to be true in only one major area. Maria, Mitchell's wife, suffered a stroke during childbirth around 1843. Afterwards she could no longer speak, but she could comprehend what was said or written to her. For the sake of preserving the dramatic conflict between Mitchell and Maria, I have left her with her voice in this story.

To be true to Mitchell's time, some of the words used in the story are archaic. Chief among these is "the Alleghanies," the term once used to describe all of the Appalachians. Some of the geological ideas expressed are no longer considered accurate, but I have left them as illustrative of the beliefs of Mitchell and his peers.

What can I learn from the life of Elisha Mitchell? That was the question I struggled with before writing this story. The answer to that question is what separates this story from a non-fiction treatment of Mitchell's life. Read on, and see what I learned from Mitchell and the mountains.

Robert Dellinger, 2003

Chapter One

Lost

My father was lost in a wide mountain wilderness and I was lost as well, not in a place but in my soul. How we each came to our time of trial is a story more easily told than understood. How we both found redemption is a matter more of miracle than of man's actions. Follow me, and see what I learned from my father and the mountains.

"Charley, it's time we were goin'."

John Stepp shook my shoulder to awaken me, but he didn't need to. I hadn't been able to sleep.

"I'm up." As I swung my legs to the floor, the lack of light told me it was still before dawn. The darkness matched my spirit. Since my father had failed to return everything had turned dark.

"Get your things together and then come on to breakfast. We've got a long way to go before this day is over."

John was wasting no time. We were headed to the Caney River settlement to look for my Pa. It would take us most of the day to get there, twelve miles up and across the height of the Black Mountains, and who knew what we would find? Everyone kept telling me that my father would be there. I didn't share their optimism. Pa had said he would meet me on Monday at the Mountain House, just below the crest of the Black Mountains. Pa was a man of his word, but he had not returned. Now it was three days later—Thursday, July 2, 1857.

When I got to the kitchen the room was already full, though it was only five in the morning. John sat at the table eating a biscuit. He was a year or two older than I was, and taller. More than that, his wisdom of the mountain ways exceeded mine by nearly two decades. In my eighteen years I had spent only a few weeks in the mountains.

"Better get to eatin', Charley," John said between gulps of biscuit.

"How are you this morning, Charles? Did you get any sleep?"

That was Mrs. Stepp, John's mother. She paused in her work over the stove, frying eggs, and turned to give me a concerned look. Her motherly affections didn't stop with her own family.

"I couldn't sleep, Mrs. Stepp, but I'm rested and ready to go."

"You've got a long walk ahead of you today. You know that, don't you, son?"

That was Jesse Stepp, John's father. He sipped coffee as he leaned against a cabinet.

"Yes, sir, Mr. Stepp. I'm aware of that."

"Listen to him, Jesse," said his wife. "He sounds just like his father."

"You're right, dear. The fruit doesn't fall far from the tree."

"Enough with the talkin'. Let Charley sit down and eat or we'll never get there."

John pointed out my plate on the table, already full of biscuits, ham and eggs. I sat down and inhaled the salty aroma of the ham and felt the steam from the hot eggs on my face. From the table I saw through the kitchen window that the sky was beginning to lighten. To the east lay the outline of the Blue Ridge, and to the north the peaks of the Black Mountains.

Men do not make mountains, but some men make mountains known. My father, Elisha Mitchell, was such a man, and he took on some of the nature of the mountains himself. I don't mean in height or mass, but in the length of his shadow, in the climate he created around him, and in the heights of perspective to which he could lift you.

Perspective—that is the great treasure of the high places—the ability to see beyond the usual. The sense of otherness in a mountain vista conquers your preoccupation with self. From the heights you can see something of the puniness of a man's efforts in relation to the vastness of creation. One can also see, across the stretch of horizon, the variety of circumstances that make up life. The storm to the south doesn't go on forever. It has an end, and over here the sky is clearing. Remember that during the stormy times.

Mountain men must expect their share of storms, and my father had his. If life in the flatlands is laced with toil and pain and uncertainty, how could it be any different in the open, elevated, and unprotected atmosphere of the Alleghanies? And what must transpire on the most extreme elevations? If my father considered this as he undertook his mountain pilgrimages, he would have counted it another valuable token in the moneybag of his adventures.

I call him a mountain man. I believe he was, but not in the usual sense of a man who grew up in the mountains or who happened to live there. No, there are many of that category of men whose only connection to the mountains is one of livelihood or birth, who may even despise the mountains because of the difficulty or isolation of living there. My father was more akin to those mountain folk who seem to grow out of the mountains, whose lives are intertwined with the hills, and who know the mountains like a friend or mate. He was more alive in the mountains than anywhere else. He was famous for the amount of trail he could cover in a day. To him a three-thousand-foot climb was a set of stairs to a fine spot for lunch. I remember once we were caught out at night in a thunderstorm. We were on the ridge top for the view, of course, and I had never been more frightened as the lightning crashed and thundered nearby. I remember to this day the look of joy and amazement on his face, reflected in the lightning, as he sat like a spectator and took in God's fireworks display. Who can draw the line between fearlessness and foolishness in such cases? I know he could never have been so foolishly happy if he had been but half again as fearful. Fear is a valuable commodity in some professions, but it counts for little with explorers and mountain men.

I'm afraid that I may be painting my subject too big. Everything I've said is true, but my father was, after all, a university professor, a part-time preacher, a full-time father full of the same faults and eccentricities as any father, and a man whose actions are mostly unknown and ignored by the world and history. His life might have remained that of the quiet academic, but instead it was elevated to notoriety by his encounters with the stark relief of the Black Mountains.

Some men love the mountains and are moved by them in ways that compare with little else in life. For such men the mountains are a magnet that draws them back again and again. They are drawn by the size of the mountains, with a scale so out of proportion to everyday existence that it cannot help but seize one's attention. They are drawn by the coolness of the mountain forests or mountaintop breezes, so longed for during the humid heat of a lowland summer.

They are drawn by the unexpected angles and unpredictable construction of the ridges and valleys, at once so amazingly God-hewn and refreshingly free of the human touch. They are drawn by the simplicity of the backwoods, which clearly illustrate what is of value and what is only vanity. They are drawn by the freshness of a mountain stream or flower. They are drawn by the God-sized view of the world that can best be seen from the top of a mountain. And where could one be more drawn, than by the view to be found on top of the tallest mountain?

In our day these attractions may seem dull and overstated, but imagine their power in an earlier time before roads or rails took men over the mountains more quickly than their minds could appreciate them. In that younger time the mountains were both unnamed and unexplored, unmeasured and unconquered, mysterious and magnificent. How blessed the man who finds such wonders in his own backyard! What fortune to find yourself alive in a time and place where the frontier is both within sight and not yet reached. Who with a yearning heart could resist such an opportunity? How much harder it is to find the frontier today.

When my father arrived in North Carolina in 1818 the frontier was within a week's journey by wagon. I'm sure he had his eye on it as he headed south from his home in Connecticut to the more unbroken ground of North Carolina. Even his work was frontier work. He was one of the first professors at the young University of North Carolina in the sleepy village of Chapel Hill. His field was mineralogy and geology. His laboratory was the entire state. Add to this his ordination as a minister and his marriage to Maria North in 1819, and you can begin to see the reach and energy of my father. It must have been an exciting time for a 25 year-old young man.

But now it was 1857, not 1819. My father was no longer the youthful professor with a new bride and a new position. He was a 64-year-old father of five with a reputation across the state of North Carolina as the expert in geology. He was the man who had proved that the Black Mountains were the highest mountains east of the Mississippi. And he had been missing for three days.

John and I started out as the first light of day began to shine over the Blue Ridge to our right. We were heading up the North Fork of the Swannanoa River. Swannanoa comes from the Cherokee word for "trail of the Suwali Indians," but some say it means beautiful or peaceful. Any other time I would have sworn to the accuracy of the name, but today it taunted me. The beauty of water, plants, and light held no attraction for me now. They were obstacles to be passed on the road to our destination.

The North Fork Valley where the Stepps live is drained by the headwaters of the Swannanoa. From the valley the North Fork flows south, joins the Swannanoa River and heads west fifteen miles to the town of Asheville. We walked up the North Fork, away from any town or settlement and into the wilderness. I call it wilderness, but it was nothing like the wilderness my father found when he first climbed the Black Mountains. The North Fork Valley was becoming a destination for those adventurous sorts of people who take tours through the mountains. Jesse Stepp provided lodging and outfitting for these excursionists who could ride or walk up a maintained trail to the Black Mountains. William Patton had even built a rustic lodge at an elevation of 5200 feet on the southern slopes of the Blacks, where a lucky traveler could now find a bed and fine food. Soon we would pass Patton's Mountain House, where I last saw my father.

"You're awful quiet," said John. "Whatcha thinkin'?"

"About things I wish I had said before Pa left. I don't think we said a proper goodbye."

"Don't give up on your Pa too quickly, Charley. You'll be talkin' to him soon enough. He's a strong man and he knows that mountain pretty well for an outlander. We'll find him over in the Caney River settlement, I'm sure."

John's words and the warmth of the morning sun coming up over the ridge cheered me as we walked. I tried to imagine what Pa would say if he were in my place, and all that came to mind was a passage from the *Gospel of John*: "walk while ye have the light." With the sun on our shoulders and the mountains rising above us, it looked like there would be no lack of light or walking.

Chapter Two

Looking Back

I was eight or nine when I realized that my father was different from other men. He was working at an old table with rocks that he had brought home from one of his journeys. He talked to himself and wrote in a memorandum book as he worked. Sometimes he poured liquid on the rocks and muttered as he watched whether the liquid bubbled or simply ran off. Sometimes he scratched the rocks or hammered them until they broke. I spoke to him and tried to pull him away from his work, but it was hard to get his attention. I pulled on his coat and asked him questions until I aggravated him so much that he cried out, "Charles, what do you want?"

"Quit playing with the rocks and come play with me," I demanded.

"I am not playing with the rocks," he shouted back, but then he caught himself. He pulled me into his lap, picked up one of the rocks and placed it in my palm. "Charles, what is this?" he asked in his most serious voice.

I thought it must be a question meant to trick me. Anyone could see it was a rock. What else could it be? Yet I thought there must be more to it than that. So I looked at the rock with the intense gaze that Pa used. I pursed my lips like he did. I turned the stone over and over and still saw nothing new. Finally I gave up and shrugged my shoulders.

"It's the backbone of the world," he declared. "It's the marrow of the mountains. It's a message from the world beneath to show us some of the secrets of God's creation. It's a map, for those who can read it, which will direct you to the wealth of the mineral kingdom. It's a piece of the puzzle of history." All I could do was look at Pa, and then at the rock, and wonder. That's when I began to sense how unique he was.

What determines a man's interests or where his heart lies, and what drew Pa to the rocks? Perhaps he was fascinated by the details of the various kinds of stone: their color and granularity, their hardness or lack of it, their fracture lines and imbedded minerals.

Maybe it was the influence of Dr. Silliman, his former professor at Yale. Sometimes I think it was the novelty of geology that attracted him. "Here," he might have said, "is a field where I can excel and make my mark." Maybe it was one or all of these things that motivated him, and maybe it was none of them. All I know is that Pa was drawn to the rocks, and the rocks led him to the mountains.

Just so one thing leads to another. Life is a string of events. Individually they may seem of little importance, but put them together and they determine the direction of your life. There are times when we struggle with decisions only to watch them turn out to be meaningless. Then there are decisions that we make with but a moment's thought that have terrific consequences. In just such a way many factors may combine to magnify the effect of a small step, and I saw this first-hand in my father's life.

Pa was known affectionately as "Old Mike" by his students at the University. They liked him on account of his wit and because he could be counted on for mercy in matters of discipline. With his New England upbringing and Yale education he was out of the ordinary for North Carolina. That pleased him. Though he was bald and graying by the time I knew him, already 46 years old at my birth, there was nothing gray about his personality. He was a forceful man at home, in the classroom, and in the public forum. Most people summed up their impression of Pa by calling him "the walking encyclopedia." I know the description fit, because my father tried to impart a large part of that encyclopedic knowledge to his children. He knew something about almost every subject, whether scientific, religious, cultural, or historical. He didn't browbeat people with his knowledge, but he was always eager to share it with anyone who was interested. Of his own memory, he said it was "like a tarred board that catches everything thrown against it."

Some people criticized my father for being too much of a generalist. There's merit in their argument, for Pa studied so many subjects that he never became a widely known expert in any of them. He never met a rock or plant that he didn't find curious and want to investigate. I've heard it said that during his early years in North Carolina he couldn't rest until he had "geologized and botanized" every corner of the state. It was his nature to cast a wide net of interests. He wasn't undisciplined, but he could be absent-minded and lacking in attention to commonplace details as such men often are. It's easy to look back and wish he were different. But Pa's weakness was also the strength that motivated him to leave his familiar surroundings and explore the North Carolina mountains.

I can't show you his photograph since he lived in the time before they were widely available. He was a large man, at least six feet tall and weighing over two hundred pounds. He had a face to match his classical training: a high domed forehead enlarged by his receding hairline, dark eyebrows set close above brown eyes, a long face with square jaws, thin lips and a Roman nose. He wore a dark suit with a high white collar and black tie.

My father was a towering man in his stature and his accomplishments. Though occasionally such men or women will rise up from great disadvantage by their own will, more often they build their character on the platform raised by their predecessors. So it was with Pa. His father, Abner Mitchell, was a successful dairy farmer in Connecticut. His great-grandfather, Rev. Jared Eliot, doctor of medicine and divinity, was well known for his studies of the natural sciences including botany and mineralogy. Rev. Eliot received a medal from the Royal Society of London for a discovery in the manufacture of iron. People say Pa favored him in appearance as well as in interests. Another ancestor, John Eliot, was known as the "Apostle to the Indians" and wrote a translation of the Bible for the natives.

Then there was Ma. How could I describe those who influenced Pa without mentioning her? He never could have accomplished his life's work without her help. Husbands and wives are supposed to support each other, each providing strengths to match the other's weaknesses, and Ma complemented my father well. She had an executive ability to match Pa's many commitments.

My mother was a rarity, as precious as a diamond, because she was willing to take her refined and polished upbringing and use it to raise a family in the rustic environs of North Carolina. Her father was a physician in New London, Connecticut, who prepared his daughter for life in the wealthy society of New England. He never dreamed she would end up in a place almost devoid of society. Instead of being dismayed at her life's turn of events, she used her background to create a social framework for our family and the town of Chapel Hill. A visitor from Connecticut gave her one of the greatest compliments she ever received when he said that our home in Chapel Hill was just like a typical New England home.

My parents first met after Pa graduated from Yale and taught at a girl's school in New London. Maria North, his future wife, was one of the students in that school. I can imagine how her handsome features and intelligence captivated him. Over the next four years Pa returned to Yale as a tutor, was ordained as a minister, and moved to Chapel Hill to take the professorship in Mathematics and Natural Philosophy. After a year of teaching at the University he returned to Connecticut long enough to marry Ma.

Once I asked my mother what it was like to leave Connecticut.

"It was thrilling and frightening at the same time," she answered. "Thrilling because of the novelty of it all and being so in love with your Pa. But very frightening because of having to leave home and family and come to a place that was so far away and so . . . different."

"How different?" I asked.

"Oh, Charley, you've seen New London and Grandmother North's home. Surely you can appreciate the contrast, even after thirty years of growth here in Chapel Hill. Think of what it must have been like then. The bustle and commerce of New London, the ease of obtaining goods, the educational level of the people, the opportunities for culture and entertainment. Chapel Hill had none of those things."

"Then why did you come?"

"You know the story of Ruth in the Bible. 'Whither thou goest, I will go.' Besides, your father can be very convincing."

"Are you glad you came?"

"Of course I am . . . now. But those first two years were very hard. Sometimes I wonder how I survived."

"Why do you say that?"

"I was very sad, Charley. I couldn't see my parents or my sisters. Your father was very busy with his teaching. It was so difficult to obtain even the necessities, and none of you children had been born yet."

"But now you're happy, aren't you?"

"Yes, now I'm happy." She smiled as she mussed my hair. But there was sadness mixed with her happiness.

Cornelia Phillips, who grew up with my sisters, said that Ma was so cheerful in the early years of our family's life. "Neat, and precise, and cheerful" was the way she put it. But that was before some of the hardships that came her way. Two children died in infancy, one before and one after my birth. She suffered a stroke of the palsy with the birth of my younger brother, who died at six months of age.

Then there were my father's trips. Ma never said it to me, but I think she came to resent his weeks away from home exploring the state. There was so much to do to keep a home and five children in good condition. Ma could get pretty quiet in the days before Pa left.

Some of my earliest memories are of our family sitting around the table and listening to stories of my parents' early years of marriage. My older sisters were usually the ones that got Ma and Pa started.

"Tell us again about your first trip here," Eliza would say. She was the youngest daughter and closest in age to me.

"Well, we had just been married, of course," Ma began. "In Connecticut. I was only nineteen at the time."

"Can you believe she would have me?" Pa asked. Mother smiled but kept on talking.

"Your father was twenty-six. He had already been teaching here at the University for a year and a half before he came back for the wedding. He insisted we get married on a Friday just to protest the superstition against it."

"And you see? There was nothing to it," Pa gloated.

"It took exactly two weeks to travel eight hundred miles from Connecticut to Chapel Hill. Our first stop was New York, where Dr. Ives welcomed us. Your father shaved off his whiskers for good in New York."

"I can't imagine you with a beard, Pa." That was Mary, my oldest sister.

"The problem was your mother couldn't stand me with it. It had to go to save our marriage."

"Dr. Ives was a wonderful host," Mother continued, "though I never have thought much of New York."

"But Philadelphia," Pa interrupted.

"Yes, Philadelphia . . . the next stop on our trip. That was another story. A wonderful city. I remember the shopping there was wonderful. And the museums. Do you remember our visit to the museums, Elisha?"

"Of course I do. Who could forget West's picture, or the natural history specimens at Peale's Museum."

"I was thinking more of Peale's portraits," said Ma.

"*Chacun à son goût*," replied Pa.

"Momma, please make him speak English," Eliza protested.

"Eliza, that means, 'to each his own.' It's time you started learning another language." Pa never quit trying to teach us.

"Tell us about sailing at night." That was Ellen, the romantic one and next in age after Mary.

"You mean on the Chesapeake," said Mother, and I could tell by her pause that it was a very fond memory, probably etched deeply in her mind. A taste of another time when life was much less complicated, and when she had suffered fewer disappointments. "It was a moonlit night, and even though it was December I was very tempted to sleep on the deck of the steamboat."

"Why didn't you?" This time it was Margaret, the middle child.

"Oh, it wasn't practical, I suppose," answered mother.

"And she didn't want to look foolish," added Pa.

"What happened next?" I asked.

"Well, after Baltimore we went up the Chesapeake to Norfolk, then by stage and boat through the Dismal Swamp into Carolina."

I had no idea what the Dismal Swamp was, and said so. Mary was quick to show her seniority and fill in my gaps of knowledge.

"The Great Dismal is a giant swamp where they dug a canal and built a turnpike beside the canal. But instead of riding on the road, you traveled on a boat pulled by two horses. Right, Pa?"

"Exactly, my dear. Are you sure you weren't there?"

"I can vouch for that, Elisha." Mother was laughing now, and that was good to see, for even then I knew that her health was not good. "But back to our story," she continued. "It was Christmas Eve, you know, as we traveled in that boat through the Great Dismal. The men were armed against bandits as we traveled through the night. Such was our first Christmas together, but my mother always told me that the first year of marriage would be the most dangerous . . ."

"Followed by the second, the third, the fourth . . ." Pa added.

"Let me tell this story, if you don't mind," Ma scolded. "After the swamp our party traveled in a cart and a gig, each pulled by one horse. There was no room for your father . . ."

"So I ran beside the gig keeping up a steady pace with the horse," Pa said, beaming. He was always proud of his stamina.

"Yes, you were quite the gentleman, but what *kind* of gentleman I was only just beginning to find out."

"And you were the most intrepid traveler," said my father.

"More intrepid than I wished to be. You see, children, after spending Christmas day resting in Elizabeth City, we spent the next day crossing Albemarle Sound in a little boat with four oars. The boat leaked more than a gallon a minute. Two of the passengers begged to go back, but your father said to push on, and so we did. You know how forceful your father can be."

"How far was it?" I asked, wondering if all men pushed on in the face of danger, or just Pa.

"Twenty-two miles," he boasted, "and seven hours of bailing, but we were never in any real danger if that's what you're thinking. I have to say this about your mother, though. If she ever gets tired of you children, I think she would make a wonderful sailor."

"And there are days when I'm tempted," she replied, but none of us were worried.

"Is that it?" I asked, thinking the story was over.

"Of course not," answered Mary, who had probably heard this many times before. "The best part is still to come."

"Let me tell it, please," said Mother, with just a little bit of annoyance in her voice. "Charley, the 'best part' that your sister refers to took place on the final leg of our journey when we took the stage from Raleigh to Chapel Hill. As he climbed into the stage, your father told the driver to 'drive well, because I've got a gun and I'm not afraid to use it.'"

"Were you afraid, Ma?" That was me again.

"Not afraid, but worried about what kind of man I had married." Here she glanced suspiciously at my father. "My worries were short-lived, though, for no sooner had your father climbed into the stage than he whispered in my ear, 'Our driver is suspected of being a murderer.'"

"I'm glad I could put your mind at ease, Maria," said Pa in his most serious voice, but that lasted only a moment before Ma and Pa and all my sisters erupted into laughter.

After settling in Chapel Hill, Pa began his explorations of the state by taking long walks through the countryside. These walks were not just for exercise. They were his best opportunity for satisfying his curiosity about the natural world. His finances were limited and he had only a few weeks free each summer while the students were away. There was no opportunity for a lengthy journey, so the country around the University became his world.

As children we often wondered why Pa took these long walks by himself. When Eliza asked him about it one day he said, "Do you miss me?"

"Yes, I do," she answered.

"But I come back every time."

"I know, but I still miss you."

"Well, why don't you come with me, then?" Pa suggested.

"You walk too far and too fast!" Eliza protested.

"Then I'll just have to walk alone," he replied in mock sadness.

He hadn't answered Eliza's question, so I asked again why he went walking.

"It's like reading, Charley. The world is God's book, and I go out to read it. Every time I go I find something new he's written. I enjoy reading it for myself and I write down the things I read so that I can share them with others."

He often took his students with him on these rambles. It was a time for teaching and an occasion for the good-humored exchange of jokes and barbs. On one occasion he led a group to a nearby pond to talk about the willows and other trees growing there. Among the students was Zeb Vance, who would later become governor of the state. Vance saw an old, decrepit mill across the water and asked in his most serious voice, "Dr. Mitchell, what do you think? Is that mill worth a dam?" I heard that got a very hearty laugh from Pa. Another time Vance told the class he had found an unusual "red stratum" in the nearby countryside. My father and the class dutifully followed Vance into the field only to find a ripe watermelon cut open and waiting for them. After that Pa could never speak of Vance without smiling.

Years later I had the privilege of attending my father's classes at the University and going on the walks as a student. I can remember only remnants of the scientific descriptions that came pouring out of him—one of my classmates said it was like trying to catch a waterfall in a thimble—but I cannot forget the joy of those times together out of doors. There was such camaraderie and humor, and Pa gave us an unforgettable example of appreciation for learning.

I remember one walk in particular. It was the first spring-like day after a very long winter. We were like little children in our enthusiasm to be outdoors, and Pa was no different. He was always out in front because of his long stride and because he knew where we were going. Some of the students kept up with him. I usually hung back with the stragglers.

"Where are we going today?" I heard one of the students ask.

"Down Morgan's Creek as far as Barbee's Mill," was the Professor's reply.

"What are we looking for?"

"Rocks and plants, of course!"

"Of course!" came the echo from the group.

"I've got a question," asked McLean.

"Ask away, then," the Professor replied.

"But it's not about rocks or plants."

"No matter. I'm a man of many interests, and you should be as well."

"What do you think causes the luminescence in faux fire?"

"You mean the *Ignus fatuus*. Rotten wood that glows in the dark. Answer that and they'll be ready to give you a professorship, Mr. McLean. All I can offer you is speculation. It might be the result of energy released from minerals taken up by the tree while it was growing, now released as the wood decays. Or perhaps it is a chemical reaction between acids in the wood and phosphorus in the soil, or vice versa. These are only theories, you realize."

"Of course," said McLean.

"What do you think about the origin of the *aurora borealis*?" asked Graham.

"Caused by the movement of electricity through the atmosphere. But as to the origin of the electricity I have no idea. It was reported to have been so bright in Paris on one occasion that the firemen rode through the city seeking the source of the blaze."

"Professor, do you agree with those who say you can judge a man by the shape of his head?"

"If they were right, Mr. Avery, then how could we ever make sense of you?"

Even Avery laughed at the Professor's good-natured jibe.

"No," Pa continued, "I've always believed that in man, as in nature, the character of the parents predicts the character of the offspring. Tell me who a student's parents are and I believe I can give you a good idea of what that man will be like when he grows up. Take Mr. Bingham here for instance. Now I've known the Bingham family for years . . . a fine family. But I don't recall the maternal side of the family. Tell me your mother's name, Mr. Bingham."

"Betsy, sir."

Everyone but Pa and Bingham burst out laughing.

"I meant her maiden name, Mr. Bingham."

I don't know whether Bingham's ignorance was real or pretended, but by the spreading smirk on his face I suspect it was more false than factual. If Pa caught on to the deception he kept it to himself. He did appreciate a good wit.

"What do you think about the debate over vultures and how they find carrion?" asked Major.

"You mean whether they find it by sight or smell. Why don't you tell us what you think, Mr. Major?"

"Well, I know Audubon's experiments showed the vultures would come to a lifelike painting of a dead cow. But others found that the birds could find carrion even when it was out of sight."

"And to which view do you ascribe, Mr. Major?"

"I believe both have merit."

"A politician in the making, I see. In this case I happen to agree with you. As I remember, those who claim the buzzard has no sense of smell did their study in the neighborhood of Charleston. How did they expect any bird to pick out a particular smell among all the garbage and smoke from the thousands of kitchens in that city? It would be like asking a drunkard to tell if a companion reeked of spiritous liquors. No, I believe if they had done their experiment out in the fields they would have discovered the buzzard can smell as well as any member of the temperance society, who can tell if a man has had a thimbleful of grog at a hundred yards."

"Is that a warning, Professor?"

"He that hath ears to hear, let him hear!" he answered.

By now we had made our way below Barbee's Mill and Pa gathered the group around the banks of the creek.

"Now we'll see what the rocks have to say," the Professor informed us as he took out his hammer and began to chip at a rock from the creek.

"And what language do they speak?" one of my fellow students asked sarcastically.

"A language all their own, which you would do well to learn."

The Professor cracked open a rock and held it up for everyone to see. It was a confusing mixture of smaller rocks of various sizes and colors that looked as if they had been cemented together.

"Who can tell me the name of this rock?" he asked as he passed it to one of the students.

The rock made its way through several hands before one of my fellow students recognized it and said, "Conglomerate!"

"Very good, Mr. Venable. Now, if you will all direct your attention to the large rock outcropping downstream, you can see an example of the familiar granite typical of the land around our University. Granite is the most plentiful of the primitive rocks. I'm referring, of course, to Werner's classification of rocks into primitive, transitional, secondary, and tertiary. He believed that this reflected the order in which the rocks precipitated out of their original chaotic mass."

"Dr. Mitchell, what do you say to those who think Christians shouldn't poke their noses into such matters, but should only study the classics?"

"I would quote *Proverbs*: 'It is the glory of God to conceal a thing: but the honor of kings is to search out a matter.' However, lest you grow too proud in your learning, it's wise to remember what Blackstone said: 'It is well if the mass of mankind will obey the laws when made, without scrutinizing too nicely into the reasons of making them.' Blackstone was talking about the laws of men, but his words apply equally well to the laws of God and nature."

Just then Pa caught a glimpse of something out of the corner of his eye. I saw what he saw, and knew what was coming, but before I could warn my classmates he yelled, "Gentlemen, a rattlesnake!"

Students scattered to the right and left and several ended up in the stream. Only those of us who were familiar with this oft-repeated prank were still standing close to the Professor as he knelt down to the ground and inspected what he had seen.

"I don't know what you're all so afraid of. It's only a rattlesnake plantain, *Goodyera pubescens*, a member of the orchid family. If you were here later in the year you could see it bloom. It's reticulated leaves look remarkably like the skin of a rattlesnake, wouldn't you agree?"

We all agreed that a bad day out of doors with Dr. Mitchell was better than a good day inside the classroom.

In 1827 and 1828 the Legislature paid Pa a small stipend to do a geological survey of North Carolina. The geology, 'pounding rocks' as he put it, didn't interest me much, but his stories about the people that he met were another matter. There was the old man named Ellwood who, like Ishmael in the Bible, had his hand against every man, refused to hear Pa preach, and spread the lie that the state paid Pa $9,000 to look at the rocks. I remember the story of a hunter, a man in the mold of Cooper's Leather Stocking, who had two wives and children by both of them. Pa talked about the balsam that could be cut out of the blisters on the bark of the balsam fir trees. This sap or resin was said to be the universal cure of the mountains. He told us about the man who searched for treasure that was taken from white men by the Indians and hidden in underground chambers. This man claimed that he was kept from recovering the treasure by the two-horned devil himself. There were the mineral-rod men, charlatans who offered, for money, to find metal ores with the help of a tree branch. "Why," Pa asked, "if such a thing could work, are not all the branches in the vicinity of a mine pulled down or stripped off?" He could never talk about these trips without going into a tirade about the endlessly repeated tale of a rich lode of lead found by a hunter in the bottom of a creek. As the story goes, the hunter failed to mark the spot and could never find it again. To Pa's scientific mind this seemed like an unfounded myth, but I'm sure it reflected a deep desire for wealth and security among the poor people of the mountains.

The survey trips back in the 1820's were my father's first expo-sure to the mountains of Carolina. That was when he originally laid eyes on the Black Mountains, though he didn't get close enough to climb them. In those days Grandfather Mountain was said to be the highest mountain in the Carolinas and Mt. Washington in New Hampshire was known as the highest peak east of the Rockies. During the survey trips Pa had a chance to view the Blacks from the top of the Grandfather, and even then it was his opinion that the Blacks were higher.

The Black Mountains were named by botanist André Michaux, the first white man to explore them. He came in search of plants for the French government. Following the lead of William Bartram, a contemporary who preceded him to the Carolinas, Michaux and his fifteen year-old son climbed the mountain he named the *Montagne Noire* in 1789. No one knows how far up the mountain he went, but it's obvious to anyone who has seen the range why he chose the name he did: the balsam firs which cover its high elevations give it a dark color that can be seen for miles. Some have called it a funereal color. To me its dark blue-green is an oasis of coolness in the middle of summer's heat and a reminder of Christmas even in July. The smell of the fir grove is freshness concentrated and opened up before your face. A few steps into the balsams and all sounds from outside are banished except for the soughing of the wind. In this cathedral quiet-ness you can hear the slightest chirp of a bird or whisper of a man.

The range of the Blacks stretches from north to south like a let-ter J twenty miles in length. It's a spur just separated from the great chain of the Blue Ridge. At the northern end stands Young's Knob, at the southern terminus Yeates's Knob. In between the ridge undu-lates up and down through a series of fifteen or more peaks, most above six thousand feet but never dropping below five thousand feet in elevation. These facts I can share with you now after many men have climbed the range and measured it, but when my father first climbed the Black Mountain in 1835 it was *terra incognita*. Then as now it was surrounded by 100,000 acres of wilderness. There was not a home in a ten-mile radius of the high center of the ridge. The nearest settlements were the North Fork Valley to the south of the range, home to Jesse Stepp and other Buncombe County men, and the Caney River settlement of Yancey County. The Caney River drains the hook of the J, running north along the western flank of the range. Here you would find the Allens, Riddles, and Wilsons—men who would play an important part in my father's explorations.

My geography lesson, like all such book learning, cannot show you the real nature of the Blacks. Without seeing it yourself you could never understand what it meant to climb the mountain without a trail and feel the change in climate between the peak and the valleys below. Yes, there are more remote and rugged mountains. True, this was no supernatural feat. But try and see the mountain as my father saw it. It was the great unknown of his day, and in climbing it he was one man acting alone and making his own way.

Chapter Three

Mountain House

John Stepp and I made our way towards the Mountain House on a well-worn trail. We climbed steadily through a forest of maples, oaks and hickories. Rhododendron and laurel, covered in pink and white blossoms, crowded the undergrowth and reached up higher than our heads. At eight in the morning the woods were alive with the sound of birds, but the only sound I heard was my father's voice saying goodbye to me five days ago.

John's voice broke my reverie. "Charley, let's go over what we know about your father's plans. Maybe it'll give us an idea about where he is."

"All right," I answered, grudgingly. I had already been over this again and again in my own mind. "He was headed for the Caney River settlement."

"What was he going to do there?"

"He wanted to talk to Mr. Wilson."

"You mean Big Tom Wilson?"

"That's right. He did say it was Big Tom."

Big Tom Wilson was a bear hunter and guide who lived at the headwaters of the Caney River. He farmed, fished, and robbed honey from the wild beehives of the Caney River Valley. But his fame, up until that time, rested on his reputation as a master tracker and hunter of the local black bears. Big Tom killed over a hundred bears during his lifetime. His wife, Niagara, was the daughter of Amos Ray, who owned 13,000 acres of land on the headwaters of the Caney River. Big Tom's work, if you can call it that, was looking after Mr. Ray's land. I suspect it was about as much work for Big Tom as looking after a candy store would be work for a child.

"What did he want to see Big Tom for?"

"He'd heard how well Big Tom knows the Black Mountain, and he wanted to talk with him about the lay of the land. He also wanted to talk with Big Tom about the men who guided Pa when he first climbed the mountain back in '35. He was sure Big Tom would have heard them talk about the climb."

"Did he say how he was goin' to get to Big Tom's?"

"No, but I'm sure he would have followed the trail."

For several years a trail had run from Jesse Stepp's house in the North Fork valley past the Mountain House and on to the southernmost part of the Black Mountains. Within the past two years the trail had been extended to a more northern peak, believed to be the highest. Now a new trail, perhaps one year old, wound its way from Big Tom's cabin in the Caney River settlement eight miles up the mountain to the high peak. John and I agreed that my father would have taken the trail from the Mountain House north for several miles to the high peak, then followed the new trail from the peak down to Big Tom's.

"Was there anything else your Pa was plannin' to do?"

"He was hoping to preach Sunday morning in the settlement."

"And he was supposed to meet you back at the Mountain House Monday."

"That's right."

At that moment we walked out of the woods and into a clearing holding a rustic two-story cabin which was the Mountain House. An excursionist sat on the portico reading a book and smoking a pipe, and smoke wafted up from a chimney, but otherwise there was no sign of life. Everything was peaceful, but my stomach churned and I felt sick at seeing this spot again. This was where I had said goodbye to Pa. I had waited here for hours when he failed to appear three days ago. I had come back here Tuesday and Wednesday, hoping for his return but hoping in vain.

"Good mornin'!" John shouted to the pipe smoker, who returned his greeting in the same fashion.

"Any news of Dr. Mitchell?" I asked.

"You mean the Dr. Mitchell that the peak is named after? Is he in these parts?"

Just then Mrs. Garenflo, who ran the lodge for Mr. Patton, came out onto the portico.

"What's the news, boys?"

"None," answered John. "We were hopin' you had some."

"Sorry, boys. I wish I did. Hasn't been a soul gone by but Mr. Hubbard here, and he just arrived from the Swannanoa side yesterday evenin'. Whatcha goin' to do?"

I told her we were heading to the Caney River settlement to look for Pa.

"That sounds like a very good idea. Betcha find Dr. Mitchell there nursin' a sore knee or ankle. Say hello for me when you see him. Do you need a bite of breakfast before you go?"

John said, "That's a mighty tempting offer, but we already ate a big meal."

"Well, ya'll be careful now, you hear?"

John said we were big boys and could take care of ourselves. As we walked on I could hear Mrs. Garenflo explaining the whole matter to Mr. Hubbard, and she sounded very despondent now, not at all cheerful.

Above the Mountain House everything in the landscape around us changed. We were leaving the deciduous trees behind and entering the evergreen forest of spruce and firs that crowned the Black Mountains. We were about 5500 feet high and still climbing.

John asked, "Whatcha thinkin'?"

I told him I was preoccupied with the way Mrs. Garenflo's mood changed after she thought we were out of earshot.

"Don't pay attention to that old biddy. She just loves to gossip. That's why she was layin' it on so thick with that fella."

I wondered to myself who was being more truthful: Mrs. Garenflo or John?

"John, what do you think has happened to my father?"

"Seems to me there's a long list of possibilities. I can't say which is most likely."

"What possibilities have you thought of?" I asked.

"Well, he could be waitin' around in the settlement to talk with someone. Big Tom goes off for days sometimes. Then again, maybe he did hurt himself like Mrs. Garenflo suggested."

"Then we should find him along the trail," I pointed out.

"Maybe," replied John. "But he may have gone on to the settlement to recuperate. Or maybe he got sick after he got to the settlement. There's one other thing, Charley."

"What's that?"

"They say it stormed bad on the mountain last Saturday."

I remembered the dark clouds I had seen after Pa left me. "What about it?"

"Maybe your Pa got caught in the storm. That would've slowed him down. He would've had to find shelter, and if it got dark he might have spent the night on the mountain. That would've delayed his trip considerably. Might've even caused him to get pneumonia. That's bad enough, but what if he got struck by lightning?"

"Your list keeps getting worse," I complained.

"You asked what I thought. Just because I thought it doesn't mean it happened. There's plenty of other things I haven't thought of that could've happened."

"That's not very reassuring," I said between breaths as we continued uphill.

"Those other things aren't necessarily bad, Charley. They're just unexpected. Life is full of the unexpected, like when you think your dog is gonna have two puppies and she has six instead."

"Or you think you might get your own horse for your birthday and you get clothes instead," I continued.

"Exactly. Or the girl you're courtin' up and marries another fellow."

"That happen to you?"

"Don't want to talk about it," he muttered.

"All right. How about this? You think it's going to be a beautiful day, but then a storm blows up."

"You've got my point," said John.

I did get the point. Pa had headed up the mountain into a storm. What had happened in that storm?

"I know what you're thinking," said John. "You think something terrible happened to your Pa in the storm. My point is, whatever you think happened probably didn't. That's the unexpected nature of life."

"I expected Pa to be back on Monday. Now it's Thursday and he's still not back. What am I supposed to expect now?"

"Charley, sometimes you just have to take what life gives you and make what you can out of it. That's how people around here survive. They're very good at takin' what they find and then makin' it suit their purpose."

We stopped to rest and catch our breath. We were on the ridgeline of the Black Mountains at their southernmost point. To our right rose the Pinnacle, the highest point of the Blue Ridge, with its pointed peak looking like a tree-covered volcano. The Blue Ridge sharply divides the Alleghany Mountains from the foothills of the Piedmont. It stretches like a natural Great Wall all the way from Virginia through North Carolina and on to Georgia. To our left the hook of the Black Mountains continued across Black Knob and then curved north towards Yeates's Knob. Rising up in front of us was Potato Top, the first in a chain of peaks that led due north from our position to the high peak. I could see no sign of human life anywhere except for John and myself.

"John, do you ever think about death?"

He looked at me with a scowl and said "I know what you're thinking and I don't agree with it. Don't go buryin' your Pa before his time."

"I'm not just thinking about Pa. Haven't you ever wondered what will happen when your life is over?"

"You see, that's the difference between you and me. I'm too busy thinkin' about what there is to do in this world to worry about the next one."

"So you believe there is life after death?" I asked him.

"Course I do. Don't you?"

"I'm not sure," I answered hesitantly.

"Well I can't believe you grew up in a preacher's house and don't believe in Heaven and Hell. Are you sure you're Professor Mitchell's son?"

I thought about telling him that being a preacher's son didn't automatically make you believe in God, but decided against it. Instead I told him I hadn't made up my mind yet.

"Well, you like to think about things, don't you?" he replied. "Think about this, Charley. Creation is all around us and it's shoutin' out that there is a God. Look at the countless trees around us, every one a testimony to the limitless imagination of God. Take in the view of these mountain ranges and then tell me there's no artist of unbe-lievable talent behind that beautiful picture. Consider how long this land has been here before us, consider eternity, and then tell me how you and I can comprehend these ideas if God didn't create us."

I looked at the mountainsides and saw the infinite variety of shapes and colors and tried to imagine how long the land had looked like this. Then I saw the trail and realized that even now the land was changing. People were coming to the high peaks and the mountains would never be the same again. My father had a hand in that change. Had the mountain turned on him because of it?

"John, where you see certainties I only see questions. Until I find out where my father is, God will have to wait."

"Fine, Charley, but it's a slow ship that sails without the wind."

We skirted around the base of Potato Top and within a mile arrived on top of the next peak. A clearing, called a prairie, covered the top of the mountain, and John and I sat down in the soft grass to rest and enjoy the breeze. The Swannanoa settlers had called this peak "Mt. Mitchell" since my father explored the area in 1835 and 1844, and for years folks had considered it to be the highest point of the Black Mountains. The trail to this peak had been cut about 1851, and a crude hut had been built on top of it three years later. One year after that T. L. Clingman declared that a peak three miles to the north was higher, and the controversy that followed his announcement caused my father return to the Blacks. I looked north to the oblong shape of the higher mountain and wondered if my father was there. That peak had been our objective as Pa and I worked our way up the mountainside over the past two weeks. We were performing an accurate measurement of the mountain as part of Pa's effort to prove that he had been the first to climb and mea- sure the high peak. He should have come this way after he left me five days ago. He should have made it to the oblong knob of the high peak and walked across the summit he first climbed twenty-two years earlier. He should have walked back across these peaks three days ago, but he had not. Now we sought my father where once he sought to find the highest mountain.

Chapter Four

Ascent

As John Stepp and I walked on toward the high peaks of the Blacks I thought about my father's initial ascent of the mountain. It took place in 1835, four years before my birth. There were two major events in Pa's life that year. The first was the death of Dr. Caldwell, the president of the University. Dr. Caldwell had been the guiding force at the University through most of its formative years. With his death Pa became the acting president of the University. Another title was added to his long list of official and unofficial jobs: professor, preacher every other week in the school services, prayer leader, bursar responsible for the collection of fees from the students, justice of the peace for the town of Chapel Hill, and superintendent of grounds for the University. He was also the father of four girls.

Never busy enough, Pa also chose that year to attempt something he had been planning for years: climbing and measuring the Black Mountains. As early as 1823 he had been encouraged to undertake the task by David Swain, an Asheville native who would later serve as governor of the state and president of the University. John C. Calhoun had also spoken with my father about his belief that the Black Mountains were the highest in the United States. President Caldwell's failing health had kept Pa occupied with University business for years. Now he finally had the opportunity to explore the Blacks.

The students were gone from the University for six weeks each summer. That was the time frame for Pa's expedition. It took a week traveling by horse-drawn wagon to reach his base of operations in Morganton. Morganton was a small town located just east of the Blue Ridge and within viewing range of the Black Mountains. From Morganton Pa headed northwest on a grand tour of the more conspicuous peaks of the North Carolina Blue Ridge.

His first stop was the Table, a squared-off outcropping of rock sitting astride the eastern rim of Linville Gorge. The Gorge itself was a marvel to behold, drained by the Linville River, running from north to south for a distance of twelve miles, rising over two thousand feet from its bottom to the top of the Table, and covered entirely by virgin timber except for scattered rock walls along its sides. To stand atop the Table and look into the gorge was to look back in time and see the world as it existed before men changed it.

From Linville Gorge Pa headed north to Grandfather Mountain. He had first climbed the Grandfather in '28, and as before he found it isolated, mysterious, and a very difficult climb. Many people had believed that the Grandfather was North Carolina's highest mountain, but Pa's measurements showed this was not the case. He recorded his impression of the climb in his diary:

> What a change from the familiar landscapes back east. The ascent of the Grandfather was mostly under cover of the trees, but here and there it would break out into the open on the back of a rock outcropping. Then you could witness the drastic change that had occurred. It was as if you had floated above the earth to an unnatural vantage point in some miraculous flying machine or heavenly ladder. Gone was the limitation of flat terrain and surrounding trees. Now row after row of mountains spread away like giant forest-green waves frozen in advance to the horizon. Looking at it you could not help but feel small, though that was as nothing compared to the sense of wonder at seeing such a great expanse of countryside.

Pa continued westward until he reached Roan Mountain, which he said had the most beautiful views of any mountain he visited. I agree with him. The Roan has the necessary height for spectacular vistas, and because it's bald over much of its summit the views are unobstructed. It didn't hurt Pa's opinion of the mountain that it is easier to climb than most or that the summit is covered in natural gardens of rhododendron that put on an unparalleled display of color every summer.

Now my father headed south to his ultimate destination, the Black Mountain. He found lodging on the road between Burnsville and Morganton at the home of Thomas Young. With Young guiding him he climbed the high knob at the northern end of the range and could see that there were higher peaks further south. Passing on through Burnsville he came to the Caney River settlement where he stayed with Samuel Austin. The Black Mountains encircle the settlement like a giant fishhook. Pa hired William Wilson and Samuel Austin to guide him up Yeates's Knob, located at the point of the hook on the western terminus of the range. Once upon Yeates's Knob, Pa and his guides used a spirit-level to determine that it was not the highest point in the range. The spirit-level is an instrument that establishes a perfectly horizontal line of sight. Looking across the level Pa could determine whether a nearby peak was above or below the elevation of his current location. From Yeates's Knob he saw that the highest knob was directly across the valley on the eastern part of the range, the shank of the hook. Wilson agreed to accompany Pa up to the highest peak the next day, and Adoniram Allen was hired to take the place of Samuel Austin.

The next day they were up early despite Wilson's fatigue—not that Wilson was happy about it. He and Allen were in no hurry to get started, but Pa was in charge and that settled it. Wilson was torn between a variety of feelings: muscle fatigue and stiffness of the joints versus a quickening of the pulse and a liveliness in his step at the thought of what they might accomplish today. His face darkened when he thought about what it would take to get to the top. Puzzlement clouded his vision when he considered why Pa was so interested in a mountain he lived beside every day. Yet he smiled at the thought of even one day's escape from the dull routine of life.

For Pa there was no such conflict of emotions. Enthusiasm and determination drowned any fatigue. The target had been chosen, and he felt certain that by day's end he would have discovered something of significance, something worthy of the time and effort, and something his family and friends would talk about for a long time.

Talk about for a long time. He remembered how his Pa would talk on and on about how proud he was of his son's work at Yale. How long had it been since he had seen his father? Too long, he thought. And suddenly he yearned for his father to be there, beside the Caney River, that he might share in the events of the day, and so that my Pa might hear those words of encouragement he longed for.

"Professor Mitchell, ain't you gonna eat any breakfast? You can't do what we're fixin' to do on an empty stomach."

Wilson's suggestion snapped him out of his daydream. "You're right, of course, Mr. Wilson. Believe me, my appetite is too good to overlook this wonderful breakfast for long. Shall we give thanks for the food?" And with that they sat down at the table and bowed their heads as Pa blessed the meal and the day. Then their plates were piled high with as much food as any outlander's supper. There were backbones and ribs, sweet potatoes and fried chicken, biscuits and molasses and fried pies. They dug into their breakfast heartily and their plates were soon empty. Even sleepy men enjoy breakfast, especially mountain men.

They traveled by foot, regretting it but knowing that their route was impassable to horses. They headed south, up the Caney River, and then turned left beyond Sugar Camp Creek. Now they were climbing in earnest. By Pa's reckoning they were somewhere around three thousand feet high in the floor of the valley. The top of the Blacks might exceed six thousand feet. That three-thousand-foot gain in elevation was only one of the obstacles they faced.

Soon they reached a territory like Pa had never seen before. Allen called it a "hell," and there was no end to the similarities between this earthly hell and the eternal one. It was an age-old tangle of laurel, a tall shrub also known as rhododendron, and it formed a nearly impassable living wall of woody branches. The rhododendron loomed overhead as high as ten feet in places. In front the branches criss-crossed like a never-ending army of soldiers with pikes held at angles to each other. Underneath they constantly tripped at the men's feet. They threatened their eyes and gouged their skin. Pa and his guides struggled through the hell for an hour or more and made little progress before they collapsed on the ground, exhausted.

"Whoever named this knew exactly what they were talking about," sputtered Pa, between breaths. "It's inescapable. It goes on forever. It tortures you. Is there any hope of salvation?"

"You won't find Heaven here, if that's what you mean," Allen said sincerely. Pa bit his tongue, but had to agree with Allen.

"I'm open to suggestions, gentlemen."

"Here's what you need," said Wilson, sounding like a confident salesman. He was pointing to a darker but open area in the rhododendron hell. Pa pulled himself to his feet and staggered over to the opening. As he bent down and peered in the opening he saw what looked like a tunnel above ground.

"What is it?" he asked.

"It's a bear track," the two guides answered in unison.

"You mean you ain't never seen one?" Wilson blurted. He was surprised, not ridiculing.

"I can honestly say I haven't," Pa confessed.

The bears had trampled down the laurels over the years so that there was an open pathway through the thicket. There were crushed laurel branches underneath and living laurel overhead, but straight ahead a narrow passage large enough for a man as well as a bear.

Wilson went first, getting down on hands and knees and crawling, bear fashion, through the tunnel.

"Let's go brougin'. Follow me, Professor."

"I'll be directly behind you, Mr. Wilson. But I would like to complain to the bear that built this trail about his craftsmanship." He puffed as he inched through the tunnel.

"What's wrong with it? I reckon it's a perfectly good bear trail."

"If it were perfect I wouldn't be crawling."

"Adoniram, I think the Professor was happier in Hell."

"I believe you're right, William."

"All I meant to say was that I had a few suggestions for the bear."

"I'll let you discuss that with Mr. Bear himself if he shows his face."

"I appreciate your kindness."

"You're welcome."

"By the by, Professor," said Allen, following behind the other two, "how fast do you have to go to outrun a bear?"

Pa was glad to pause from his crawling and consider the question. "I don't know, Mr. Allen. How fast?"

"Oh, not too fast. Just a little faster than William and me." The two guides laughed hard at Pa's expense, but he was chuckling, too.

"Very good, Mr. Allen. I will be sure and tell that one to the students next term."

"Hey, Adoniram," said Wilson, "I don't know about you, but I'm not plannin' on runnin'. I didn't bring this rifle to turn and leave like a dog with his tail between his legs. If a bear does poke his nose in this tunnel, his skin will soon be drying on my porch."

"Just make sure you're shooting ahead of you and not behind you," warned Allen from the rear. "I wouldn't want it to be the Professor's or my skin on your porch."

"Mr. Allen," asked Pa, "what do you call a man who makes a mistake in front of a bear?"

"Besides dead? I don't know, Professor. What's the answer?"

"Em-bear-assed."

"Oh, that's bad. I've always said that puns are the lowest form of humor. Don't they teach you any better down there in Chapel Hill?"

It was extremely slow going. The bear trail followed the ridge-line, which meant taking a direct route to the top. In this case direct meant steeper. There was no chance to take a more gradual sideways ascent. Underneath the climbers the ground was rocky and covered with branches the bears had trampled down. On their backs the guides carried rifles, food and water, and my father's barometer: a narrow tube of metal and glass about three feet long and filled with mercury. As they climbed in altitude the temperature fell steadily, about three degrees for every thousand feet. The sky grew more and more cloudy. Soon they were in the clouds. The only brightness in their journey was the joking of the guides and the pink-white blooms of the laurel and rhododendron over their heads. Even the flowers were dimmed by the swirling mist that clung to every natural and human artifact it touched.

Each hour Pa would stop and set his barometer upright on the ground. He would note the height of the mercury column, measured in inches, as well as the temperature.

"So what does it say, Professor?"

"It's not saying anything just yet, Mr. Wilson."

"Sounds like the silent treatment I get from my wife," kidded Allen.

"I know exactly what you mean," Pa agreed. "But the barometer doesn't have a temper. Would you like me to explain how it works?"

"Be my guest. I'm all ears," Wilson answered.

"Why, William, I've been tryin' to tell you that for years," kidded Allen.

"Ignore him, Professor. Consider class to be in session."

Pa didn't hesitate. He came to measure the mountain, but teaching was his *raison d'etre.* "Well then, gentlemen, the first thing to remember is that air has weight."

"Very little weight," offered Allen.

"Actually a substantial weight, but one doesn't realize it because the air pushes out from inside us as well as pushing down upon us."

"I always knew you were full of air, William."

"You're the one who's all puffed up, Adoniram."

"The weight, gentlemen, is pushing down on the reservoir of mercury in my barometer. As we climb higher, it pushes down with less force. As a result, the column of mercury is shorter at the higher altitude."

"So that's why you're gettin' smaller numbers as we climb higher," observed Allen.

"Exactly."

"So how high are we?"

"I can't tell you that. The readings I take here must be compared with those taken at about the same time in another location, a location nearby where the height above sea level has already been determined."

"What's the reason for that?" asked Wilson.

"Well, because the barometric pressure in any location isn't constant. It fluctuates from day to day. No one knows why, but it seems to be related to the weather."

"That makes sense. Why, I've always told Adoniram I could tell the weather according to my rheumatism. Isn't that right, Adoniram?"

"Yes, but you also told me that you can only pickle beans when the moon is waxing full."

"It's the gospel truth."

"Well, I beg to differ, William. What about you, Professor? Do you believe in plantin' and pickin' by the moon?"

"I've always planted my potatoes and beans in the ground and not in the moon. Shall we get back to the lesson?"

"Sorry, Professor. Carry on." But the guides eyed each other with the look of men who were considering the next point in their debate.

"Now, the readings I take as we climb today will be compared with readings taken by a colleague in Morganton. I've already determined the elevation of Morganton to be 968 feet. A mathematical formula will allow me to use the two sets of readings to determine the height of the Black Mountain."

"Could you make a guess about how high we are?"

"I've done that already, Mr. Allen, and I would say that we are at least five thousand feet high at this point."

"With a long way yet to go."

And with that knowledge and an exchange of glances the three men resumed their climb.

It's a cruel trick of mountains that the top often seems close at hand, when in reality the crest of the mountain is hundreds of feet away, hidden by the gradual upward slope. So it must have been for the Yancey men and Pa as they struggled up those last hundreds of feet and hundreds of minutes. Sometime in the afternoon they left the rhododendron behind and entered a thick balsam fir forest. Their path was now less obstructed but no less steep.

"Professor, I know I've said it before, but we've got to be near the top now. These fir trees only grow near the ridge top."

"I know you're right, Mr. Wilson. Here comes Mr. Allen. Perhaps he's found something."

Allen had scurried further ahead to do some scouting. On his return he reported the ridge crest was just ahead.

"This way will lead us to the top. Follow me and we'll be there before you know it." He was out of breath but grinning a big bearded grin.

"What did you see?" asked Pa.

"I shan't spoil it for you. Come see yourself."

Wilson didn't hesitate. Pa caught one more breath, secured his fur cap on his head and lumbered up the slope after the two guides. They used the tree trunks to grab onto and hoist themselves higher, as if going rung by rung up the mountain. Finally, they came to a point where there was nothing higher ahead, only the other side of the mountain sloping down and clothed in firs like the side they had just ascended. To the left the ground also sloped down, but to the right it rose gently. Wilson and Pa followed Allen up the rise three hundred feet. Now they found themselves huddled together in the cold mist, surrounded by dark balsam firs, and on a point that sloped away in every direction.

"What do you think, Professor?" Allen asked, having had more time to catch his breath.

"I think you've led us to the top, and I'm thankful to be here."

"I'm thankful there's no more climbing to be done," added Wilson.

"We've got to get a view somehow," said Pa, wanting to be sure this was the highest point. "We'll have to do what I did before on the Grandfather Mountain. Help me climb this fir tree so I can get a better look around."

Allen and Wilson hoisted Pa up the likeliest-looking tree. Harsh winds and winters had stunted the firs, so there wasn't far to climb. Once near the top, he looked out upon a sight as virgin as the timber, a blanket of greenish black firs laid out across a narrow ridge running north and south. But circumstance was against the explorers, for the foggy mist of the mountaintop limited the visibility to a few hundred feet.

It was too exposed and precarious to stay up in the tree for very long. Convinced that there was no higher peak nearby, my father climbed down from the tree and squatted against its trunk. Wilson and Allen took turns climbing the lookout tree, but neither could spot any familiar features or higher peaks through the mist. The guides waited for Pa to catch his breath, but Allen's curiosity finally overcame him.

"Well, Professor, what do you think?"

"I think it's time for a barometric reading."

Wilson and Allen shook their heads at each other as Pa set up his apparatus.

"23.807 inches. 58 degrees."

"And what does that tell you?" asked Wilson, not expecting a useful answer.

"It tells me that if the pressure back in Morganton is in the usual range of about twenty-nine inches of mercury, then we should be close to six thousand feet in elevation, perhaps higher."

"So are we on the highest mountain in these parts?" asked Wilson.

"Gentlemen, we may be on the highest mountain within the boundaries of the United States. Mt. Washington in New Hampshire is 6,234 feet in elevation. We could be higher. I won't know for sure until I return to Morganton."

Wilson and Allen congratulated each other and discussed what to do next while Pa looked with a naturalist's eye at the wilderness scene surrounding him. He noted the dominance of the balsam firs, which crowded out most other trees on the peak. The effect of the harsh winds or winters had sculpted the tree branches so that they pointed away from the wind. There were juncos in abundance—the familiar snowbirds of winter. Back home they had been gone for months, yet here they were in the middle of summer. It struck him that climbing five thousand feet in elevation was like taking a long journey north to New England.

"Professor, hadn't we ought to be movin' on?"

Wilson's prompting brought Pa's attention back to the nature of their situation. The thermometer might say fifty-eight degrees, but the wind and moisture said it was colder. None of them were adequately dressed to spend much time on top of the mountain.

"Right again, Mr. Wilson. The prospects of locating a higher peak than this one today seem very unlikely. I'm not sure I have the strength for it anyway. Let's start back."

"Shouldn't we make some kind of mark or sign that we were here?" asked Allen. "Seems a mighty far piece to come and leave nothin' to show for it."

"I've already thought of that," said Pa. He climbed back up the tree, pulled out a piece of shingle, some nails, and a rock hammer, and began to hammer the shingle onto the trunk.

"What's on the shingle?" asked Allen.

"My initials. Would you like to climb up and add yours?"

"Adoniram, don't believe we've got time for it," said Wilson. "Professor, we'd better be going."

"All right. I'm through." Pa was quickly down the tree and with little more than a glance over their shoulders the three men were off the peak. Except for the obscure letters "E. M." on a fir tree there was no evidence they had ever been there.

Chapter Five

On the Peak

John and I could find no sign of my father as we crossed the high peak.

"Don't you think it's odd?" I asked. "My father has walked across this mountaintop time and again, but you would never know he's been here."

"People call the mountain Mitchell's Peak. Don't that count for somethin'?"

"A name," I said. "A name that can be taken away as easily as it's given. I'd feel better if there was some proof he'd been here." And I thought how ironic it was that my father could not be found on his own mountain.

"I see," said John. He sat down on a fallen tree, whether to rest or enjoy the view I couldn't tell. "You're not worried about your Pa's posterity. You're wantin' proof of his existence."

"That's right. Even a footprint or a piece of his clothing would do. Right now it's as if he's fallen off the edge of the world."

"Some people would say we are on the edge of the world." He thought about what he'd said, then added, "Sorry, Charley."

He was right, except this wasn't the one and only edge of the world. It was one of many edges I could see from the height of the peak. Running north and south of us was the undulating edge of the Black Mountain range. Far to the north but still visible was the broad edge of the Roan Mountain. Intersecting the Blacks on a line from the northeast was the Blue Ridge. In the distant west I could see the many-edged Smoky Mountains.

"I count it a blessing that we haven't seen any sign of your father," John offered with his gaze on a distant peak.

"How can you say that?" I asked.

"Cause it means he's still up and around somewhere else while we sit here blabberin'." John wasn't one to waste words or time, so when he didn't immediately get up and head down the trail it surprised me. "What's your Pa like, Charley?"

"He can be difficult at times," I told him.

"Any father can be difficult. What exactly do you mean?"

"He has high expectations of his children, and I don't think I'm able to meet them."

"What kind of expectations?" he asked.

"Doing well in school, for instance."

"And you didn't do well in school?"

"I did well," I answered, "but not the best."

"And you felt you had to be the best?" John asked.

"I felt that was expected of me."

"I see," said John. "You know, sometimes you put more pressure on yourself than your parents do."

"I don't know about that," I replied. "All I know is that it's hard to be the son of a prominent professor."

John leaned back and chewed on a stalk of grass. "So how does your Pa handle bein' famous?" he asked.

"Oh, I don't think he considers himself famous. He knows he's not well known outside of North Carolina. But he does long for attention and recognition."

"Who doesn't?" said John.

"Right, but I think Pa sees his chance for recognition fading as he gets older. That's why he's so determined about his claim to the high peak. When he first came here I think it was just for the scientific curiosity and the thrill of the exploration. He was surprised to hear people call the mountain Mt. Mitchell. But over the years I think that name has become more and more important to him."

"I've met a few other people like your Pa. Ambitious people. Always got to be doin' somethin', never happy unless they're busy accomplishin' somethin'. I think they're all lookin' for some kind of reward, but they're the ones who get things done, and I say give 'em their reward. They've earned it."

"And what about you, John? I take it you don't consider yourself one of those people."

"No, not me. Let me just look after myself. I don't want the cares of the world. Just give me the sticks and a rifle and I'll be a happy man."

"The sticks?" I asked.

"You know—the woods, the hills. What about you, Charley? What kind of person do you want to be?"

"I haven't decided," I told him, and that was the truth. I knew what kind of person Pa wanted me to be, and for some reason that made me want to be someone completely different. But I wasn't sure I could be happy living for myself alone.

"Is that all you've got to say about it?" John asked.

"For now. Shall we move on?"

"My thoughts exactly."

With John in the lead we climbed down the northern slope of the peak and took a sharp left turn. I might have missed it without John showing me the way. We were finally on the trail to Big Tom's and the Caney River settlement, where all my hopes of finding my father now rested.

Chapter Six

The Return

A cavalcade of the Mitchell children chased Pa's wagon through the town as it returned to Chapel Hill in the summer of 1835. I can imagine how my sisters must have jumped and yelled at seeing my father again. Mary would have been 12, Ellen not quite 10, and Margaret 7. Ma would have run out to see what the commotion was about. Perhaps she carried one year old Eliza with her and said a silent prayer of thanksgiving when she saw it was her long-absent husband returning home. Pa would already have two armfuls of daughters as he climbed down from the wagon, with another hugging him from behind as he and Ma kissed. Then my sisters would have been untangled from Pa, and Eliza passed to one of her sisters, before my parents could finally embrace one another.

"Maria, my love, it's so good to be back home." Pa picked her up and swung her around once. "I have missed you so much."

Ma was half crying and half laughing. She had a serious look on her face, but she was too overjoyed to be entirely cross. "Elisha Mitchell, don't you ever leave me alone with four children for that long again!"

"Maria, you are the most valiant and talented woman in all the land. Who else would I leave them with?"

Ma was just about to launch a verbal assault on my father when she realized his sarcasm. "Mr. Mitchell, if you only knew how close I have come to losing my sanity, you would not be standing around making jokes. I think I should pack up and go visit my family in Connecticut for a few weeks and see how well you manage with three rambunctious girls and a baby."

"You're right, of course. I'd be completely lost. I will never have your talent or patience."

"Flattery won't get you very far today."

"Then how about presents?"

"Presents?" asked the girls, swarming around my father anew.

"What did you get us, Pa?" asked Ellen.

He asked them to be patient and then reached into the back of the wagon for a box. "All right, girls, I knew it would be hard to please all three of you, so I got several different gifts. First of all, some pretty stones from a mountain stream." Here he held up a smooth pearly river rock made of quartz. As he predicted there were oohs and ahhs, but one of my sisters cried out "I don't want a rock!" Next he showed them three spools of ribbon in different colors. This was a success with all three girls, who began talking about how nice it would look on their dolls or in their own hair. "Finally," said Pa, "something very special." He opened his large hand and showed them three small fir cones.

"Where did they come from?" asked Mary.

"These came from a tree on top of the tallest mountain." And as he said it his eyes were on my mother. She said nothing, but slowly her eyebrows raised up and the corners of her mouth broke into a smile.

"So you were right," she said quietly.

"Yes!" he shouted loudly, and in a moment their arms were around each other again. "Maria, I'm only sorry you weren't there with me."

"I believe you, Elisha. And believe me, I would love to have been there with you. Isn't that right, girls?"

They answered dutifully, "Yes, Mama," but their minds and eyes were on their presents.

"So how tall is it?" my mother asked.

"According to my calculations, 6,476 feet. Over two hundred feet higher than Mt. Washington. It wasn't a very easy climb," said Pa. "I believe you would have had a bit of a struggle."

"Moi?"

"Yes, you. Though it did have its enchanting moments. I believe you would have especially enjoyed crawling up the mountain on hands and knees in the footsteps of an old bear . . ."

"Elisha!"

". . . and finding just the right tree to hide behind when performing those necessary functions, while just out of sight of our guides."

"No thank you."

"Well, see there. You were better off here all along."

"You think you're so smart, but I still say it will be a long time before you go off without me."

Then Pa remembered something. "We're forgetting your presents, Maria." He hurried back to the wagon.

"You're still trying to make me forget the trials of the last month, and I know it," she replied.

"Maria, don't be so cynical. Do you really doubt my sincerity?"

Ma wasn't sure how much to trust him, but she decided to withhold judgment until after seeing the presents.

Pa handed her a box that she unwrapped, revealing several different fabrics including a calico print. Pa could see that she wasn't overwhelmed with the gift.

"I don't suppose one of the fir cones would make you appreciate my present more, would it?" He held it out to her, but she looked at it scornfully. "You know, Maria, there is one more gift in the wagon, but I think I might need your help with it."

Ma suddenly perked up. "Elisha, are you holding back on me?"

He just laughed and pointed out a tarpaulin in the back of the wagon. She pulled it back and saw a very handsome mahogany work stand with several drawers and brass mountings.

As she admired it Pa said, "I thought you could use it by your chair next to the fireplace."

Ma was beaming. "It's beautiful. It will be perfect for my papers and writing materials. Thank you so much, dear." And then she gave Pa a very sincere hug and kiss.

That evening there was celebrating in the Mitchell home. The Mitchell and Phillips families gathered together to welcome my father home and hear more of his journey. Reverend James Phillips was a fellow professor at the University. His children and my sisters were constant playmates.

"You know, Elisha," said Professor Phillips, "it's too bad that Dr. Caldwell couldn't be here to enjoy your achievement."

"You're right. I miss him a great deal. I couldn't help but think of him one night when we were up on a ridge after dark. The view of the stars was incredible. If he'd been there he would have begun building an observatory right on the spot."

"What else did you see on your trip?" asked Mrs. Phillips.

"You would have loved the flowers. The laurel and rhododendron—those are evergreen shrubs that grow at the higher elevations—were in full bloom. I've never seen such a variety of whites and pinks and reds. Whole sides of mountains would be covered in thick growths of the shrubs. The local people call them hells."

"Whatever for?" she inquired.

"Because you feel like you can never get out of them once you walk in. They say hunters have actually been trapped in them for a week or more. I didn't tell you, Maria, but at one point in our climb through the rhododendron hell on the Black Mountain we came upon a clearing beneath a shelf of rock. I lay down there to catch my breath, and I thought to myself, 'I'm going to die right here where I lay.'"

"You were kidding weren't you?" Ma asked anxiously.

"Only half kidding, dear. I've never been so tired in my life. I don't think I ever worked as hard moving stones on my father's farm as I did walking up that mountain."

"Did you see any bears?" Professor Phillips asked.

"No, not this trip. We saw plenty of bear signs, but I think the "old man of the mountain," as they call him, is rather shy of human contact. You can't blame him the way the local men are always after him for his hide and meat."

"You look like you ate your fill, Elisha," kidded Mrs. Phillips. "What do you think, Maria? Looks like they fed him well in the mountains."

"Elisha eats his fill wherever he goes. You don't have to worry about him starving." She reached over and pinched the side of Pa's stomach.

"I did eat well, in fact," Pa agreed. "Though I didn't always ask what I was eating. The mountain families don't have much but they've learned to do well with what they have. The specialty of the house was usually potlikker."

"What's that?" asked Ma.

"A soup or stew. They start with a piece of ham. Depending on what they have it may be as little as a piece of fat or a bone, or a jowl if they have it. The ham is cooked in a pot for several hours and then a cabbage is quartered and added to the pot and covered with water.

Greens are used if they have no cabbage. Peppers are used to season the broth. It's always served with corn bread for sopping up the broth. Very tasty."

"I'll take your word for it," said Professor Phillips.

"And you'd have to try the gritted bread, James."

"What's that?"

"It's a delicious corn bread. But instead of using dried corn meal they grate fresh ears of corn and make a milky batter from it. It's rather sweet and very different from the usual corn bread. Sticks to your teeth a bit."

"All this talk of food has my mouth watering," said Mrs. Phillips.

"Well, I don't have potlikker or gritted bread," said Ma, "but let me go see what kind of refreshments I can muster up."

James Phillips asked, "Elisha, have you thought about how you'll publish your findings? I'm sure your account would be of great interest to other geologists and to all the people of North Carolina."

"What would you suggest? I've thought about it, but I don't know how to proceed. I have such a limited amount of data. I'd feel better if I had more than one measurement from the high peak."

"What are the prospects of your getting back there for another measurement?"

"Perhaps in another two or three years," wondered Pa.

"Perhaps," said Phillips, "or perhaps it will be five or ten years, and perhaps someone else will do it before you return."

"James," said my mother as she returned with tea and biscuits, "what are you carrying on about? Has Elisha done something to upset you?"

"Don't worry, Maria. It's what he hasn't done that I'm carrying on about. I'm trying to get him to go ahead and publish the results of his fieldwork. He feels like he doesn't have enough measurements yet."

"What do you think, dear?" asked Pa.

"Well," my mother said, "do you believe that your measurements are accurate?"

"As accurate as they can be under the circumstances. Accurate enough."

"Would the findings be of interest to other people?"

"Well, I think . . . of course they would be!" affirmed Pa. James Phillips nodded in agreement.

"Are the results significant?"

Pa and Phillips shouted out at the same time, "Definitely!"

"Do I want you going right back up that mountain again? Let me answer this one, Elisha. Definitely not! Therefore, I suggest you proceed with the publication of these significant and interesting findings *post haste*." With that Ma sat down and began pouring tea.

"Well done, Counselor Mitchell," applauded Mrs. Phillips. "Does Elisha always listen so well to your arguments?"

"Ha! That will be the day," my mother answered.

"Well, you've convinced me this time, Maria. Not that you had a difficult task to begin with. I want to tell everyone what I've done, but I don't want people to think I've made all this up or that I don't know what I'm talking about. It may be hard for some people to believe that the tallest mountain east of the Mississippi is in North Carolina."

"Well, let them get used to the idea," said Professor Phillips.

"I think we're making too much of all this," said Ma. "It's likely that the only ones who will take notice are your fellow professors. The common man may not even take heed or hear about it."

"Which brings us to the method of publication. You should write a summary for the newspaper," Phillips suggested.

"Why the paper?" asked Pa.

"It will be quicker. You know how long it can take to get something into one of the scientific journals. And the readership will be much greater for one of our state papers. It's a local story. I think they will be very interested in it."

"I agree," said Mrs. Phillips. "It's a very good idea. Don't you think so, Maria?"

"I do. And Elisha, don't think of it as only benefiting you. It will bring credit to the University, and as the work of a minister it will also bring glory to God."

"I'm convinced," Pa announced. "I'll begin work on a report tomorrow."

It was late that night, after the guests had gone and all my sisters had been put to bed, before my parents could finally have some time alone. It was a loving reunion, I'm sure, but knowing Ma I imagine she had more to say about Pa's absence.

"I meant it when I said I didn't want you to be gone so long again, Elisha."

"I know, dear. I don't enjoy being apart from you, either. Almost every day I was away I thought of the trip you and I made through the mountains last year . . . the places we saw, the people we met . . ."

"So we agree. No more long trips without me."

He did not answer immediately.

"Elisha, what are you thinking?"

"I'm thinking I don't want to make a promise I can't keep. You're asking me to abandon my most promising area of study. How long will I be a prisoner in Chapel Hill?"

Now my mother was silent.

"It's not forever," she finally replied. "The children won't be children for long. I wouldn't mind going with you again . . . and don't worry, I won't be trying to go up every mountain you climb. But can't you at least promise that you won't be going away for a while?"

"Of course I can, dear," Pa agreed and kissed her. "Now, how long is a while?"

Pa's report appeared in the *Raleigh Register* that November. The article detailed his exploration and measurements among the North Carolina mountains and his claim that the Black Mountain, at 6,476 feet, was the highest mountain east of the Mississippi. Ma's prediction that few people would notice proved entirely wrong. Papers in major cities reprinted the article. In addition, Governor Swain, the new president of the University, became the chief booster promoting the attachment of Pa's name to the high peak. My father received a measure of fame that, while unexpected, was welcomed by him.

Chapter Seven

Happiness

I was born in 1839, the same year that Pa's father died. I've often wondered how the combination of those two events affected him. Pa already had four girls, but having his first boy must have been a memorable event. I hope I'm not being presumptuous. I've never had children myself, but people tell me it's a wonderful thing.

Some folks believe that the good and bad events in life balance each other. When things are going well, these people are always looking over their shoulder for something terrible to happen. They would point out Pa's 1839 events as perfect proof of their theory. I'm not convinced. It seems to me there are plenty of exceptions to their rule. How about the man or woman, and we've all known them, who suffers one horrible calamity after another? Sometimes it's their own fault, sometimes not. Then there are folks, and I count myself among them, who go through life with one blessing piled upon another. Not that bad things have never happened to me, but the good has certainly exceeded the bad.

All this talk of good and bad reminds me of the story of King Croesus and Solon. The Greeks had a very different attitude about the mixture of good and bad events in a man's life, and this story illustrates it well.

King Croesus was a very rich man, the one of whom we say "as rich as Croesus." One day the great Athenian lawmaker Solon came to visit him. Solon was as famous for his wisdom as Croesus was for his wealth. The king put on a show of his great riches for the sake of his visitor, but Solon was not impressed.

Then Croesus asked Solon, "Who would you say is the happiest man in the world?"

The king thought that Solon would surely say that Croesus was the happiest man. Instead Solon replied, "Tellus of Athens."

The king was shocked. "Who is this Tellus?" he demanded.

"An ordinary man, sire, who lived in a flourishing country with sons who were both good and handsome. Tellus saw his sons grow up and have children of their own. After a life of simple blessings and comforts, he ended his days in the most heroic and glorious fashion. It happened that the Athenians were at war with a neighboring city. Tellus came to the aid of his countrymen, helped them defeat their enemy, and died courageously in battle. After his death the Athenians gave him their highest honors."

Croesus remained dumbfounded following the story of Tellus. "How is it, Solon, that you count my wealth and position of such little value when judging my happiness?"

"Oh, King," Solon replied, "do not ask me to judge you until I hear that your life has ended happily. For now let me call you fortunate. The only man who is truly happy is the man who possesses all the advantages of health, good children, good fortune, and who ends his life well. You would not proclaim a victor before the race is over, and life is too uncertain to call a man happy before his life is done."

The story might have ended there, but it did not. Some time later King Croesus was defeated in battle by Cyrus, who condemned Croesus to death. As the flames of execution licked at Croesus' feet, he cried out "Solon! Oh, Solon!" Cyrus was overcome by curiosity and freed Croesus in order to find out more about this Solon. When Cyrus heard the story, and saw the truth of Solon's wisdom proven in the life of Croesus, he pardoned Croesus and gave him a position of honor in his court for the rest of his life.

During the year of my birth Pa's article on the Black Mountains was published in Silliman's *Journal of Arts and Sciences*. Professor Silliman had instructed Pa in geology at Yale. That same year David Swain, former governor and now president of the University, convinced Roswell Smith to put "Mt. Mitchell" on his *Geography and Atlas* as the "highest point east of the Rockies." In addition to all these accomplishments, the University of Alabama granted Pa an honorary Doctorate of Divinity. My father, like Croesus, no doubt reflected on these successes and saw only good. Was he a happy man as a result of the events of 1839? I will cast my vote with Solon and say it was too early to tell.

What is happiness? Ask a hundred people and you will get a hundred answers. Ask an individual if he is happy himself, at that moment, and if he's honest he will have no trouble answering. Like many other things in life there's a great deal of difference in the theoretical and practical aspects of happiness.

Some people think happiness depends on circumstances and others don't. No matter what you say, life has a way of revealing your heart. You plan for a big event and look forward to it, only to fall ill and find yourself unable to go. You are not happy. Another person suffers trial upon trial but remains optimistic, even joyful. What makes the difference?

During my father's lifetime I struggled with happiness. No, let me correct that. I struggled with unhappiness. Happiness was somewhere else, a place I was trying to find. Now I know that happiness, like a mountain view, depends on perspective. How far can you see? If you're stuck in a thicket of circumstance that limits your view to a day, a month, or even a year it can be pretty hard to see where happiness lies. But get above the tree line for an eternal perspective and joy spreads out before you like the Piedmont stretching east of the Alleghanies. It spreads out before you but you've got to walk through it to claim it.

Happiness is such a temporary condition. I'm always glad to have it, but if I have to choose between happiness and joy I'll take joy. Joy is a lot harder to come by but it lasts a good long time. Happiness falls into your lap by accident but then gets up and moves on like a cat looking for a better scratch. Joy moves in to stay for a spell like your best dog that's true to you even when you ignore him. Happiness will make the day as bright as sunshine while joy warms you like a crackling fire in winter. Happiness runs away at the first sign of trouble but joy stays by your side even in adversity. Happiness comes with gain or achievement; joy grows with relationships. The two make a great pair, but if you've got to choose between them choose joy. My advice is don't worry about finding happiness. Let it come to you. Concentrate on cultivating joy.

Pa was busy that year constructing what he called "stone fences" around the grounds of the University. Everyone else calls them rock walls, and it's odd to think that something so ordinary has become one of his most enduring legacies. In the '30's there was still a lot of livestock living around the University. These goats and cows and horses often wandered onto the school grounds and tended to ruin any plantings that were done to beautify the school. Governor

Swain wanted to do something to fence out the animals and my father gave him the idea of the stone fences so common in New England.

One day my father was working on a preliminary section of the stone fence when a visitor stopped to inspect his work. "Professor, are you planning to give up teaching and take up the stone mason's trade?"

Pa looked up from his work to see the lanky figure of Governor Swain standing beside the newly crafted section of wall. He wiped the dirt from his hands on his work clothes as he stood up to greet the university president.

"No, Governor," Pa replied, "though I'll admit I'm dressed for the part. What do you think of my design for the wall?"

"Very attractive, Elisha." Swain prodded the stones with his hands and feet. "And sturdy, too. Much stronger than I would have expected without some form of mortar between the rocks."

Pa patted the wall affectionately. It stood about three feet tall and two feet across and was made of local fieldstones. "Exactly right. The rocks are fitted together so that they can't move, and the weight of the upper rocks makes the whole wall more stable. Not having to use mortar makes the construction much more economical."

"I think it will work perfectly to keep out the animals, and it's attractive. My only concern is your having the time to complete the work along with all your other responsibilities."

"Don't worry, Governor. I built this section as a demonstration to get your approval. I'll be supervising the men who do the work but I won't be doing much of the building myself."

"I'm glad to hear that. You've got more important things to attend to, though I don't doubt you could do it if you had to. Where do you find your energy, Elisha?"

"I'm happiest when I'm busy," answered Pa.

"I've noticed that," Swain replied. "I still wonder if you would-n't be happier if you had been picked as president of the University rather than me."

Pa chose his words carefully. "We've talked about this before, Governor. I know you and I had our disagreements to begin with . . ."

"I remember," said Swain.

"But that was only because you didn't understood how much time I gave to my different duties as professor and bursar and grounds superintendent. As I said then, the trustees chose the right man for the job. I served as acting president long enough to learn what it takes to be president. And as you said, I have more important things to attend to."

"Still, the position must hold some attraction for you. You're a man of ambition. I know you'd like to leave your mark on the world."

"Like this stone fence?" Pa asked with a grin.

"I doubt you'll settle for this pile of rocks," Swain answered.

"You're right, you know." Pa hefted one of the rocks in his hand as he sat down on the wall and looked across the university grounds. "There are my students. They'll leave bearing some mark of my influence."

"No doubt," agreed Swain.

"But I can't deny that I find myself craving recognition at times. As for posterity, is there anything any of us can do to guarantee our place in the history books?"

"If there is, let me know," Swain said and laughed. "In the end I think all you can do is carry out the job you're given to do with your utmost ability. The rest is up to chance or circumstance." He paused and then sat down on the wall beside my father. "Do you think a man has to be famous to be happy, Elisha?"

"Some men may feel that way," answered Pa, and his eyes followed the path of the unfinished wall west to the imagined walls of the Blue Ridge Mountains.

Chapter Eight

Connecticut

When I was five years old Pa returned to the Black Mountain. It was his final stop on a geological tour through the western counties of the state. Looking back I wonder why he went there last, since it was the site of his most famous accomplishment. Perhaps he was putting it off as long as possible—further testimony to the difficulty of the climb in those days.

I have to speculate because Pa went alone. Standing by Ma's side and holding her hand, I watched her cry as he left. The days that followed were somber ones that grew more tense until the morning I awoke to find Ma packing my clothes in a travel bag.

"Where are we going?" I asked her.

"To visit your grandmother North," she answered energetically.

"While Pa's away?" This was not at all like my mother, especially considering her health. She had suffered a palsy when pregnant the year before and had not fully recovered. The baby, my brother, had died at six months of age.

"Yes. Your Pa expects us to take care of ourselves while he's away, and that's just what we're going to do." She sounded almost cheerful, and in hindsight I know it was the cheer of one who has decided to put her troubles behind her and move on with life.

"Does Grandma know we're coming?"

"No, she doesn't," she said as she stuffed more clothes into the bag, "but she will be very happy to see us just the same. Now, get out of bed, young man, and let's get you dressed and fed so we can be on our way."

I thought this would be the greatest adventure of my life. I couldn't remember traveling outside of North Carolina, and I had heard so many tales of Connecticut and my grandparents.

"Who will we see, Ma? Who will be there besides Grandma North?"

"I expect we will see Aunt Eliza . . ."

"Is that who Eliza is named for?"

"Yes."

"And will we see Aunt Ellen who Ellen is named for?"

"Aunt Ellen died last year, Charley."

Ma's sister and father had both died the previous year. I had forgotten about Aunt Ellen's death.

"I'm sorry, Ma."

"It's all right, dear. I have too many brothers and sisters for you to remember them all. We should see Uncle Erasmus."

I had no brother named Erasmus, and for that I was grateful.

"What about Grandma Mitchell? Will we see her?"

"We'll have to wait and see about that, Charley. Her home is a long way from New London even if it is in the same state."

"How will we get there?"

"By coach and boat. It will take nearly two weeks to get there, so you'll have plenty of time for questions. Why don't you save some for later and go finish getting ready so we can get started."

She didn't need to encourage me. I was ready to leave right away. But my enthusiasm for travel faded in the days that followed. Hour followed hour without any sign that we were getting closer to Connecticut. I enjoyed traveling by boat much more than riding in a coach. At least you could walk about in a boat. People were stuffed in a coach like pickles in a jar. The road bumped you about until you were sore, dust flew in the windows, and there was no way to escape an unpleasant travel companion. On the boat deck I could find my own private place, there was no dust in the cool breezes that blew past, and the views of the surrounding country were wide open. Best of all, because it was summer, I got to sleep out on the deck under the stars, as Ma had wanted to do on her first trip to Chapel Hill. One night as she lay on the deck beside me we talked and watched the stars as the boat steamed across the Chesapeake.

"What star is that?" I asked as I pointed to a star that lay directly ahead of us.

"That's the North Star. If you can find that star you'll always be able to tell which direction is north."

"That's a good direction, isn't it?"

"Why do you say that?" she asked.

"Because that's your family's name . . . North."

She laughed and it made me smile to hear it.

"You are a very funny boy, Charley. I think you have your father's sense of humor."

"Is that a good thing?"

"Oh, yes. That's a very good thing."

"How else am I like Pa?"

"Well, people say you look like him, and you're smart like him, but I think it's too early to say if you're like him in other ways."

"Like what?" I pressed her.

"Do you like rocks, for instance?"

"No, I don't," I quickly answered.

"All right," she replied. "Do you like the mountains?"

"Yes," I said without reservation.

"Do you like to teach?" she asked.

"Ma, I'm too little to be a teacher."

"I know," she said as she tickled me, "I'm teasing you. But teaching is very important to your father." Then she sat up and looked away from me. "When you grow up and get married will you go away and leave your wife alone for weeks at a time?"

I didn't know if she really expected me to answer the question. I knew what Ma wanted me to say, but I didn't have any idea whether I would ever get married. I decided to change the subject.

"Ma, does Pa see the same stars we see tonight?"

"He does if he's looking at the sky tonight."

"Why?"

She looked at me with the weary look of every mother who has heard that question too many times. With five children, she had grown tired of it many years ago.

"The sky is very big," she dutifully answered, "and Earth is small, so the sky looks very much the same wherever you stand on the Earth. However, if you travel very far to the north or very far to the south, you would see some stars that we can't see here."

"Well," I asked as I pursued a childish theory, "if Pa can see the same stars we see, why can't we see him?"

"Oh, Charley," Ma almost wailed, "what ideas you come up with. You never cease to amaze me. Well, let me see. How can I answer your question? The truth is, now that I think about it, you might see your father if there was a big enough mirror high enough in the sky and enough light to carry his reflection. But your father is so far away that his reflection in the mirror would be almost invisible. And there is no mirror big enough to do what you are suggesting."

"Don't you wish you could see him?"

"Of course."

"What would you tell him?"

"I'd tell him to come home! I'd say, "Dr. Mitchell, your wife and son miss you terribly." I'd tell him to say goodbye to the mountains and come back where he's needed."

"And would he come?"

"I don't know. I asked him not to leave, but he did anyway."

"Are you mad, Ma?"

"Oh, Charley," she sighed. "Why are you asking me these questions? These are problems for adults, not children." I thought she wasn't going to answer, but then she continued. "Yes, I'm angry. I'm angry that your father leaves and expects me to carry on just as before, with all of the responsibilities and none of his help. I'm angry that he thinks nothing of the risks in his journeys or what it would mean if he were injured or became sick. It upsets me that he seems to think the mountains are more important than his family."

"But they aren't, are they?" I offered in agreement.

"No, they're not."

"Then why does Pa think they're so important?"

"That would be a good question for you to ask him," Ma said, "but since you can't I'll try to do it for him." She paused a moment to look at the stars, then continued. "The first thing you must remember is that when people grow up they set goals for themselves, things they want to do."

"Like going outside to play in the creek?" I asked naively.

"No, not like playing. These are serious things. It could be something practical such as building a house or building up a farm. It might be writing a book or getting an education. Some men want to do things that no one else has done before. Some try to do something that will make them rich or famous."

"Does Pa want to be rich or famous?"

"I don't think he believes that he'll ever be rich, Charley. That is not the life of a professor. Though I dare say that there isn't a man or woman alive that wouldn't like to be better off than they are. As for being famous, I think your Pa does want to be well known and respected. His work in the mountains has brought him attention, and I can understand why it pleases him to go back there."

"Is that wrong?" I asked.

"No, it's not wrong, but sometimes your father's goals and my goals interfere with each other, Charley."

"Pa wants to study the mountains and you want him to help you at home."

"Something like that. I want the best for our family. Your father is very important to this family and I want to be sure he's around for many years. To be fair to your father, I'm sure he sees the work he does as being very important to all the people of North Carolina, and I'm sure he believes that anything that benefits him will benefit our entire family."

"I thought Pa just liked being in the mountains and in the woods."

"Oh, he does, Charley, he surely does. You're exactly right about that."

"And what about you, Ma? Do you like it, too?"

"Your father and I have spent some wonderful time together traveling through the mountains, but I don't believe I appreciate them the same way that he does. No, I think I'm much more interested in people than your father, and he's much more interested in the rocks and the plants and the trees. Now, that's enough talking for tonight. I'm tired and ready to get some sleep."

With that she kissed me goodnight and turned over and was soon still. I lay awake and watched the sky and imagined I saw the stars outlining the shapes of mountains. I looked for Pa among those mountains and could not see him, unless he was the shooting star that fell towards the west.

* * *

In the days ahead we passed in succession through America's largest cities: first Baltimore with its hillsides coming down to the harbor, then Philadelphia with its lofty church spires along the Delaware River, and finally the constant movement of people, goods, and ships that was New York City. Each one seemed gigantic to me, who knew nothing larger than our village, and each one seemed to exceed the last in size and activity. Strangest of all, for one who had always lived landlocked, was to see how these cities thrived upon the water's edge or on an island jutting far out into the waters.

In New York City we found rest and refuge in the home of Dr. Ives, a physician friend of Ma's father. He provided lodging for my newlywed parents when they first made their way to North Carolina in 1819. Though older, gray, and bearded, he was as energetic as any young man. After we unpacked and rested a bit he invited us to go on a carriage tour of the city, and soon we were riding down the busy avenues with the doctor as our personal guide.

"I can't believe how much everything has changed since I was here last," my mother exclaimed.

"Oh yes," Dr. Ives agreed, "this city is constantly remaking itself. You remember the great fire of '35?"

"I read about it."

"Over six hundred buildings destroyed. One quarter of the business district. The entire area was rebuilt within a year. People like to say that a different New York is created every ten years, and they are not far from the truth."

"And how do you feel about that?" asked Ma.

"I don't like it very much at all. You know how we older folks are. Change is hard on us. I look around and all the places I knew as a child or young man are gone. The fields where I played are now streets and neighborhoods. The streams have been filled in for more roads. The restaurants where my wife and I used to go are no longer open. In many cases the buildings that housed the restaurants no longer exist. It's just like my personal life. All my old friends are dying and the places we used to go die with them."

Having never seen the city before, I couldn't understand what Dr. Ives was talking about. For me it was one amazing revelation after another. The streets we rode down were full of people and carriages. There was an endless variety of noises, not the least of which was the sound of human voices speaking a jumble of words which were completely unknown to me. Dr. Ives overheard me asking Ma about it.

"That's German, my boy. The men we just passed were German immigrants. They say there are over 40,000 Germans in the city now. In addition there are 100,000 Irishmen, and I don't know how many Chinese. Those are just a few of the languages you hear on the streets."

"How many people live here now?" my mother asked.

"Who can say for sure? There are so many immigrants each year. Twenty years ago there were probably only 200,000 people in the city, but now there may be three or four times that many."

Just then Dr. Ives turned the carriage and headed down towards the water. My curiosity rose as I saw the masts of many ships ahead. Soon we were heading down the road that traveled right beside the water. To the right of the muddy street was a row of buildings, but to my left a line of ships of every shape and size stretched out of sight. Most of them had tall masts rising high like bare trees, so many that it seemed a forest of dead trees had sprung up out of the water. Their bowsprits jutted out over the street above us like giant spears.

"That, my boy," the doctor indicated with a wide wave of his hand, "is the East River. And this is South Street, the street of ships. Here the produce of America leaves for foreign shores and the bounty of the world comes to ours."

As we rode down the street I tried to recognize the various boats tied up at dock or making their way across the East River. The giant ships caught my eye first.

"Those are packet ships," instructed Dr. Ives. "The largest one, the *Liverpool*, displaces over one thousand tons."

"What's a packet ship?" I asked.

"They carry people and mail and other cargo across the Atlantic," my mother answered.

There were ferries shuttling back and forth across the river, carrying people to and from the growing community of Brooklyn. I recognized the steamboats with their single or double smokestacks, but the ones I saw here were far larger and finer than the one we took across the Chesapeake Bay.

"Those steamships carry passengers to England," Dr. Ives pointed out. "They can cross the Atlantic in ten days, half the time it used to take. Everything is happening more quickly these days, including travel. They're building a sailing ship now that is supposed to travel to China and back in seven or eight months."

"How is that possible?" Ma asked.

"Shape of the hull. Very sharply angled in front to reduce friction. Of course they'll sacrifice cargo space, but speed is of the essence it seems."

"So you live surrounded by change," Ma commented. "How do you cope with it?"

Dr. Ives laughed out loud. "I'm not sure I do cope with it very well, Maria. But every day I remind myself to expect the unexpected. And I'm never disappointed."

Dr. Ives directed the carriage away from the waterfront and back into the heart of the city. "There are a few more changes I'd like to show you," he told us.

Soon we were on the wide avenue called Broadway. Looking down it I saw the high steeple of a large church in the distance.

"That's Trinity Church. It's been entirely rebuilt since '39. Across the park to our left is City Hall."

"Look at that!" I cried out. In the middle of the park a plume of water shot fifty feet straight into the air.

"That fountain took a lot of work and money, Charley. The water you see there has been brought all the way from the Croton River, forty-one miles away."

"They brought the water forty-one miles for a fountain?"

"No, no, no, my boy," corrected the Doctor. "The water was brought for our drinking and bathing, so we wouldn't have to depend on our foul well water anymore. The fountain is meant as a celebration of the accomplishment. Now, straight ahead on the left is P. T. Barnum's American Museum."

The building the Doctor pointed out was painted bright white, covered in giant colored pictures of the attractions inside, and topped by many flags.

"What kind of museum is it?" asked my mother.

"Oh, unlike any museum you'll find anywhere else. Mr. Barnum is an entertainer more than a historian or naturalist. Inside his museum you'll find a mermaid from Fiji . . ."

"No!" Ma exclaimed.

"Yes, and a bearded lady . . ."

"Doctor Ives!"

"It's true, Maria. He's from Connecticut, you know. Barnum, I mean."

"I don't believe it!" Ma concluded.

"That he's from Connecticut, or that there's a bearded lady in the museum?" But before Ma could answer the Doctor turned and winked at me.

"And people pay to see this?" Ma asked in disbelief.

"Indeed they do," insisted the Doctor. "Along with the model of Dublin, the Siamese twins joined together since birth, and General Tom Thumb, a man only twenty-five inches tall."

Ma just sat there with her mouth open.

"Did I mention the fireworks and balloon ascents from the roof?"

"What's a balloon cent?" I asked.

"Ascent, my boy. It means rising up into the air. Imagine a great bag or sack with an opening at the bottom instead of the top. The air inside is heated and the balloon ascends or climbs into the air while still secured to the building below. You can ride in it."

"Can we go see it, Ma?"

"Not this trip, Charley," and she glared at Dr. Ives as she said it. He just smiled back.

"Let's move along, then," said the Doctor. "Here on our right is the Astor House Hotel, owned by John Jacob Astor, the richest man in America. Eight hundred rooms."

"Eight hundred? Where do the people come from?" Ma wondered aloud.

"From America and the world, Maria. Businessmen by and large. The world is coming to America and America is coming to New York. And here," the Doctor pointed as he spoke, "is how those people will all be talking to each other."

We pulled up in front of a building which was unremarkable except for a number of wires running from the building and then along a series of poles beside the street.

"It's called the telegraph. Messages are sent through the wires by means of a code, dots and dashes, which are translated back into words at the end of the line. Latest invention of Mr. Morse."

"And how fast does the message go?" Ma asked.

"Miles in the blink of an eye."

"Do you think we will ever have such a device in North Carolina?" she asked longingly. "It would be wonderful to communicate so quickly with my family in Connecticut, or with Elisha when he's away."

"I'm sure you will have it one day, Maria. It's too amazing not to spread across the whole country. Now, there's one more thing I'd like you to see. If you and Charley will step out of the carriage, I'd like you to walk down to the next building and look in the windows. I'll stay here with the carriage."

Dr. Ives helped us down from the carriage and pointed us down the sidewalk. A few steps brought us to a storefront with many windows and large letters across the top of the building.

"What does it say?" I asked.

"Brady's Daguerrian Miniature Gallery," Ma answered in a puzzled voice.

I was too busy looking in the windows to ask what that meant. The most lifelike pictures I had ever seen caught my eyes. I did not know any of the men or women in the pictures, but if they had been life-size I would have thought they were real.

"Ma, who painted these?"

"I don't believe they are paintings. They're much too detailed. I think these pictures were made with a machine that automatically captures the picture on glass."

"Is that magic?" I asked.

"No, it's not magic, but it is amazing."

Just then a bearded man in a broad-brimmed hat walked up to Ma and said, "Excuse me, ma'am."

"Yes, may I help you?"

"If you wouldn't mind. I'm a reporter for the *Aurora*, and I wondered if you would answer a few questions about the Gallery."

"A reporter? I'm not sure if I can be of much use to you. We're from out of town, and I've only just this minute looked in the Gallery. I haven't even been inside."

"That's fine. I'm just asking people for their impressions of the pictures. Where are you from?"

"North Carolina," Ma replied.

"You've come quite a way, then. Did you come to see the sights of the city?"

"No, we're on our way to visit family in Connecticut."

"I see," the reporter commented as he wrote in a small notebook. "That your husband by the carriage?"

"No, that's Dr. Ives, a family friend. My husband is back in North Carolina."

"Tending the farm?"

"Oh, no, he's a professor, not a farmer. At this moment he's somewhere in the mountains of North Carolina. Perhaps you've heard of him. Dr. Elisha Mitchell."

"He found the highest mountain," I added proudly.

"I haven't heard of him," the reporter confessed, "but what's this about the highest mountain?"

"My husband climbed and measured the Black Mountain in North Carolina in 1835, and proved it was the highest mountain east of the Mississippi."

"I thought Mt. Washington was the highest," the reporter countered.

"I'm afraid many people still mistakenly believe that, Mister . . .?"

"Whitman. Sounds like you might have an interesting story to tell, Mrs. Mitchell. Why don't you . . ."

Just then Dr. Ives walked up. "I'm sorry to interrupt the conversation, but we'd better be going now. I can't leave my carriage on the corner any longer. If you'll excuse us." He bowed slightly to the reporter and gently lead Ma by the arm back toward the carriage.

"It was a pleasure to meet you, Mrs. Mitchell," the reporter shouted as we walked away. "I hope you enjoy Manhattan!"

Once out of the reporter's hearing the Doctor confided his real motive for retrieving us. "I wasn't as worried about my carriage as I was about rescuing you from that man."

"We were fine," Ma insisted. "Did we have some reason to be worried?"

"No, not really. Did he say whom he worked for?"

"I think he said the *Aurora*."

"Just as I suspected. The *Aurora* is one the city's many penny papers, cheap publications that cater to the crowds seeking sensational stories about the worst sort of people and behaviors. I thought it best to end the interview before you found your name printed across the pages of such a paper."

"But surely I have nothing to say that would interest the type of readers you just described."

"Probably not," agreed Dr. Ives, "but it's not beyond the papers to make up the details they need to add thrills to their stories."

Soon we were back at the Doctor's home, a quiet sanctuary after the bustle of the city. Dr. Ives and my mother seemed much more relaxed once inside. My thoughts returned to the forest of ship's masts I had seen along the East River and the endless parade of persons traveling the boulevards of the city. My visions of this new world were brightened further that night by a powerful light that swept across the rooftops of the city, bright as the moon itself and coming, Dr. Ives told me, from Barnum's American Museum.

I lay awake and listened to my mother and Dr. Ives as they brought each other up to date on all that had happened in the past twenty years. Soon their talk turned to my father.

"Do you have any idea where Elisha is right now?" Dr. Ives asked.

"Not really. He's somewhere in western North Carolina. He usually covers hundreds of miles in his survey trips. He also talked about returning to the Black Mountains. For all I know that's where he is tonight."

"Have you ever thought of returning to this part of the country?"

"We've talked about it. In fact, Elisha has had offers from some of the northern universities."

"Good offers?"

"Yes, very good," Ma asserted. "But we've always turned them down."

"May I ask why?"

"In the beginning it was because Elisha was so committed to improving the University, and because he was fascinated by his explorations of North Carolina. Now it's because we feel like Carolina is our home."

"I think," said the doctor, "that your husband is very much an individual, and a man who likes to make his own way. I doubt very much if he'd be happy bumping elbows with mobs of people every day or going where someone else had already gone. It's the nature of our country today, wouldn't you say? 'The new spirit abroad . . . young, restless.' Isn't that how the papers put it?"

"Yes, I'd say that describes Elisha, except for the part about being young," Ma answered.

"Well, we're none of us getting any younger, my dear, though I'd like to think that youth is all in the mind. Shall we call it a night? I believe you'll want to get an early start in the morning."

I pretended to sleep as Ma came in and kissed me goodnight. When she lay down beside me it comforted me. *Don't leave me alone*, I thought. *That must be how Ma feels when Pa leaves her.*

* * *

Early the next morning we continued our journey. I was glad to be out of the city. New York had been exciting, but too noisy and crowded. Traveling through Connecticut was like being back home. There were forest-covered hills with small villages snuggled against them. Villages like our own Chapel Hill, yet somehow finer. The whitewashed buildings were brighter and cleaner. The roads were smoother. There were neat fences everywhere, and no town was without a church.

"Why?" I asked Ma. "Why is it prettier here?"

"It is pretty, isn't it?" she wistfully agreed.

"Are people richer here?"

"In some ways they are. There is wealth that goes beyond money, Charley, and we have no shortage of that kind of wealth in Chapel Hill, but when it comes to money I think Connecticut is better off."

"Why is that, Ma?"

"Well, there are lots of reasons."

"Like what?"

"Schools, for one thing. Connecticut has a long tradition of good schools. Then there are the rivers and the ocean. They make it easy for farmers and others to get their goods to cities like New York and Boston. And Connecticut doesn't depend on slaves like we do in the South."

"Why does that matter?"

"Every time a farmer in the South gets a little money he uses it to buy another slave. Here that same farmer uses the money to buy land or a barn or some machinery. I think he becomes richer that way, and I think he's a harder worker."

"Was your Pa a hard worker?"

She smiled at the thought of her Pa. I know she was still hurting over his loss, but remembering him now brought a light to her face.

"Oh, yes, he was a hard worker. But he wasn't a farmer, you know. He was a doctor, and doctors have their own kind of hard work to do. Don't be afraid of hard work, Charley, and don't expect somebody else to do your work for you."

The final days of our journey dragged by as if they had no end. All my desire for adventure was drowned by fatigue. Then, when I felt I could take no more and lay exhausted in my mother's lap, I heard her say, "Look, Charley, it's home!"

I sat up to see a bustling village by the sea. The ebb and flow of people and merchandise reminded me of New York City on a much smaller and more comfortable scale. Factories and warehouses crowded many of the streets, but the roads themselves were so wide that they looked nearly empty despite the people and carriages traveling through them. Out in the Thames River, many ships lay at anchor. These were not like the steamships or packet ships I had seen before. These were whaling ships, and according to my mother the town owed all its prosperity to these ancient-looking and weather-beaten craft.

A final carriage ride brought us to a quiet street lined with tall elm trees. The trees stood guard in front of stately houses with tall columns that looked like Greek temples I had once seen in a drawing.

"This is Whale Oil Row, and there's my home," said Ma.

"Is this where Grandmother lives?" I asked in disbelief.

Ma nodded as she helped me out of the carriage. An elderly woman was waiting for us at the door with a very surprised and happy expression on her face. Ma whispered, "That's your Grandmother North."

There were many hugs and tears, along with exclamations of "What in the world are you doing here?" and "It's so good to see you!" and "Can this be little Charles?" Once inside the house I sat upon my grandmother's lap and took it all in: her mellow voice which sounded as though nothing could unsettle her, the sweet smell of her perfume, the bright whiteness of her clothing. She looked back at me and smiled.

"Well, Master Charles, what do you think of your old grandmother?"

I looked at my mother for some hint about how I should answer this question, but she only smiled and raised her eyebrows to prod me to make some reply.

"I like you very much, Grandmother North," I finally answered. "You smell like flowers and you're very clean."

My mother and grandmother both burst out laughing. Grandmother had to put me down to keep from bouncing me out of her lap with her belly-shaking chuckles.

"Oh, Maria, what a funny boy you've raised."

"He's not trying to be funny, mother."

"I know, but sometimes that is the best kind of humor. When I think of some of the things you said as a child, my dear, it still makes me chuckle."

Grandmother's easy laughter won my heart immediately.

"All right, Charles, what do you think of New London?" Grandmother was almost laughing in anticipation, but I couldn't think of anything funny to say.

"It's very different from home, but so were all the other places we saw on our trip."

"He means Baltimore, and Philadelphia, and New York," added my mother.

"I can imagine," Grandmother said, "that those cities must seem unbelievably large compared to Chapel Hill. Did they frighten you?"

"No, ma'am, but I wouldn't want to live there. I didn't see any good places to play."

"Is that so. Well, I dare say you wouldn't have that problem here in New London. Wouldn't you agree, Maria?"

"Yes, mother. I had a wonderful time growing up here."

"What did you do when you were a little girl, Ma?"

"Lots of things. My sisters and I would go for boat rides on the Thames and pretend that we were floating down the actual Thames River in the original London, with Sir Walter Raleigh and Queen Elizabeth and William Shakespeare. Or we'd go on family trips to the beach in the summer."

"I think you spent more time at Buttonwood Corner than either of those places, Maria."

"You're probably right, Mother."

"What's Buttonwood Corner?" I asked.

"A street corner in town," Ma replied. "It's called Buttonwood Corner because of the Buttonwood tree that grows there."

"Did you like to climb the tree?"

"No, silly, girls didn't climb trees. Not in town, anyway. We went to Buttonwood Corner because that's where everything happens in New London."

"You know," Grandmother added, "the abolitionists gather there now to preach their sermons against slavery. Before them it was the temperance movement. There always has been something going on at that corner. You should have been there in '39 when the *Amistad* was brought to New London. I never have heard such arguing in my life as what went on between the different parties in that dispute."

"I'm not surprised. The politics may change but the love of controversy never goes away. I don't remember many arguments happening there when I was a girl. We went there because that's where we could always find our friends."

"You mean boyfriends don't you, Maria?"

Ma laughed and rolled her eyes back. "Oh, Mother, that does take me back. Whatever happened to . . ."

"John Wells?"

"Yes, John Wells! Oh, it's been so long since I thought of that boy. What is he up to these days?"

"He's married and lives in New Haven. He's a lawyer, I believe."

"It's hard to imagine him a respectable lawyer!" Ma declared.

"Yes, isn't it," Grandmother agreed. "But then who would have thought you would end up in a small town in the backwoods of North Carolina."

"It isn't the backwoods," argued Ma. "Still, when I think about what I imagined for myself as a girl, and what my life has turned out to be . . ."

"Yes, dear?"

"Well, life is full of the unexpected, isn't it?"

"Yes it is, Maria. I still wake up each day expecting your father to be with me and wishing me a good morning."

There were tears in Grandmother's eyes and Ma reached over and hugged her and held her a long time. "I miss him, too, but I think I've grown more used to being away from him over the years."

"Well, I don't envy you that. I'll take my tears as welcome payment for the many years we had together. It is difficult learning to live without him, though." Grandmother paused for a moment, lost in the thought of her husband, then suddenly snapped out of her reverie. "Charles, come here."

She motioned for me to come back to her while she reached for something on the table beside her.

"This is a something that belonged to my husband, your Grandfather North." She held one arm snugly around my waist as she spoke. "His name was Elisha, just like your father. He was always wanting to see you, you know. You would have liked him, and I'm sure he would have been proud of you."

"What do you have in your hand?" I asked.

She opened her hand slowly and there lay a large golden watch and chain. "Your grandfather wore this pocket watch almost every day he worked, and he told me that he wanted you to have it one day."

I held the beautiful metal orb in my hands and admired its heavy coolness and the intricacy of its face. "Ma said that grandfather was a doctor."

"That's right. He was especially interested in the eyes and he began the first infirmary for eye diseases in the country, right here in New London."

"He must have been smart."

"Oh, he was. I dare say that both you and your mother inherited a lot of your smarts from him."

"And from Pa," I added.

"Yes, and no doubt from your Pa as well," she agreed. "I'm sorry your father couldn't come with you to visit me."

"He's too busy trying to become famous," I informed her.

Grandmother looked very surprised at my comment and Ma was suddenly talking as fast as she could.

"What he means is that Elisha is gone exploring the mountain counties again, Mother."

"I see," she answered dryly.

"I was trying to explain to Charley why Elisha is so interested in the mountains, and I'm afraid he may not have understood everything I said."

"Oh, I wouldn't be so sure of that, dear. I think he understands very well. What else do you have to say about your father, Charles?"

"He's more interested in rocks than in people. That's what Ma says."

By now my mother was burying her face in her hands.

"Maria, I always knew you would make a good teacher for your children, but I never imagined some of the things you would be teaching them."

"Mother, things are not as Charley makes them sound."

"I'd say it sounds as if there is some disagreement between you and Elisha regarding his explorations."

Grandmother turned back to me and asked, "Charles, would you like something to eat or drink?"

I nodded enthusiastically, and she led me to her kitchen and found some biscuits for me to eat and poured a glass of water. She suggested I sit in the kitchen and enjoy the refreshments while she and my mother talked. I figured she wanted to be alone with Ma, but I was willing to do what she said for the sake of the biscuits.

"Now, Maria," I heard Grandmother saying from the other room, "tell me about you and Elisha."

"It's not as bad as you're thinking, Mother."

"And how do you know what I'm thinking? All I know is that my daughter appears without warning, without her husband, and with her son who is convinced that his father is only interested in rocks and being famous."

"You're exaggerating."

"Perhaps I am," Grandmother said. "Why don't you help me understand what's really going on?"

For a long time there was silence, then I heard the sounds of Ma crying quietly and of Grandmother comforting her. After another long silence Ma finally spoke through her sobs.

"I thought I was so strong, moving to North Carolina with Elisha the only person I knew, making a home there, surviving my grief when our first boy died in '28. When we lost Charley's little brother and Father last year, I still held on and believed that I would see better days, but now . . ."

I waited for Ma to finish.

"What, dear? Doesn't Elisha love you anymore?"

"No, Mother, that's not it. I'm sure he loves me as much as ever."

"Then what is it?" Grandmother asked.

"I'm afraid," my mother answered.

"Afraid that he'll leave you? You just said he loves you more than ever."

"No, I'm afraid that I'll lose him . . . that something terrible will happen to him on that mountain. For all I know he could be there right now, and I can't stand the thought of what could happen to him. I know it's not a rational fear, but every time he leaves me I feel like I may never see him again. I can't explain it, but that's the way it is."

There was more crying and I peeked around the corner to see Grandmother holding Ma and rocking her gently in her arms.

"There, there, my dear. It's going to be all right. My girl is trying to carry all the weight of the world without letting anyone know how she's hurting." Grandmother stopped rocking and stroked Ma's hair. "Maria, I think I understand a little of the reason for your fear."

"What is it?"

"You've lost so much in your life already . . . your babies when they died so young and now your father's death. Well, it's no wonder you fear losing something . . . someone . . . so dear to you."

"It's true, Mother. I watch him go out that door on one of his trips and I swear a part of me dies."

"And that explains your resentment of Elisha as well," Grandmother added.

"What do you mean?" Ma asked.

"Maria, it doesn't take a great deal of discernment to see that there's more than fear in your heart. There's bitterness there as well. What I picked up from Charles is only what he's heard from you. Now, tell me the truth. Isn't that so?"

"Yes, you're right. I've been upset at Elisha for leaving me alone."

"And who can blame you? Your health is not what it used to be and you've still got Charles and a home to look after . . ."

"Exactly," Ma agreed.

"But what are you going to do with your anger, Maria? Are you going to let it fester until it destroys what remains of your health? Do you no longer love Elisha?"

"Of course I love him, Mother, but what do I do with my resentment? I've talked with him about it. He knows how I feel. He knows how I worry."

"And what does he say?" Grandmother asked.

"He says I have nothing to worry about. Honestly, Mother, he still thinks he's invincible. He has the mind of a twenty-year-old in the body of a fifty-year-old."

"He's a challenge, dear, but so was your father. It's part of the nature of men to take risks and it's also the nature of women to try and reduce those risks. I know he's not perfect, dear. No man is."

"I don't expect him to be perfect."

"Are you sure?" Grandmother asked.

"I'm certain. You don't stay married for twenty-five years if you expect perfection."

"Fair enough," Grandmother conceded. "So if you put up with his imperfections then he must have some good qualities that you admire."

"Of course he does. You know that I well as I do. What are you getting at?"

"I'm trying to get you to think about your blessings for a while, Maria. I know I'm not telling you anything you don't already know, but humor me and tell me something about Elisha that you can be thankful for."

As Ma paused to think about her answer I wandered back into the room. When she saw me she held out her arms and gathered me in. She kissed me on the cheek and said, "I'm glad for the children he's given me, and that he's a good father."

"How is he a good father?" Grandmother prodded.

Ma looked a little annoyed at Grandmother, but she answered the question. "He provides well for us and makes sure the children have every opportunity to learn. He sets high standards for them and encourages them. He gives them a good example of faith in God."

"And is he a good husband to you, dear?"

"Yes, he is. He's faithful to me. He always comes back, even if he does go away for a while. He comforts me when I'm hurting. He shares his dreams with me. He tells me that he loves me."

I looked up to see that both women were smiling now.

"There, isn't that better?" Grandmother asked. "Doesn't your mother have such a pretty smile, Charles?"

"Yes, ma'am."

"All right, Mother, I will try to have a more positive outlook."

"That's my girl. Remember, Maria, Elisha isn't a bird you can put in a cage. You might keep him safe for a while, but in the end he'd only resent you. Give him his wings. He won't be with you every moment, but he will keep coming back."

My mother seemed in much better spirits in the days ahead, and she laughed more than I had heard in months. Grandmother and I came back from a walk one afternoon to find her smiling as she read a letter.

"Who is the letter from?" asked Grandmother.

"It's from Elisha. He's back in Chapel Hill."

"Well, now you can put your mind at ease. What does he say?"

"He opens with a poem by Cowper:

> T'was in the glad season of spring
> Asleep at the dawn of the day
> I dreamed what I cannot but sing
> So pleasant it seemed as I lay."

"Whatever does he mean by that, dear?"

"He means that he couldn't help but write to me. When he wrote these lines he was still in the mountains, getting ready to preach at a church. He was feeling guilty about writing me when he should be preparing his sermon."

"Well, isn't he the romantic. He does love you, Maria."

"You're right, Mother."

"What else does he say, or is it too private?"

"No, it isn't. He says, 'I rode yesterday along the same roads that you and I took ten years ago when we toured the mountains together and were on our way back home to our children. I thought of you with every familiar sight I passed, and longed to see you. We were so happy then, Maria. It would please me so much to know that you were happy today.'"

"Times are different now, aren't they, Maria?"

"So much has changed over the years. Ellen married . . ."

Ellen had been the first of my sisters to marry, and that only six months before.

". . . my health fading, Father gone . . ."

"We should be thankful we can't see the future. But every age has its trials and triumphs."

"Do you really think so, Mother?"

"Yes, I know so. You may be discouraged right now, but I guarantee you that there will be happy days ahead. Now, why don't you finish reading your letter to me."

"Elisha talks about climbing the Black Mountain again. He says he hopes this will be the last time."

"There, things are looking up already."

"He says he was surprised to find that people are actually calling it Mount Mitchell now."

"So he's getting a little of that fame he longs for, after all," Grandmother commented.

"Listen to this, Charley," my mother said, "your father is describing his walk up the mountain. 'July 8, 1844. I went up the Caney River, then up one of its branches, over the Pine Mountain ridge, then up another creek, across another ridge and up a third creek. All this took me until noon and I still had most of the mountain in front of me. I didn't reach the top until four o'clock, but was back to the Caney River by sundown. Came down most of the way by jumping from rock to rock along the creek and managed to get thoroughly wet by falling in the creek several times. It also rained heavily. Slept on wet moss on the wet ground in my wet clothes. I've never been so exhausted in my life.'"

"Do you think Pa had a good time?" I asked.

"Knowing your father, I'm sure he had a wonderful time, despite his complaints about the weather. It's a wonder he hasn't caught pneumonia, though."

Grandmother North asked how Ma knew that Pa was back in Chapel Hill.

"He says so at the end of the letter. 'August 9. Back home. This letter is more than a month old now, but better for the aging. Ellen informed me of your leaving for New London. I have sent money to Henry Purser, No. 10 John Street. Spend only what you have to, for I have none to waste. Ever coming home? Love, E.M.'"

"I believe he misses you," said Grandmother.

"Yes, I'm sure he does, as I miss him."

"When are we going home?" I asked eagerly.

"Soon, Charley."

"But you've only just gotten here," Grandmother protested.

"I know, Mother, but think how long it took this letter to get here, and how long it will take us to get back."

"Is this the same Maria that arrived here so sad and upset?"

"All right, I admit it," Ma stated. "I was very upset when I left Chapel Hill. And I still won't agree with Elisha going off without me for weeks at a time every summer . . . but you've helped me remember why I love him, and I do miss him, Mother."

"I'm glad to hear it, dear, and I wouldn't want it to be any other way. Of course you've got to be getting back home, but before you go, do we have time for one more family get-together?"

"Yes, of course."

"Good. We won't have you leaving without a going-away party."

And so, on our last evening in New London, as many of the North family as lived nearby gathered together for a farewell dinner for Ma and me. Uncle Erasmus was there along with his wife, and Aunt Eliza came as well. Much was said that I did not understand, but it was clear that Erasmus didn't think much of our new home.

"Come now, Maria, you don't really like it as much in Carolina as you pretend, do you? I mean, all that tobacco, pitch, turpentine, and pine trees? What is it that keeps you down there? I'm surprised you haven't figured out a way to get Elisha back up here years ago.

Tell him to give up on stomping around the mountains and come back to Connecticut where he can make a real name for himself."

"I think Elisha is a pretty strong-willed man, Erasmus," said Eliza.

"Must be very strong-willed to keep Maria away from us," he agreed.

"Are the people as poor and ignorant as they say?" asked Eliza.

Ma ignored Eliza's question. "You assume I would want to come back to Connecticut."

"Well of course. Wouldn't you?" asked Uncle Erasmus.

Ma didn't answer. She had a painful look on her face.

"Sis, do you mean you would rather live in Carolina?"

"It's not as simple as that."

"What does that mean? Surely you know what you do or don't like?"

Ma looked at Grandmother as if looking for help. I saw Grandmother nod and then say, "Erasmus, do you remember when you were a just a young man, not yet married . . ."

"I remember it well. It was not that long ago, as I remember."

"And you were in love with two women, as I remember."

He looked at his wife, then back at Grandmother. "So I was."

"And you came to me one day and said, 'Mother, I'm in love with two women, and I can't decide between them.' And do you remember what I told you?"

"Yes, I remember. You said, 'You can't keep them both or you'll lose them both.' You needn't say anything more, Mother. I know exactly what you're trying to say. It was the most difficult decision of my life." He paused and squeezed his wife's hand. "And the most rewarding."

Then he looked at Ma. "Sorry, Sis, I understand now what you were trying to say."

Ma nodded to show that she accepted the apology, but I was still upset at her brother.

"Uncle Erasmus, I don't see why you make fun of our home," I complained. "It's not very different. We eat the same food and everyone talks about the same boring stuff. Maybe the plates are nicer here and people wear fancier clothes, but that's the only difference."

"I'm sorry," said Erasmus. "I didn't mean to insult your home."

"And what's so special about Connecticut, anyway? It sure looks nice, but it's pretty where we live, too. And as for what you said about my Pa, he came to Carolina so he could do something no one had ever done before. I know your Pa did that, too, but what about you? Have you ever done anything that no one else did before?"

"Well, I . . . I . . . I guess not, Charles."

Suddenly I noticed that everyone was looking at me. Everyone but Erasmus, that is. He was staring down at his plate. No one was talking, either. Ma was stroking my hair and looking very pleased, and I noticed Grandmother North was smiling as well.

"I think Charles has wisdom beyond his years," she said. "It seems Maria has made as good a home in Carolina as she could have made here. I think the differences we notice don't really matter that much. Wouldn't you agree, Maria?"

"Yes, Mother, very much."

"Well, I feel a fool," said Erasmus.

"Not the first time," teased Grandmother.

"Oh, don't worry about it," Ma said sincerely. "We all take pride in the place we call home. There's nothing wrong with that. I still love New London. I wish I could have both New London and Chapel Hill. The fact is, Erasmus, if you had talked to me about Carolina just a few days ago, I would have agreed with you completely."

"I don't understand," he said.

"It may seem strange, but coming back here has helped me appreciate home more."

"Is that an insult?" asked Erasmus.

"No, of course not. It's Mother who helped straighten me out."

"Thank you, dear," said Grandmother.

They hugged each other and Eliza came over and joined in.

"Must you go back so soon, Sis? It seems like old times to have you back again. This house feels very empty at times without you and Father."

"I really wish I could stay, but I know Elisha needs me back at home. And I want so much to see him again. You understand, don't you?"

"Of course I do. You be sure and remind him how lucky he is to have you."

"I'll tell him you said so."

* * *

Looking back at our trip I can see things that were hidden from me as a child. My mother always praised the benefits of our home in North Carolina, but she never told me how much she gave up in leaving New London. It wasn't just family and friends. It was wealth and comfort and the prospect of a certain station in life. The awareness of that sacrifice helped me realize that Pa carried quite a burden in bringing my mother to Chapel Hill. It was impossible for him to provide for her according to the standard she had known in New London. Though he never said so, he must have longed to give her more of the finer things in life. I imagine it chafed him to be unable to do so.

Our journey home was like a journey back in time. Though we were traveling back to the familiar, it seemed strange now to be leaving the cleared landscapes and crowded cities of the northeast to enter the woods and villages of Carolina. The scenery wasn't the only thing that changed as we headed south. The people were dressed differently and they moved at a slower pace. Yet none of these rural and antique appearances discouraged me. I rejoiced at seeing them again, for it meant that home was near.

There was no one to meet us when our stage arrived in Chapel Hill. The town was bustling with students returning for the start of the fall term. It was late in the afternoon as we walked across the grounds of the school, and it was still hot with little breeze to stir the September air. Ma walked slowly and seemed to be taking in every bit of the scene, though she had walked past this spot for over twenty years. We were headed towards Pa's office in South Building to see if he might be there, and had stopped to rest in the shade of an old poplar tree, when all at once we saw him burst out of the building, running and yelling, "Maria!" He vaulted over one of the stone fences and didn't stop running until he had Ma in his arms.

"Thank goodness you made it back," he said, beaming.

"It's very good to be back . . . home." Ma said it with conviction and satisfaction.

"You don't know how glad I am to hear you say that. I was beginning to wonder if you were having second thoughts about coming back home."

"Really? Well now you know a little of how I feel when you're gone. But . . ."

Ma tried to continue, but couldn't seem to find the words, and there were tears in her eyes.

"Maria, what is it?" Pa asked. "Tell me what's wrong."

Ma was still unable to talk. She took my hand and Pa's hand and smiled through her tears, and kissed Pa on the cheek, and finally said, "Nothing's wrong. Not one thing. You're back home safely, and I'm here with you, and I know without a doubt that this is exactly where we are meant to be."

Pa didn't quite know what to make of Ma's earnest confessions. He stared at her intently with a bit of worry on his face, then abandoned his concerns, laughed out loud and picked her up off her feet.

"My turn!" I yelled.

"Charley, my boy," he hollered as he put Ma down and scooped me up. "Welcome home, and thank you for taking such good care of your mother. How does it feel to be such an experienced traveler?"

"Tiring," was all I could say.

"Then let me give you a ride," he replied. He shifted me up onto his shoulder, took Ma's hand, and led us towards home. I felt like I was in the trees looking down on everything around me including my mother and father.

"Hey, I can see the whole world," I informed them. "I bet I could see your mountain from up here, Pa."

"I doubt that, Charley. It's a little too far away to see, even if you are on top of the world. But do you see anything else of interest?"

"I see home," I answered, "and there's nothing nicer."

There's nothing like a journey to make the glories of home shine forth. I had seen the great cities of America, its wealth and prosperity, its energetic drive for progress, its masses of people with more being added each day, but I had seen nothing that I wanted.

Everything I desired was waiting for me in Chapel Hill: my family and friends, the quiet lanes to walk down, the woodland paths to explore, the creeks to fish in. I looked at my parents as they carried me toward our house and knew it was their hard work that had helped make this village such a wonderful home.

In my memory I look back on the grounds of the University and see three buildings surrounding a rectangle of grass and trees not more than one hundred yards across. It is such a small plot of land, yet so much of importance has happened there over the years. The cities may be full of people and commerce, but it is the villages that claim the prize in my eyes. There every man counts for something and because of that almost every man and woman does something worthy. Like the border between woods and field they are a place where all the variations of life meet and mix and thrive. They are close enough to the cities to benefit from their advances yet close enough to the country to flourish in the fertile loam of the frontier. Such was our home.

Chapter Nine

Clingman

What giant things come from small beginnings. A seed falls to the ground, and though tiny produces a towering tree. An invisible germ is passed to an unsuspecting person who develops a deadly case of pneumonia. Two strangers exchange a passing glance, which leads to conversation, romance, and love. So the small leads to the great, and this may work for good or for evil.

In the fall of 1855 Thomas Clingman went for a walk and then wrote about it. For most people this mattered little, but for my family his walk shook the world. His steps were like an earthquake because he walked across the peaks of the Black Mountains and wrote that my father had failed to measure the highest peak.

Who can judge what is truly significant? Even regarding my own interests, my judgments change with time and experience. How much more difficult to say what really matters to another man. Remember that before you decide the merits of measuring and naming mountains.

Thomas Clingman who walked along the Blacks was a former student of Pa's, having graduated from the University in 1832. He graduated first in his class, but he was no shy bookworm. He was an ambitious, driven statesman who became a lawyer and then a political fixture in western North Carolina. Clingman was a big man with bigger goals.

I can't think of him without being reminded of Pa, yet for every similarity between the two of them there was an equal distinction. In the end I came to see him as a nearly perfect foil for my father. Clingman was the student and Pa the Professor. Clingman was the native Carolinian with Indian blood and Pa the well bred New Englander. Clingman was a politician with eyes on the highest offices, but my father never attempted politics. One bearded, one clean-shaven. One in the prime of his manhood, one in his golden years. Both were large men with their eyes on the high peaks and on public recognition, so I suppose it was inevitable that their paths would become entangled in the laurel thickets of the Blacks.

Mitchell's Peak

It was a different mountain when Clingman climbed it twenty years after Pa. A horse trail extended all the way from the North Fork Swannanoa Valley to the southern peaks of the Blacks. Clingman went to the peak at the end of this trail, a peak the locals felt was highest and which they called Mitchell's Peak. He measured the pressure with a barometer, just as Pa had done, then struck out along the ridge of the Blacks to another peak three miles north. He took another reading there and found that the pressure measured .19 inches lower than before. Each .01 inch of drop in pressure represented an 11-foot gain in elevation, so Clingman claimed that the more northerly peak was 209 feet higher and was in fact the highest peak in the range.

We were sitting down to eat lunch several weeks later when Pa stormed into the house very upset.

"Maria! Maria!"

"Elisha, what's the matter?" She set the food on the table and headed to the door, but Pa was already striding quickly into the dining room. His face was strained, and he was out of breath.

"Look at this article from the *Asheville News that* Governor Swain gave me today. It's written by Thomas Clingman to Joseph Henry of the Smithsonian Institution, and it describes an expedition he made along the peaks of the Black Mountains."

"What's so remarkable about that? More and more people are making excursions there."

"What's remarkable is that Clingman claims to have measured the highest peak, and he says I have never been there." With that Pa threw the paper on the table and slumped into his chair. His eyes were somewhere far away, but Mother's eyes were on him and her face was tense. I reached for the paper, just beating Margaret to it.

"When did this happen?" Margaret asked.

I read quickly to find out as many details as I could. "According to the article it was on September 8 of this year. Let me read it to you. 'My dear sir' . . . he's addressing Mr. Henry of the Smithsonian . . . 'you know there has been controversy for some time regarding which is higher: the White Mountains of New Hampshire or the Black Mountains of North Carolina. Professor Mitchell has proven, it appears, that part of the Black Mountain is higher than

Mt. Washington, the highest point of the White Mountains of New Hampshire.'"

"What does he mean by 'appears'?" Pa objected. "Does he mean I never demonstrated beyond doubt that the Black Mountain is highest? And this business about dividing the mountain into parts . . . he's only trying to reserve the highest part for himself."

"Aren't you being too hard on him?" Ma asked.

"I don't think so. Keep reading, Charley."

"He says conversations between the two of you lead him to believe that you had never measured the highest part of the mountain."

"There!" Pa shouted. "See what I mean. He's making up conversations to suit his own purpose. How could he possibly conclude that I had not been on the highest point?"

"But you and Thomas have spoken about the mountain, haven't you?" asked Ma. "And didn't you have some doubts yourself about whether you'd reached the highest part of the mountain when you first climbed it?"

"Thomas and I have talked," Pa answered curtly. "When he was a student we shared ideas about which mountain might be highest. But that was before I ever climbed the Black. Since he graduated we rarely see each other. We can't have written more than a few letters to each other over the past twenty years. I never remember telling him I had not been on the highest part of the mountain. And as for my doubts, I can assure you I had no doubts after climbing the mountain in '44."

I read on. "Clingman says that it was so difficult to climb the mountain twenty years ago that you couldn't reach certain parts of the range or be sure of your position. That's true enough, isn't it?"

"The facts are true but his conclusion is wrong. It was difficult, but that did not keep me from reaching the high peak."

"I believe you," Margaret said as she bent over Pa and hugged his neck.

"Thank you, dear. I appreciate your support, but I'm concerned about the opinions of the uninformed people who will read this in the papers."

"Clingman gives you credit for your previous measurements of the mountain," I offered.

"And then slights my efforts by saying he believes my measurements understate the actual height of the mountain."

Ma, Margaret and I looked at each other and agreed wordlessly that it would be difficult to mollify Pa's anger. He could be as hard as any rock when he encountered opposition to his ideas. It was plain to see now that his personal identification with the Black Mountain had crystallized into diamond-like hardness over the past twenty years.

I read through the article quickly, searching for some weakness in Clingman's claim. I thought I had found one.

"He says the barometer readings on the two peaks only differed by nineteen-hundredths of an inch. How can that be held up as proof that one peak is higher than another?"

"That nineteen-hundredths of an inch amounts to over two hundred feet of elevation. That might as well be a mile when it comes to these kinds of investigations."

"Maybe his measurements were inaccurate," Margaret suggested.

"No, he confirms the reliability of his instrument. No one will question his readings. The only question is whether I was ever on the peak he has now shown to be the highest."

"Let's hear his description, then," suggested Ma. "Read it out loud, Charley."

"All right." I returned to the article. "A short ridge runs northwest from the Pinnacle on the Blue Ridge to the Potato Knob on the Black Mountain range. From there it is one mile north to Mt. Mitchell or Mitchell's Peak, a half-mile further to Mt. Gibbes, then a descent for one mile to a point five hundred feet lower than Mt. Mitchell. Next one climbs a hill shaped like a sugar loaf to within 150 feet of the elevation of Mitchell's Peak, only to descend again. The trail proceeds up and down in a northerly direction for two miles, until one finds himself in a natural grassy meadow with magnificent views. From this meadow or prairie it is only necessary to climb a few hundred feet to reach the summit of the high peak, covered in balsam-firs stunted by their exposure to the elements."

"How does that fit with your recollection?" Ma asked my father.

Pa was red and stuttering in his exasperation. "By his description . . . the peak I climbed . . . the one the locals call Mt. Mitchell

. . . would have to be at the very southern end of the range, with his high peak three or four miles farther north. It's impossible for me to believe I was that far south."

"Could your memory be mistaken? It has been nearly twelve years." Ma was braver than I thought to suggest such an explanation.

Margaret was quick to come to Pa's defense. "Ma, whose side are you on? You sound like you believe Mr. Clingman."

"I'm only trying to help your father understand why Thomas might believe he had been on a different part of the mountain. He and your father have always had the highest regard for one another, and I would hate to see that lost because of rivalry or a misunderstanding."

Pa took a deep breath and let it out. "You're right, of course, Maria." We all relaxed a bit. "Thomas is a good man, and has been a friend. I'm sure this is something that can be worked out amicably."

"How?" I asked.

"I'll write Mr. Henry at the Smithsonian Institution, and lay out my understanding of the situation. I believe that Thomas will withdraw his claim to the high peak when he understands that I was there before him."

"Will you have to go back to the Black Mountain?" I asked.

"Charles, there's no need to suggest that right now," Ma replied pointedly, and I could see that Pa felt the hardness in her voice as well.

He reached over and took my mother's hand reassuringly. "Don't worry, Maria. This is something that I should be able to correct with a letter or two. Now, I think I'd better be returning to class, and so had you, Charley."

"What about your dinner?" asked Margaret.

"Thank you, but it's time to be going, and I'm not the least bit hungry. See you all at supper."

He kissed Ma and headed out the door quickly. The house was quiet again, but it was the quiet of uncertainty.

Before the week was over Pa had written his reply to Mr. Henry at the Smithsonian. He shared the letter with us one evening before posting it. It was November and a fire was blazing in the study fireplace as we sat and listened. Pa recounted how he and the guides had climbed Yeates's Knob in '35 and viewed the entire eastern ridge of the Black Mountain in profile. They had decided which of the numerous knobs and peaks was highest, settling on one which was "conical and covered on top with a prairie." They headed towards this peak the next day, but Pa indicated that when they arrived on the mountaintop they found themselves on a knob covered with the balsam fir tree. He concluded that they had ended up north of the desired target.

Next Pa described his ascent of the mountain in '44, coming from the town of Burnsville in the north once more because he was certain that the high peak was far from the southern end of the mountain chain. This time, he said, he was not disappointed in reaching his goal.

Pa concluded that the local mountain people had, in his absence, given his name to a more southerly peak which he had never visited. "I would be honored," he read, "to be in that illustrious company of men who deserve to be named among the peaks of the Black Mountain. Men like Clingman, who for breadth of experience among the Blacks deserves it more than any, or Gibbes, or Swain. But do not give my name to a mountain which I never visited and for which I possess no claim."

"Well spoken," commended Ma as we all applauded.

"Thank you. I think it will do," my father replied. "I've asked Mr. Henry to share the letter with Thomas Clingman. With any luck this matter will be straightened out in just a few weeks."

But the weeks turned into months and Pa's hopes were disappointed. Rather than agreeing with my father's arguments, Clingman wrote back that Pa should revisit the mountain so that he might see for himself where the high peak lay. Clingman insisted that Pa's description of the mountain only confirmed his belief that Pa had never been on the high peak.

One afternoon I came in from class to find Pa and Governor Swain sitting in the study in serious conversation. As I passed by the Governor called me in.

"Charles," he said, "I'm trying to talk some sense into your father. Lend me your support here a minute. Don't you think it's time he published a reply to Clingman's report?"

"Yes, sir," I answered. I wasn't about to disagree with the University president.

Pa responded quickly. "Governor, if you had given me a chance, I would've told you that I've already prepared an article for publication."

"Good, I'm glad to hear it. Where are you submitting your article?"

"I was thinking about asking the *University Magazine* to print it."

Swain was not enthusiastic. "No disrespect to the *University Magazine*, but do you think that will have much effect? How large can its audience be?"

"I don't know," Pa admitted. "I was thinking more of its official standing and the ease of getting the article published."

"Think about this, Elisha. John Hyman at the *Asheville Spectator* would love to print your article.. in Clingman's own town . . . in the very heart of the region where the controversy occurred."

"Why would he?" I asked.

"Because he's a Whig, Charles, and extremely partisan. Since Clingman switched to the Democratic Party, Hyman likes nothing more than to find reason to criticize him."

"And how will Clingman respond to that?" Pa asked, squirming a little in discomfort.

"It's politics, and he's a politician. He's used to it."

"I know you speak from experience, Governor, but I don't want this to be a personal attack."

Swain smiled. "That's why you're a professor and Clingman is the politician. But let me warn you, he's an expert in rhetoric and debate. Did he hesitate to publish his report in a notable forum? No, he published it in the nation's capitol!"

"And in the *Asheville News*," I added.

"Exactly!" shouted Swain. "A paper as partisan in its support of the Democrats as the *Spectator* is in support of the Whigs. Clingman has already brought the debate to Asheville. You didn't start it, Elisha. He did."

Pa frowned as he thought about Swain's words, but before long the frown gave way to a look of determination. "You're right. This debate needs to be brought before the public, and Asheville seems the best place to do it. Would you a write a letter of introduction to Mr. Hyman to accompany my article?"

"Not that you need one, but I'll be glad to do it," replied Swain.

The *Spectator* printed Pa's article in June of 1856. Once again he stated his view that he was north of the high peak in 1835 but reached it in '44. He claimed this was the same peak now described by Clingman as the highest point in the Black Mountain range. The peak called Mt. Mitchell by the locals was too far to the south and was not the mountain he had climbed on any of his previous visits. The reaction to the article was predictably mixed: each man's supporters held their ground and the debate continued. But the next volley, fired by Clingman, blasted large holes in my father's case. Clingman's reply was printed in the *Asheville News* in July and also circulated widely as an eight-page pamphlet. The congressman seized on inconsistencies in Pa's account and used them with a lawyer's skill to ridicule Pa's claim to the high peak.

I came into the dining room late one morning during the summer recess to find my mother and Margaret intently reading a newspaper.

"What's so interesting?" I asked.

"It's an article by Clingman in the *Asheville News*," Margaret replied. "He's answering Pa's statements in the *Spectator* last month."

"What's he say?"

"Nothing that Pa liked."

"So he's seen it already?"

"Oh, yes," my mother answered. "He brought the paper home last night. If you'd been up earlier you would have seen how upset he was. I'm afraid Congressman Clingman doesn't exactly fight fair in this letter."

"Can I read it?" I begged.

"Wait your turn!" Margaret demanded. "Listen to this. 'Though I have no doubt that Professor Mitchell did ascend the Black Mountain from the Caney River valley, he never describes whose house he left from or the names of the men who guided him. How can one confidently accept the conclusions of a man whose descriptions are so vague?' Ma, he's as much as calling Pa an idiot."

Ma was just shaking her head, weighed down in her certainty that nothing good could come of the continuing conflict.

"What else does he say against Pa?" I asked Margaret.

"He says that in 1846 a surveyor named Blackstock found a long piece of wood with a groove in it on Mt. Gibbes. The surveyor supposed it had been used by Pa as a water level and left there by Pa on his 1844 ascent of the Blacks. Clingman says that proves Pa was far south of the high peak in 1844, since Mt. Gibbes is right beside the peak the locals call Mt. Mitchell."

"That doesn't sound good. Does he say anything more?"

"He says it would be difficult to change the name of the current Mt. Mitchell since it has been known by that name for nearly twenty years."

"Sure he doesn't want the name changed," I charged sarcastically. "He's more than willing to leave that as it is and claim the name of Mt. Clingman for the high peak."

"Margaret, read the last part to him," Ma requested.

"All right. 'I regret that this controversy has arisen between Professor Mitchell and myself. If the Professor will return to the mountain, I am certain that he will see with his own eyes that he has never yet been upon the highest peak. If he ever was there, he has never described the high peak with any degree of accuracy.'"

"No wonder Pa was upset," I said.

Ma was shaken. "Upset is not the word, Charley. He was angry, of course, but he was almost frantic. I think he feels betrayed . . . and fearful."

"What's he afraid of?" I asked. "Not Thomas Clingman?"

"No, not him. He's afraid of losing his reputation and his claim to the Black Mountain. Your father is a proud man, and though he may be important here in Chapel Hill, the truth is that his reputation is limited. His fame, if you can call it such, rests upon his measurement of that mountain."

She was right. Pa feared that he might lose a dear possession. If he had made other significant discoveries, held some high office, or written a noteworthy book, then this loss might not seem so great. But he had achieved none of these things, and Pa wanted the recognition that any of them might bring him. It's easy for me to say he should have felt a sense of accomplishment for all he meant to our family and the University, but in the end what matters is how he felt about it.

Mitchell's Peak

I had never seen Pa in such a frame of mind as he was in the days that followed the publishing of Clingman's July article. Older members of the community said they had seen Pa in a similar mood before, but not in years. They recalled the debates in the newspapers with Bishop Ravenscroft during Pa's early years in North Carolina. There had also been a disagreement with Professor Green, who wanted to allow the students to attend church in the community rather than at the University. They all agreed that his temper now exceeded anything they had seen before.

We expected Pa to write a quick reply to Clingman's attack, but day followed day with no new article. He said little, muttered to himself often, and lost all of his usual sense of humor. Nothing that any of us did seemed to affect his somber mood. It finally got to Ma one evening at the dinner table. No one was talking, the only sound was the clinking of spoons in the soup bowls, and Pa kept looking at the table with a glazed expression. Suddenly Ma threw down her napkin and spoke sternly.

"Elisha Mitchell, I've had enough. It's been two weeks, and I'm tired of seeing you like this. Now get on with whatever it is you're going to do."

Pa didn't answer. Margaret and I knew exactly what was going on, but Pa was still in a daze.

"What's wrong, Maria? What are you talking about?"

"I'm talking about the terrible mood you've been in ever since you read that article by Thomas Clingman. Look at yourself. You wander about like a crazy man talking to yourself all day. You don't smile. You don't talk to us. You're lost in another world, a world of worry and bitterness to look at you."

"It's true I've been preoccupied," Pa admitted.

"And it's time you got on with life," Ma continued.

"This debate is about an important part of my life," he argued.

"And this family is also an important part of your life," she insisted.

Margaret saw they were at an impasse. "Pa, listen to her. This argument with Clingman is wearing you down. You haven't been yourself at all lately, and if it keeps up I'm afraid it might hurt your health. Whatever you're going to say to Clingman, go ahead and say it and then get over it. We want you to be the man we've always known."

He wouldn't look at us. I'd never seen him so sad, or at such a loss for words. Ma reached for his hand and squeezed it, then said softly, "We will always love you, dear, no matter what mountains are or are not named after you. *You* are our mountain, and always will be."

And Pa smiled, only a little at first, but then widely, and then he laughed. And we all came out from behind the shadow of our mountain man into the warmth of the sun, and I saw Ma glowing in the rays of that sun and knew that she was a mountain as well, the Grandmother Mountain to his Grandfather, the sturdy Table to his sharp Hawksbill, the green and flowered Roan to his sometimes dark and cold Black Mountain.

"I've been a fool," Pa confessed. "I've been so upset by that article from Clingman that I've become obsessed with answering him. I'm sorry. Believe me, I'm just as ready as the rest of you to put it behind me." He smiled as he held tightly to Ma's hand with both of his. But then his smile disappeared and his voice trembled. "It's just that when I think about all that I've invested in that mountain . . . the weeks of vacation spent getting there and back . . . my own money used to finance the trips . . . the sweat I've poured out climbing those hills . . . and when I think of all that effort being shoved aside because a man spent one day there walking along a trail someone else had made, I just . . . I just . . . ."

His voice trailed off and he never finished the sentence. It looked as if he might give in to his obsession, but just as we began to fear that we had lost him he smiled again and said, "Don't worry. I'm back with you. I'm going to write a reply and then move on to other things, and that includes paying more attention to all of you."

"And just how soon can we expect this letter to be finished?" my mother asked warily.

"Surely by Christmas!" Pa declared.

"Elisha, I'm warning you . . ."

But Pa was laughing before Ma could finish. "I'll start on it tonight. I promise."

He kept his word and before the week was over he had finished his reply. It was published in late August as the students were returning to town from their summer recess. It was much talked about, and for good reason, because it was unlike anything he had ever written before. His article was not a scholarly report on the Black

Mountains; it was a personal attack against Clingman. It yielded no evidence of the admiration that Pa once held for his former student. Instead it dripped with sarcasm and barely concealed loathing for the Congressman. Pa had held back none of the emotions with which he had struggled for weeks. He loosed them in print, which only hardened and sharpened them. The words revealed a man I saw only on occasion and always dreaded: the cynical Elisha Mitchell. I read and wondered why Ma had not done something to alter the harsh tone of the letter. Then I remembered how stridently she had commanded Pa to write, and understood how difficult it would have been for her to raise any objection that might hinder his effort.

I was not the only one who felt uncomfortable with the language of the letter. Dr. James Phillips, Pa's long-time friend and fellow professor, cared nothing for the political posture that had been promoted by Governor Swain. He made that point clear as he visited with us one evening after the publication of Pa's letter.

"I hear that your article is being reprinted in pamphlet form," Phillips remarked as my parents, Margaret, and I sat awkwardly in the study.

"Yes, that's true," Pa replied. "Some of my supporters offered to pay for the printing. If Clingman can go to such lengths, so can I."

"That's true enough," Phillips hesitantly agreed.

"Come now, James. Tell me what's on your heart. You didn't come over for chitchat, did you?"

Phillips had suggested that he and my father speak alone about the letter, but Pa insisted that there was no need to hide the discussion from his family. Dr. Phillips now had the awkward burden of speaking about a delicate issue in front of his friend's family.

"All right, Elisha, I'll try and be as honest with you as I can, but remember that I'm speaking to you as a friend . . . not an enemy."

"I understand that. Go ahead."

"I think you've erred in making such a personal attack on Thomas Clingman," Phillips charged. "Do I have to say it, Elisha? It wasn't a Christian thing to do."

"I was speaking the truth, James. I don't believe there's any fault in that. What in particular are you objecting to?"

Phillips pulled out the article and his reading glasses and quickly found one of the lines he considered offensive.

"Here, Elisha. You say that Clingman falsified documents in order to make his argument. You're calling him a liar."

"That's nothing more than what he's already said about me!" Pa answered hotly.

"Even if he did, does that make it right for you to do the same?"

Pa began to shout back, then caught himself. "You're right. His error would not give me the right to do the same. But you're assuming that I was mistaken when I claimed he falsified documents, and I wasn't mistaken!"

"Explain that," Phillips asked.

"As I said in the article," Pa continued, "Clingman quoted me as saying that I had taken the ridge between the north and middle forks of Caney River to the high peak. That much is true. But on his own he added the parenthesis, 'or Cat-tail,' after the word 'north,' implying that I claimed to have taken the ridge just south of the Cat-tail fork."

"And is that wrong?" asked Phillips.

"Yes, it's wrong!" Pa was exasperated, but he took a moment to compose himself and then continued. "James, let me give you a geography lesson. There are several streams that run down the western side of the Black Mountain. They generally run towards the west and empty into the Caney River, which runs north. Between each of these streams there are ridges . . . sometimes one and sometimes more. The Cat-tail fork is the most northerly of the streams that empty into the Caney. The north and middle forks which I mentioned are below the Cat-tail. If I had meant to say the Cat-tail fork I would have said so. My guides lived at the Cat-tail fork, and they would surely have called the fork by that name if we had crossed it. Clingman is changing the names to confuse his readers, just as he has confused you. I wasn't on the ridge below the Cat-tail fork, but that's what he wants you to believe."

"I see," Phillips said without confidence. I was having a hard time following the argument as well.

"Let me give you another instance," Pa continued. "Clingman quotes me again, saying that I claimed the high peak lies at the head of the Caney River. He then goes on to criticize me for vagueness. In fact what I said was that the high peak lies at the head of the Caney River . . . several miles north of the southern end of the Black

Mountain. He's taking my words, carefully editing them, and then using them to attack me."

"I can understand why you're upset at him, Elisha. I just meant to say that I didn't think it was in keeping with your character to make such a personal attack upon him."

"I explained to you how he falsified my accounts . . ."

"I'm not talking about that. I'm referring to your calling him 'wicked, unjust, and not worthy to be trusted.'"

Pa's face reddened, but to his credit he considered all his friend had to say before replying. "I'll grant you that I may have gone too far in attacking him personally."

"Good," Phillips declared.

"But," my father continued, "I want to remind you how he took the letters I sent him privately, which I never published, and then published those letters himself with the excuse that I had intended them for publication."

"Very unfair," said Phillips.

"I was speaking from memory in those letters. I hadn't been able to review the written report of my journey. But Clingman took pieces of those unpublished letters and used them to ridicule me."

"Elisha, I can't argue with what you've said. Your position is entirely reasonable. But I'm speaking to you as a friend, with your interests at heart. The arguments you're making in the papers aren't good arguments. They are only making you look foolish in the eyes of the public."

"Are you serious, James?"

"Listen to him, Elisha." It was Ma's first comment during the entire discussion.

"All right," Pa said. "Go ahead."

"First of all there's the description of the high peak itself. You began by describing it as a conical peak with a prairie on top, but now you've changed your own opinion on its appearance, and your description coincides with Clingman's. The conical peak you originally described is felt to be a likeness of Mt. Mitchell, not the high peak."

"How well could you describe something you haven't seen at all in twelve years, James? I couldn't accurately describe the Asheville courthouse to you, but there's no doubt that I've been there. But go on. What's next?"

"There's the whole business about the location of the county line. You insisted that the high peak was near the Yancey-Buncombe line . . ."

"When the state established Yancey County, the legislation said that the county line ran across the highest point of the Black Mountain."

"But now we know that the county line is actually several miles south of the high peak . . ."

"Yes, I know," Pa interrupted. "It actually crosses at the Potato Knob at the very southern end of the range."

"Why does that matter?" Margaret asked.

"Because," said Phillips, "Clingman uses that misconception to imply that your father was really at Mt. Mitchell, near the county line, instead of on the high peak further north."

"As much as I hate to admit it, your points are good ones. Is that all of them?" Pa asked hopefully.

"I'm afraid not. There's one more problem," said Phillips.

"Carry on, then," Pa said with a wave of his hand.

"It's the subject of your guides. You don't have any testimony from your guides, Elisha. With it your case would be much stronger, but without it the public will be more doubtful."

"You're right, of course. One of the things I plan to do is try and contact them. I do have one small problem there, however."

"What's that?" Phillips asked.

"I don't remember the names of the men who guided me in '35."

"How can that be?" Phillips exclaimed.

"Really, James, do you have to ask that?" It was Ma again. "You should know how absent-minded Elisha is."

"The fact is I didn't write their names down," Pa admitted, "and over the years I've just forgotten."

Dr. Phillips sat there with his mouth open and said nothing. I was shocked by Pa's revelation as well.

"It's been over twenty years," Pa said in self-defense. Everyone was silent. "Well, James, what are you suggesting I do? Concede the argument to Clingman?"

"I think you should stop arguing in the papers."

"Here, here!" Ma agreed.

"And do what instead?" Pa demanded.

"Honestly, I don't know. But your present tactics aren't working, Elisha. Anything would be better. Perhaps you need to give it some time before pursuing it further."

"I'm afraid time only works in Clingman's favor," Pa stated. "The more time, the more maps are printed with Clingman's name on them."

"I know what you're saying, but each exchange in the paper seems to be hurting you more than helping you."

Dr. Phillips' words were prophetic. It was Clingman who recorded a guide's testimony before Pa, and that led to another exchange of arguments in the papers which did more to damage my father's case. Clingman interviewed William Riddle, who had led Pa to the mountaintop in '44, and Riddle said that Pa had indeed left a water level on the mountain. It was Riddle's opinion that he and Pa had been on the peak known as Mt. Mitchell rather than the high peak identified by Clingman.

Interest in the Mitchell-Clingman debate was widespread, and the University discussed it as much as any other part of the state. It was bound to enter the classroom, so I was not surprised when McLean brought it up one morning after one of my father's mineralogy lectures.

"Excuse me, Dr. Mitchell, but could I ask you a question?"

"Yes, Mr. McLean."

"Well, we've all been reading the exchange of letters between you and Congressman Clingman."

"So I've finally gotten you to read then?"

When the laughter died down McLean replied, "Yes, sir. As I was saying, the entire class has been reading the letters in the papers . . ."

"Class, is this true? All of you have been reading the papers?" There were nods and verbal assents all around. "And without actually being given an assignment? Well, this is a day to remember. Mr. McLean, please continue. This is getting more interesting by the minute."

McLean wasn't sure how to proceed, but he tried anyway. "Dr. Mitchell, my point is, the arguments you and Congressman Clingman have made in the press haven't really settled the issue. The arguments go back and forth, and I personally believe you have made excellent points in your letters . . ."

"Thank you, Mr. McLean."

"But the debate still goes on. The public and the press don't seem satisfied that either of you has made a fully convincing case."

"The press," replied my father sternly, "will never be satisfied. They love a good fight and would be happy to see it go on forever."

"Or at least until the public grows tired of it," interjected another student.

"Exactly," agreed Pa. "Now, Mr. McLean, back to your point. I agree that the debate has gone on much too long. I would be more than happy to see it end. Did you have a suggestion regarding how to end it?"

"Well, yes, now that you mention it." At this the entire class burst into applause and the surprised McLean looked like he didn't know whether to take a bow or flee. Pa just leaned back against his desk and grinned.

"Go on, Mr. McLean."

"You need to go back to the mountain."

Suddenly the entire class was cheering, I along with them, and Pa stood now with his arms folded across his chest and his mouth half-open in consternation. He soon broke out of his reverie and motioned us back into our seats. He scratched his neck for a while then asked us all, "Why do I need to go back to the mountain?"

I could guess what Pa was thinking. It would take a week of unpleasant travel to get to the Blacks, some period of time in the area of the mountain, then another week to get back home. Most of his precious summer would be gone. There was the expense of the trip, and there was the matter of my mother's reaction to his being gone again. He needed a very good reason to go.

McLean gave him his reason. "You could perform a more accurate measurement of the elevations of the peaks. Everyone agrees that the barometric method employed up until now is not entirely accurate . . ."

"There were very good reasons why I used the barometer, Mr. McLean."

"I understand, sir. With no trail up the mountain you had no other choice. But now you could run a line of levels up the trail from the Swannanoa Valley. I believe a more accurate measurement would prove once and for all that Mitchell's Peak is the highest mountain east of the Mississippi."

The class was quiet as we waited to see how Pa reacted to McLean's idea. Pa was busy scratching his neck and looking down at the floor. After some awkward moments he looked up and said, "Mr. McLean, I am intrigued by your suggestion. I will give it my due consideration, and I appreciate your thoughts on the matter." Then, lest we take the matter too seriously, he added, "And I especially appreciate that you have all taken to reading outside of your assignments. Class dismissed."

McLean was the center of attention after class. There must have been a dozen of his classmates congratulating him and questioning him as he exited. I waited around until all the other students had left, then walked up to Pa.

"So, Charley, I saw you clapping and cheering with all of your classmates. You must think McLean's idea is a good one."

"Well, I believe he's right that a more accurate measurement would be helpful."

"Have you thought about how long it would take to run a line of levels to the top of the Blacks, even with a trail?"

I had to admit I had no idea, so my father explained the process. The measurement would have to begin at a benchmark of known elevation. In the case of the Black Mountains, that would probably be somewhere in the Swannanoa Valley at an elevation three to four thousand feet below the peaks. Pa said a survey for railroad work done in the valley should provide a benchmark. A leveling instrument with a spirit level and a rod with ruled measurements on it were the only equipment needed. One man operated the level, sighting through it or across it to take a reading from the rod held upright by his assistant. The rodman would begin at the benchmark. The leveler would set his instrument some fifty to one hundred feet up the mountain and take a reading from the rod on the benchmark, determining the height of the leveling instrument. The rodman would then take a new position some fifty to one hundred feet above the leveler, and another reading would be taken. This process added time but increased the accuracy of the measurements. Now it was the rodman's turn to stay put, at a position called the turning point, while the leveler carried his instrument up the mountain beyond the rodman to a new instrument position where the whole process was repeated. This would continue methodically up the entire mountain. The height of the readings was added to the height of the benchmark to determine the elevation of the mountain.

"Charley, I'm not sure how long it would take to run a line of levels to the peaks. It might take weeks."

I told him I knew there were other obstacles to the trip. Then I asked him if that meant he wasn't going.

"I didn't say that," he said emphatically. "I was sincere when I said I would consider it. But Charley, don't mention this to your mother." He squeezed my shoulder as he said it.

I didn't tell Pa, but I wanted him to go back. I wanted to go with him. I was waiting until he made his decision before I began lobbying him for that privilege.

In the weeks that followed there were many who urged Pa to take McLean's suggestion and return to the Black Mountains. The proponents ranged from the washerwomen at the school to Governor Swain. Some of them made very strong arguments, but countering them all were the practicalities of the trip and my mother's strong opposition.

I understood her reasons. I'd heard her tell Pa on several occasions that it would be too much of a strain on him, that they could not afford it, and that she was not ready for him to be gone again for weeks. It seemed the matter was at a stalemate. Time went by without any further discussion of the trip, and eventually it faded from my thoughts.

Chapter Ten

Christmas

Soon it was December and classes were dismissed for the Christmas holiday. The Mitchell's gathered together for a Christmas unlike any we could remember or would ever know again. The last of our family had arrived only briefly before snow began falling. Ellen and her husband, Dr. John Summerell, had just ridden in from Salisbury and we accused them of bringing the snow with them. Mary and her husband, Richard Ashe, lived in Chapel Hill and were already present along with Margaret and me. The only ones missing were Eliza and her husband, who could not come from their home in Texas.

The Mitchell clan settled in and watched the snow fall endlessly. It was the worst winter storm that our town could remember. Travel was out of the question. Outdoor activities were very limited due to the bitter cold, but indoors the warmth of family ties and Christmas spirit melted away the wintry chill and gave us an unexpected present: time together to reflect on the past and our hopes for the future.

Ma and Pa were in high heaven to have their house full again. Though she tired easily, Ma happily scurried from one chore to another. Pa held court with the men in the study, where Margaret was likely to be found as well. We covered every topic obscure and popular, from Buchanan's presidency to Thoreau's *Walden*, from John Brown's abolitionist attacks in Kansas to the Dred Scott case, from California's gold to our very own Christmas tree. The Christmas tree was Margaret's doing.

"A tree, dear? Inside?" was all Ma could say.

"What kind of tree?" asked our resident botanist.

"Any kind of evergreen will do," answered Margaret. "A pine, or holly, but I thought a cedar would look best."

Soon a three-foot cedar sapling was mounted and perched on a table in the study. Margaret went to great effort to decorate it. She wired small candles to the branches and made strings of holly berries that wrapped around the tree. There were also ribbons and paper flowers and gilded paper stars. Everyone admired it.

"It smells wonderful, and I love all the colors," said Ma.

"I've never seen a tree look so beautiful," admired Pa, "but where did you get the idea?"

"From *Godey's Lady's Book*. Haven't you seen their article about the Christmas tree, Ma?"

"No, I must have missed that one."

"They had an illustration of Queen Victoria and Prince Albert with their tree. It's all the fashion now."

"I like it," said Pa, "and imagine how it would look and smell if you had one of the balsam fir trees from the Black Mountain."

"You're hopeless," said Ma, throwing up her arms and heading back into the kitchen.

It wasn't long before the talk in the study turned to the Clingman-Mitchell controversy. All of the arguments were debated again, and the papers were thoroughly criticized for their role in the affair. It was a very partisan group, of course, and the outcome of the discussion was never in doubt. Everyone agreed that Pa should not give up his claim to the high peak. There was also agreement that Pa had nothing to gain by further debate in the press.

"Then what should I do?" he asked in frustration.

Everyone was silent. Pa's brooding countenance told me he had ideas of his own, but he was keeping them to himself. We heard Ma's voice calling from the kitchen, "All right, everyone, it's time to stir the plum pudding!"

The Mitchell siblings and Pa all rose up in unison, leaving Mary and Ellen's husbands sitting alone and baffled.

"Come on, then," Ellen coaxed as she took John Summerell's hand and pulled him from his chair.

"What's the occasion?" asked John.

"Everyone has to take a turn stirring the pudding. That includes you as well, Richard."

"Is it that much work to make this pudding?" asked Richard.

"No, silly. It's tradition. And you've got to stir from east to west in honor of the wise men."

The rest of us were already in the kitchen taking our turn. Pa took a few extra turns with the spoon, "for good luck," he said, before turning it over to John.

"What goes into this plum pudding?" he asked as he stirred.

"Thirteen ingredients," Ma told him, "one for Christ and each of his disciples. But there aren't any plums in it, John."

"Really? What is in it, then?"

"Raisins, currants, spices, and suet among other things."

With that John turned up his nose and handed the spoon to Ellen.

"Have you put a coin in it, Ma?" Ellen asked.

"Of course, so don't forget to make your wish."

"Coins, too? This is a very strange recipe, Mrs. Mitchell," said John.

"Not at all. You make your wish while you stir, and if you get the coin when the pudding is served your wish will come true."

"I made my wish," said Pa.

"And what was it, dear?" asked my mother.

"Can't say. Might spoil my wish."

"Well, I think I know what it is anyway."

"And are you telling your wish, Maria?" he asked.

"I don't mind if I do. I wished for health and happiness for all our children, and that includes John and Richard."

Everyone was pleased with that, and hugs were given all around.

"You know the Puritans banned plum pudding," stated Pa.

"Is that so, Mr. Encyclopedia?" kidded Margaret. "Did they think it was that bad?"

"No, they thought it was lewd."

"Lewd pudding?" questioned Richard. "What's next, obscene pastries?"

"You laugh, but they were very serious about it," Pa continued. "That's what comes from too much thinking about the law and too little knowledge of grace."

"Here, here!" I added. "Let's hear it for grace, and more plum pudding!"

Ma herded us all out of the kitchen with comments about too many cooks and too little room. Pa and I ended up in the dining room looking out the window and watching the snow pile up.

"Charley, what are you going to do after you graduate?"

It was that question again, the one I couldn't answer. My solution to the unanswerable question was to avoid it, to postpone it, to ignore it if possible, but my father made sure that would never happen.

"Pa, I don't know any more now than the last time you asked me. How did you decide what you wanted to do?"

"I did what I found exciting."

"Studying rocks?"

"I'm not saying you have to do what I did. I'm saying devote your life to whatever it is that interests you. What is that, Charley? What is your heart's desire?"

"I like to read," I told him. "I'd love to travel and see the world. But I don't believe there's much pay in that."

"No, I'd say not. There does have to be some practicality to your profession, meeting a need as it were. You've got to find where your interest meets the world's need, and then you'll have your life's calling."

He made it sound simple, but I didn't have a simple answer. Fortunately the entrance of the rest of the family interrupted us.

"Dinner will be ready soon. I've just got to rest," Ma sighed as she eased into a chair.

"You're wearing yourself out," said Pa. "You know the girls are more than willing to help if you'd let them."

"We've offered," said Margaret.

"Repeatedly," agreed Mary.

"I know," Ma said, "but some things you just like to do yourself. You can all help clean up after the meal. I will definitely let you do that."

"Dr. Mitchell, how many more years are you planning to teach?" asked Richard.

"What's that?" Pa replied with a shocked expression.

"Are you thinking about giving up your teaching position any time soon?"

Pa's face looked paler than a moment ago. "What do you mean?" he fired back. "I've no intention of giving up teaching. Why should I? Maria, do you know any reason I should quit teaching?"

Ma looked at Richard, then at Pa. "Of course not," she said reassuringly, "and what would we live on if you did retire?"

"Exactly," Pa asserted. "Professors aren't rich, you know. It takes everything I earn to keep this household going. No, I'm afraid retiring is a luxury I could hardly afford at this time."

His concerns about money were real, but Pa couldn't admit that the thought of retiring threatened him emotionally. What was he if not a professor? The controversy over the Black Mountain had shaken his prestige, but the idea that one day he would have to give up his beloved work of teaching was beyond consideration.

"Well, is anyone hungry?" Ma's question rescued my father from his foreboding thoughts. We all testified to the strength of our appetites and soon were carrying bowls heaping with food to the dinner table. All cares were forgotten for the moment as we gathered for the feast. There was bread, a roasted goose, potatoes, apples, and of course the notorious plum pudding crowned with a sprig of holly. After everyone was seated we joined hands as Pa gave the blessing.

"Dear Father, we thank you for once again bringing us all together. Thank you for safely guiding us through another year. We remember Eliza and Richard and ask that you be with them as they are apart from us. For our shortcomings we ask your forgiveness, for our trials we ask your comfort, and for the blessings of this meal we give you thanks. Amen."

The brief silence after the blessing was quickly replaced by the clatter of plates and spoons. Conversation drifted around the table as if following the bowls of food. The feast began with a flurry but slowed bit by bit, like a clock winding down, as everyone reached that point of satisfied fullness. Golden lamplight bathed everything, including the sparkle on my glass. I looked up from the glass to my family, and saw them as if I had never seen them before. I don't mean to imply any strangeness; they were familiar to me. But I recognized things that had been invisible before. Perhaps it was because I was older. Or it may have been the close quarters forced on us by the storm. But I think it had more to do with genuine interest. I sensed that this time was passing and I wanted to know my family, in this moment, that I might not lose them.

I looked at my sisters. Beautiful and romantic Ellen, in love with love and blessed with a well-matched husband in Dr. Summerell. How happy she was tonight as she whispered to John and praised Ma's cooking and warned my father against eating too much. Mary sat next to Ellen, and tonight I saw her strength for the first time. It was born out of a struggle of will with my father that had lasted many years. The struggle was over, but Mary's strength remained and would steel her through many difficulties. Across from her sisters and next to Pa sat Margaret, the only unmarried daughter. So intelligent, so well educated and capable and so much like Pa. I thought of all she might accomplish if she were not so constrained by society.

Then I looked at my mother. She was happy now, not like years before when she thought she would never be happy again. She was also older and looked aged beyond her years. The stroke had been hard on her and she was losing her hearing. Yet all these things were as nothing to her in comparison to the joy she felt tonight.

Pa was the hardest one to capture with a glance. He was laughing and joking, as happy as Ma to have the family together, and enjoying all the duties and privileges of his position as lord of the table. But there was also a distance in his gaze when no one was talking to him. His thoughts were not all with us, and it was easy to imagine where they wandered.

The land that lies between expectation and reality can be a cruel one. Pa was in that country now and finding it to be a trackless wilderness as thick as jungle and as dry as desert. He knew where he wanted to go, but getting there was proving to be harder than expected. Just when he thought his journey was almost over, he found himself lost and without a trail to follow. It was easy to see his expectations: recognition in the community, something for posterity, and financial security. The reality was that the jungle and desert threatened to keep him from several of his goals.

"Who's ready for plum pudding?" asked Ellen.

I could see John turning up his nose, but that didn't stop Ellen from giving him a small serving. The dish was emptied without difficulty despite John's reservations. It really was delicious and deserved every bit of suspicion the Puritans gave it.

"All right. Who has the coin?" asked Pa, disappointment on his face.

"Here it is," I said, and held it up on my spoon for all to see.

"You're always the lucky one!" Margaret complained.

"And what did you wish for?" my mother asked.

"For wisdom in the choices I need to make."

"Now that's a wish I'll second," declared Pa. "Maybe we should put a few more coins in that pudding and pass it around again."

"Pudding's all gone," John noted thankfully.

"No matter," exclaimed my father. "Pass me those potatoes. They'll do."

"Elisha, quit picking on the boy," scolded Ma. "You've just forgotten what's it's like to be a young man trying to make decisions about the rest of your life."

"I haven't forgotten, Maria. I was only joking."

"That's all right," I answered. "I can take it, and I can give it, too. I was just thinking of a way to get back at Pa."

"That sounds like fun. I think I could come up with a thing or two, myself," added Margaret.

Cheers of agreement came from all around the table, even from John and Richard. They had, after all, been my father's students at the University before they married my sisters.

"Wait a minute," cried my father. "I don't think this is very fair, everyone attacking me at once."

"Oh, you're a big boy," teased Ma. "You can take it."

"I'll start," said Margaret with a smile. "I remember a time when I was helping with one of Pa's chemistry classes."

Margaret often assisted with experiments in the chemistry courses. There weren't enough materials for each student to do the experiments, so the class watched a demonstration. Margaret often performed the experiments while Pa lectured.

"On this day," Margaret continued, "Pa told me to mix certain chemicals together for the experiment, and I told him his instructions didn't sound right. He insisted that I mix the chemicals exactly as he requested, so I did, and the next thing I knew the mixture exploded onto the ceiling."

"I still say that I asked for the correct chemical but you grabbed another one by mistake." Pa was insistent.

"I'll go next," said Ma.

"Et tu, Maria?" moaned Pa.

She ignored him. "Your father was always getting plant specimens from one place or another. People knew of his interest and
would send him seeds or cuttings, sometimes from distant countries.
Well, one time he received some seeds from a botanist friend. The
botanist said they would produce the most beautiful flowers, so
Elisha planted them, and they grew, and grew, and kept growing,
until they became these enormous trees that took over the garden."

"The princess tree!" proclaimed Mary.

"*Paulonia* to be precise. And the flowers were as beautiful as
advertised," my father argued.

"Oh, they were, but they were too much of a good thing,"
said Ma.

"My turn," I said. "I was the one that started this, remember?"

By now Pa was looking at the ceiling, pretending to be upset at
our anecdotes, but in reality he was enjoying all the attention.

"I was remembering the time the comet came."

"Oh, yes, the comet," came the reply from all around the table.

"Pa insisted that we get up early in the morning so we could see
the comet, declaring how wonderful it was to see a comet, and how
spectacular it would be. So we all got up at . . . what time was it . . .
four o'clock in the morning? Yes, four o'clock in the morning, and we
tramped outside in the cold, and what did we see? Something wonderful? Something spectacular?"

"A smudge!" shouted Margaret.

"A little blur," indicated Ma.

"All right, all right," Pa protested. "I'll admit it wasn't what I
expected. But Maria, you remember the comet of 1811, don't you?
Wasn't that a sight you'll never forget? That's what I wanted the children to see."

"It's all right, dear. No one's perfect."

"I don't remember ever claiming to be perfect," Pa pouted.

"May I add my bit?" asked John.

"By all means," encouraged Margaret.

"Oh, I know what you're going to tell," whispered Ellen.

"So do I," sulked Pa.

"Well, for the benefit of those who don't know or who have forgotten, I was remembering the first time I came calling at the
Mitchell home, hoping to do some courting, actually. Believe me

when I tell you I was intimidated . . . coming to call at a professor's house . . . calling on his daughter. Well, you didn't disappoint me, Professor. You sat me down and interrogated me like I was a stranger you'd never met before rather than a student you'd known for several years. Then you started to tell me how I'd have to behave around Mary . . ."

Mary and Ellen exchanged knowing glances.

". . . and how she was your first child, and what a fine girl she was, and I had to interrupt you several times before I could make you understand that it was Ellen I'd come to see."

"Is that true?" asked Richard, laughing.

"Unfortunately," Pa replied slowly.

"Oh, dear, see how well you entertain us?" my mother teased.

"Glad to be of service," Pa replied. "Now, if everyone has had their turn, may I say something?"

"Please do, dear, though I think you'll have a hard time matching what we've already heard."

"Oh, I could come up with quite a few blunders this group has committed in its day, but what I have to say is serious."

He looked serious, and that put a sudden uneasiness in all of us. Had he made some decision?

"Now relax, all of you. You look like I'm about to announce my own death. When I said 'serious' I didn't mean bad. I was just thinking . . ."

He paused to look out the window as the last light of day illuminated our snow-covered village.

"I was thinking in another year it will have been forty years since I arrived in Chapel Hill to begin teaching. With the exception of Maria, none of you were even born at that time. Imagine that."

He paused again as the impact of that realization sank in. He took Ma's hand and smiled at her.

"What pioneers we were, Maria."

"We were, indeed," she agreed. "No place to buy furniture . . ."

"Or books . . ." added Pa.

"Or food!" remembered Ma.

"Yes, we did have to travel a ways to market back then, didn't we? Well, times have changed, and in many ways for the better.

What changes are in store for the future? I wish I knew. But I do feel that changes are coming. How does the poem go? 'But at my back I always hear, time's winged chariot hurrying near.' And more than that, I hear the angry voices of men on both sides of the slave issue who won't be satisfied until their cause is satisfied. I cannot see how they will both be satisfied. Well, I didn't mean for this to be a talk about slavery."

"What did you mean it to be about?" asked Margaret.

"About you and your future! I intend to give you all some sage advice."

"He's been doing that my whole life," Margaret whispered to me.

"I heard that, Margaret. You aren't too old to learn something new, are you?"

"No, sir," she sighed.

"Good. Then listen to what an old man has to say. First of all, never stop learning . . . Margaret!"

"Yes, sir."

"Why should you be satisfied with knowing a little bit about something, or even a lot about one particular thing, when there are so many things of interest in the world. Every day I set out to learn more than I knew yesterday."

"Everyone knows that about you," noted Mary.

Pa ignored her. "For the same reason you shouldn't be satisfied with knowing just one place. Your mother and I gave up a lot to come to Carolina. Family, money, prestige, but I don't regret it at all because of what we've gained in return."

"Neither do I," added Ma. "It was hard at first to be so far from home, but I wouldn't give up the friendships we've made here for anything. It's been the perfect place to raise all of you. And when I see how much the school has grown, and the part your father and I had in that . . . well, I don't think we could have ever done anything like that up north."

"My point exactly," said Pa. "And whatever you do, stay with it. Don't give up when things get hard. What you see here at the University didn't happen overnight. If you could see what it was like when I first came in 1818, compared to now, you'd have no problem understanding what I mean by the importance of perseverance. There have been several times when I was tempted to quit because of the stupidity of some trustee's plans, or the difficulties of a financial panic, or the decline in enrollment due to the Nullification crisis, but I didn't. I'm glad I didn't, because now I can look back over these forty years and see how much the work has prospered."

"Thank you, Dr. Mitchell," said John.

"Oh, I'm not asking for thanks or recognition, John. I've enjoyed almost every minute of it. I've led a privileged life. When I think about the opportunities I had in the early years to explore the state, doing what I loved best, getting paid a little for it . . ."

"A very little," complained Ma.

"The fact is, Maria, I might have done it for nothing. But here's my point. It's been an exciting forty years because we've lived near the frontier, on the edge of what's new in the world."

"Then why stop here, Professor?" asked Richard. "Why not head all the way to the real frontier, beyond civilization?"

"I'll leave that to you and your generation. Maybe I'm soft but I happen to like a little civilization. Then again, I'm not sure you realize how much we've civilized Chapel Hill in the last forty years."

"I can vouch for that," Ma stated emphatically. "Years ago this was the frontier. Now it's moved elsewhere. The frontier can be a very unforgiving place, Richard. Don't forget that, and don't forget about the needs of your family if you consider moving them to such a place. But someone has to be the first, don't they?"

"Yes, ma'am," Richard agreed.

"That's my challenge," Pa declared, "to each of you. Be the first. That doesn't mean that you have to be the first to go to a new place. I don't mean that you have to be in first place, either. Be the first to do something that hasn't been done before. Try something that no one has tried to do before. Be willing to step forward and take responsibility for something that no one else is willing to do. If you don't do it, it might not get done. Don't be afraid to try. You won't always succeed, but I can tell you this: if you don't try you have absolutely no chance of success."

"Seems like success has its own share of difficulties," Richard pointed out.

"True enough. I think every worthy effort, every great accomplishment, is attended by more than a little grief. Those who step forward are the easiest targets. They make the difficult decisions. They take responsibility, which I mean as a compliment, but in taking responsibility they also take on a certain weight of care. It's bound to affect them, whether it's in lost sleep or gray hairs . . ."

"Or lost hair," I threw in.

"Was I talking about myself?" Pa pretended innocence as he wiped his hand across his large bald forehead and crown. "Of course I was," he concluded with a big smile.

"But there's a danger of trying to do too much," stated Mary. "You can demand too much of yourself."

"You're right. That is a hard fence to walk, and I can't stand here and say I always came down on the right side of that fence."

"Think about all the nights that you spent sleeping in South Building, instead of home, so you could keep an eye on the students. Maybe you should have been home more of those nights."

"Maybe I should have," he admitted.

"And I don't know if you've thought about it," Mary continued, "but people who demand so much from themselves also demand a lot from others."

"Speaking from experience?" Pa asked with a smile.

"Yes, from experience," Mary answered, but without smiling.

"Guilty as charged. Are you ready to jail me, or may I plead for mercy?"

"Oh, Pa, be serious!" she said and threw her napkin at him. But now she was smiling.

Pa put his arm around her and said, "I'm sorry, Mary, for not always being there when you needed me, and for sometimes being too demanding."

"I love you, Pa, and I'm not sorry you set a high standard."

"And I'm proud of you for always reaching that standard."

"Thank you."

"Well, that's enough preaching," Pa concluded.

"Then I'd like to say a few words." It was Ma. "It's Christmas, and I feel like we should do something more to celebrate. My family never observed Christmas very much as I was growing up . . ."

"Neither did mine," added Pa.

"But I feel like we ought to do something. We've got much to celebrate, not only Jesus' birth but all the blessings God has given this family. I want to remember those who are no longer with us but who meant so much to us, such as my father and Elisha's father. I want to thank God for all you children and what you've meant to me. Thank you for your obedience and hard work, and for sticking together as a family even when times were hard. Now, can someone suggest something we can do to celebrate the spirit of Christmas?"

"You sound like a character out of Dickens' *Christmas Carol*," said Ellen.

"Good, then," replied Ma. "That book has made me appreciate Christmas much more."

John spoke up. "Why don't we sing some Christmas carols, Mrs. Mitchell? I could teach you some that you might not know."

"You may have to teach me most of them, but I'd like to try."

"As long as you lead, we'll follow," offered Pa. "And if it looks like I'm singing very quietly, just be thankful."

"All right. Let's try *God rest you merry Gentlemen*."

Singing is a fine example of what's good in life. It's not a competition but a community effort to join together and harmonize in the fullest sense of the word. It doesn't matter what the final product sounds like. It's the spirit of the singing that counts. Our family was quite a study in human nature as they sang that evening. Ma was trying so sincerely to learn the songs. I could tell Richard Ashe had no heart for it though Mary was prodding him as best she could. John was the leader, in voice and directing, with Ellen right beside him with her eyes on him intently. Margaret and I were paying more attention to the others than to the songs, and Pa . . . well, he was Pa. He was the standout even if he couldn't sing. He gave himself to the performance with all his usual energy and passion, acting out the words with dramatic gestures and occasionally bellowing an off-key note. Even in singing it was hard for Pa to take a small role.

"I've got a special verse for you, Dr. Mitchell. Now help me to sing it, everyone. Same tune."

John led and we all followed as best we could, singing with hearts full of appreciation and with many hopes for the coming year.

"God bless the ruler of this house,
and send him long to reign,
And many a merry Christmas may live to see again;
Among your friends and kindred
that live both far and near—
That God send you a happy new year, happy new year,
And God send you a happy new year."

Chapter Eleven

Decision

Sundays were always a solemn day in our house, but Sunday mornings were also a time of excitement and expectation. Sunday services were the highlight of the week. That may be hard to believe today, but in those days we were hard pressed to find any kind of entertainment. Music recitals of relatives are an exception I'll ignore. That someone would put in great time and effort to hold our attention for a solid hour, and for free at that . . . well, it was an event. And sometimes the preachers succeeded very well in their efforts.

My father was not the most eloquent of preachers, or the most riveting, but he always backed up his sermons with a convincing argument. What he lacked in style he made up for in the amount of content he delivered. Pa did not sermonize with the emotional abandonment of the fire-and-brimstone preacher. Instead he persisted in piling argument upon argument until the listener surrendered to the weight of Pa's conviction.

This sermon was to be different, though. I could tell it as we rode to the church on that sunny spring morning in 1857. Pa was more reserved than usual. Most Sunday mornings he and Ma or Margaret would be in deep discussion about some philosophical or theological topic. Today he was quiet. Margaret and my mother had to carry on the conversation by themselves.

"Margaret, have you noticed how quiet your father is today?" Ma was speaking to my sister but she was trying to get Pa's attention.

"Yes, ma'am," said Margaret. Then she was more to the point. "Pa, why *are* you so quiet?"

"What's that? Quiet, you say? Sorry, I'm just going over my sermon in my head."

"Must be a very important sermon," remarked Margaret.

"Well, they're all important," replied Pa. "I'm just not as confident of this one."

117

Ma spoke up for all of us. "Elisha, you've been preaching for nearly forty years. Why are you losing your confidence now?"

Pa looked a little embarrassed. "I'm not worried about my delivery, dear. It's the content I'm unsure of. I haven't preached on this topic before. But that's enough about my sermon. You'll hear it soon enough. Let's talk about something else. Margaret, what do you think about the Supreme Court declaring the Missouri Compromise unconstitutional?"

And with that Pa resumed his typical go-to-meeting discourse. Soon we were at the church where Pa took his place in the pulpit and the rest of us found our seats in the pews. But something about Pa's appearance that morning struck me. Perhaps it was the lighting, or the stark white interior of the church, or the strain in his face. Whatever the cause, he looked older and more frail that morning. I doubt there had been any sudden change, but for some reason the effect of the passing years was suddenly evident. Pa cleared his throat and began.

"My text for today is the 121st psalm. Please stand as I read.

"I will lift up mine eyes unto the hills,
from whence cometh my help.
My help cometh from the Lord,
which made heaven and earth.
He will not suffer thy foot to be moved:
he that keepeth thee will not slumber.
Behold, he that keepeth Israel
shall neither slumber nor sleep.
The Lord is thy keeper:
the Lord is thy shade upon thy right hand.
The sun shall not smite thee by day,
nor the moon by night.
The Lord shall preserve thee from all evil;
he shall preserve thy soul.
The Lord shall preserve thy going out
and thy coming in from this time forth,
and even for evermore.
"You may be seated."

Pa did not immediately begin his recitation of the sermon, which struck me as a change from his usual method. He was pensive and seemed to be fidgeting with his sermon booklet.

"Brethren, I hope you will bear with me in today's sermon. It is a new subject for me and one that weighs somewhat heavily on me because of its relevance to my own personal situation."

These words were spoken without any reference to the sermon booklet, another change from his routine.

"The psalmist begins by looking up to the hills that loom ahead of him as he travels towards them."

Now he was reading and I relaxed somewhat.

"And what do these hills or mountains represent? Surely there are times when they signify the difficulties or obstacles which we face each day. Some are trivial, small hills such as a blister on the foot or a dinner that is accidentally burned. Others are true mountains, as when a loved one dies. These major difficulties tower over us in imposing fashion. They frighten us so that we cry out, 'from whence cometh my help?' Who among us has not faced these mountains of loss, financial ruin, sickness, drought, and death? Consider God's grace and mercy towards you, Christian, that you do not face these mountains alone. How we should pity those poor souls, lost and without God, who must face such trials on their own."

I counted myself among those souls lost and without God. My parents, even Margaret, had patiently explained my need for salvation. I accepted the reason in what they said, but I had never been able to accept my need for it. I didn't think of myself as a poor soul. On the contrary, I felt I had lived an almost charmed life. It wasn't that I didn't believe in God. I was almost certain that I did believe. But I didn't know what God had to offer me or what I needed from him. The trials Pa was talking about seemed awfully unlikely to me. What seemed real was the prospect that I was going to live a very dull and unsatisfying life if I became a Christian.

"The hills," Pa continued, "are not always so intimidating. Sometimes they do not take from us what we hold dear, but instead keep us from reaching or obtaining that for which we long. They become barriers that limit our efforts and thwart our plans. We make our plans and say we will do this and that, but as James tells us, we should say, 'if the Lord wills.'

"Finally, brethren, some hills are not deadly, nor are they barriers to trap us, but they are trials set up to challenge us. In overcoming them we prove our faith and gain a glimpse of a brighter future. In exercising our faith to climb them and reach the pinnacle we grow stronger in our faith. Each mountain thus conquered becomes a stepping stone to a greater mountain. As we overcome these successive challenges we come closer to the ideal the Deity has set before us: being perfect, even as Christ is perfect."

I wasn't convinced of the need or possibility of perfection. It seemed that just being good would occupy a lifetime. But I was intrigued with Pa's mountain allusions. Was there a worldly as well as a spiritual application to this sermon? I wondered where in the mountains he was headed. To the pinnacle, no doubt, but which one?

"I wish it were as easy to attain perfection as it is to speak of it. Experience teaches us otherwise. One reason we often fail to scale the heights is that we do not ask for help. The Psalmist cries out, 'from whence cometh my help?' Brethren, when you are faced with trouble, do you cry out to God for help? I don't question whether you seek God in the truly great struggles of life . . . though even here there are those who fail to seek his aid . . . but I wonder if you seek God's help in all the daily difficulties you face, both great and small. I'm afraid many among us seek help in the wrong places. Some rely on their own wisdom, but who among us is as wise as God? Some try to escape their troubles with strong drink, only to find that 'wine is a mocker.' Some believe that charm or beauty will make a way through their trouble. Beauty and charm will fade like the flower, which is here today and withered tomorrow. And let us not forget pleasure, which so many employ as a means of escaping trials. Pleasure has many forms, and within the bounds set by the Deity, pleasure is a wonderful gift of grace. But pleasure as a means of escape, whether pleasure in money, food, or the flesh, will always fall short of delivering us from trials."

What about fierce self-reliance and independence? I thought. That's what I see in the people around me. Is that good or bad? Shouldn't a person do everything they can in their own strength before turning to God for help? If there is a God, I don't think he would want us to come running to him, like a spiritual infant, with every problem we face.

"No, brethren, only God is a trustworthy and reliable source of help in our days of trouble. God is able to overcome the mountains in your life because He is greater than they are. He is the creator of everything in Heaven and on earth. He is able to provide everything we need.

"The Deity is trustworthy because he is ever watching over us. He neither slumbers nor sleeps. He watches over us at all times, whether day or night. He is with us in all places, wherever we may go. He is with us whether our journey, or our life, is just beginning or is in its final stages. He shall preserve thy going out and thy coming in.

"Look, brethren, at the surpassing greatness of our helper. He is the keeper of Israel, of an entire nation, and yet he is also the shepherd of each one of you though you are the smallest sheep in his flock. Our helper not only protects us; he refreshes us as shade refreshes in the heat of day. How close is our helper? As close as your right hand."

If God was so close, why did I feel so far from him? Part of me said it was God's fault, that he wasn't there or didn't care. But another voice, almost as loud, asked, "When have you really tried to talk to God?"

"Brethren, I cannot stand here and pretend that no hurt will come into your life despite God's help and protection. Your experiences and mine teach us otherwise. The message of the psalmist is that even the greatest of evils are powerless to harm our souls. Neither the sun by day nor the moon by night . . . the Lord shall preserve thee from all evil.

"Psalm 121 is called a pilgrimage psalm because the pilgrims making their way up to Jerusalem sang it. It is also a fitting song for those of us who are making our way to heaven. Death is the final mountain we all must face. The promise of the psalmist is that if we do not look at the mountain, and fear, or look to our own strength, and fail, but instead look up to God . . . then he will lead us over the mountain to Glory."

The emphasis and placement of the words signaled the end of Pa's sermon. My heart sank because it seemed that the whole sermon was leading up to a decision by Pa about returning to the Black Mountains. Then it struck me. Pa should have been stepping down from the pulpit, yet there he remained, fidgeting with his sermon booklet again and looking unsure of himself. What he was up to? Then he spoke.

"Now, friends and neighbors, forgive me if this is an inappropriate forum for what I am about to say, but there has been a matter lying heavy on my heart for some time. God has finally led me to a decision on the matter, and I wanted to share it with you."

Everyone was quietly looking at each other and wondering what the announcement could be. My heart was in my throat, for I was sure that Pa had made a decision about returning to the mountains.

"You know that Congressman Clingman and I have been disagreeing for months now about the measurement of the Black Mountain. The matter has dragged on much too long, and still there seems to be little prospect of an end to it. Therefore, I have decided to return to the mountain once again to perform a more accurate measurement and prove once and for all which is the highest peak. I bring this to your attention here and now because I would value your prayers for the successful completion of this endeavor. Thank you."

With those few words a corner was turned in Pa's life. He picked up his sermon booklet and stepped out of the pulpit into a changed world. As he came down I could see his eyes were on Ma. I looked over and saw that her face was drawn and pale. Margaret was holding her arm. The song leader immediately started the congregation in a verse of Psalm 100, following the routine of every other Sunday. But one look at Ma told me this was not going to be like any other Sunday.

"All people that on earth do dwell,
sing to the Lord with cheerful voice.
Him serve with mirth, his praise forth tell,
come ye before him and rejoice."

The congregation sang, but not my mother. Her mouth was closed and her eyes were upon the floor.

"Know that the Lord is God indeed;
without our aid he did us make:
we are his flock, he doth us feed,
and for his sheep he doth us take."

Was my mother questioning God for allowing her husband to make the decision to return to the Black Mountains? She did not seem to be resting in the assurance that God would provide for her through this difficulty. How hard it is to be an obedient sheep.

"O enter then his gates with joy,
within his courts his praise proclaim;
let thankful songs your tongues employ,
o bless and magnify his name."

I sang the words, but singing I saw those who did not sing, and who stood with no joy on their faces: my father, mother, and sister. My own rejoicing at Pa's decision quickly turned to regret as Ma's despair pricked my conscience.

"Because the Lord our God is good,
his mercy is forever sure;
his truth at all times firmly stood,
and shall from age to age endure."

The comforting words seemed without their effect today, failing to comfort me in my unbelief, or my mother in her disappointment, or Pa in the realization of his sudden strain with Ma.

After the service there was a line of church members wishing my father well. My mother was not at Pa's side but was with Margaret and a small group of ladies. They all understood how she felt about Pa's decision. I stood alone and apart lest I be called a partisan of either group.

It was a long and very quiet ride back home. Pa tried to start a discussion with Margaret but didn't get very far with it. I wasn't about to get into the line of fire of this simmering war, so I kept my mouth shut.

Back at home Ma headed straight for the sitting room and Pa followed her slowly. I admired him for not running away from the fight. Margaret and I were out of eyesight but not out of earshot as they began to discuss Pa's decision. Ma fired the first shot.

Elisha, I don't understand why you feel you have to go back."

"Maria, they're saying I was wrong, that I made a mistake, that I didn't know what I was doing. How can I just sit back and let them say those things about me?"

She must have known from the strain in his voice that his mind was set. When his mind was set it was like flint, and whether wrong or right he could not be derailed from his course. But that did not help her see around the many dangers that rose up in her imagination.

"Elisha, what is a sixty-four year old professor doing preparing to climb up such a mountain? I don't love you any less for it, but I can see the wrinkles around your eyes and your gray hair. You think you're immortal, but you're not. You don't realize how risky . . ."

"Maria, I have been up that mountain several times already." His temper was rising now. "I've been there. I know what it's like. And I don't think it's risky."

"You have always underestimated the danger in situations. You believe God will get you out of any situation you put yourself in. But how do you know it isn't tempting God to go back there? What purpose does it serve to go back?"

"Maria, when my life is done how will they remember me? As the man who almost found the highest mountain? The man who tried but failed to measure the Black Mountain? That's not the way I want history to remember me. That cannot be the measure of my life."

"Then what about me," she said, playing her highest card. "Do you care more for that mountain or for history than for me?"

"Maria, you know . . ."

"What if I lose you to that mountain? What would God say about your responsibility to your family then?" And with that she trumped even herself.

That slowed the preacher in Pa down. It was some time before he answered her. "I will not shirk my responsibility to you or to God. But what is my responsibility in this situation? Isn't it responsible to protect my reputation?"

"Your reputation is beyond assault, Elisha."

"That isn't the impression I get from the papers."

"What do the papers know?" she said, trying to encourage him.

"Not nearly enough, but what they say is gospel truth for most people." His voice was bitter.

"Then it's settled." Her voice cracked and she turned away.

"Yes. I've made my decision." There was no triumph in his statement. The words were flat. He could tell she was crying even though he couldn't see her face.

"And when will you leave?"

"In June, after classes are done and graduation is over."

"Just as all the other Junes . . ."

"I thought I would take Charles with me."

I could tell by the silence that she had been caught off guard. What was going through her mind? I imagined she already feared for my safety. Why wasn't she protesting about my going? Then I realized she might be counting on me to help keep an eye on Pa.

"I want you to take Margaret also."

So that was it. I was to watch Pa, and Margaret was to watch me.

"Fine."

"You've been thinking about this for some time, haven't you?"

"Little else," he admitted.

"I know."

And so the battle ended. I don't say the war, for when people hold such strong and differing opinions they don't forge a treaty. The best they can hope for is a truce. If this truce held, it would be in spite of Pa's determination to have his way and because of Ma's determined loyalty to the man she loved.

Chapter Twelve

Journey

Mornings are a time of unlimited possibilities and expectations, especially summer mornings as the sun rises warm and clear. The weather doesn't hold you back but invites you on to whatever activity you consider. The air itself invigorates you with the sense that, this morning, you could do anything. How much more intoxicating that feeling becomes on a morning when you have no responsibilities before you, but only a clear blackboard and a desire to be going. Such mornings are the birthplace and incubator of wanderlust.

On such a morning there is no such thing as an obstacle. Instead there are only elements of adventure, whether a rutted road, a swollen river, bad food, dust, eccentric companions or indigestion. These are the flavorings of a delicious stew of the spice of life, seasoned well so as to stick long in the memory and provide the substance for many future stories.

The morning of our departure had arrived. The graduation ceremonies were over, and with them my University days. My father's teaching duties for the year were also done, and I could see in his eyes that he was already tasting the adventures, as yet uncooked, which lay before us. The conflict with Ma was gone from his thoughts, another obstacle overcome on the road to his journey's end. As upset as he had been before, so much more was he cheered now by the thoughts of travel. His cheerfulness was contagious, and I admit I was overcome by it. I was just as ready to be on the road.

Ma didn't want us to linger long. Her old fear still followed her, and knowing she couldn't change Pa's mind she was eager to see the painful goodbye pass. Yet she could not let us go without one more warning. Pa promised that he would be careful, and said that he'd asked Mary to be sure and look in on her. With one more hug and kiss for all three of us, Ma sent us on our way.

I love the open road because of the possibilities that it offers. Even as I grow older and cling more closely to the comforts of home, I'm still easily moved to pack up my bag and take to the open road.

I'm moved by the excitement of new places, by renewed acquaintance with familiar faces, by the escape from familiar drudgery, and by the opportunity to postpone responsibility. Yet which one of us can truly elude responsibility? It is the debt that must be paid. Sometimes, however, debts can be postponed, and we were eager to escape ours by heading as far west as possible in a day's time.

Travel in those days was nothing like today, when locomotives carry us tens of miles per hour. Our one-horse wagon did well to make twenty-five miles a day. Then there was the problem of lodging. The inns or ordinaries of those days had a terrible reputation. The wise traveler avoided them whenever possible. Fortunately Pa knew a host of families across the state, connections through the University, who were willing to shelter us as we made our way west from Chapel Hill to Salisbury and on to Morganton and the Asheville area.

Heaven help you if it had rained recently. Then the roads became a quagmire. The wagon could easily mire up in the mud, requiring a variety of measures to free it. Many a fence rail has been "borrowed" for just such an occasion. If that failed your only hope was to find a farm nearby where help could be sought. So it was that we found ourselves mired one morning early in our journey. All our efforts to dislodge the wagon from a pit of mud had failed. Pa went to a nearby farmhouse and returned with two horses and several slaves that belonged to the farmer. The slaves went to work quickly in a way that told me they had prior experience with removing mired wagons. In just a few minutes they had us back on the road again.

As we rode on I couldn't get the slaves off my mind. They looked strong and healthy enough, but their clothes were worse than homespun. Even though Pa had been kind and thankful to them, their expressions had remained cheerless and resigned.

"Pa, why do we allow slavery?"

"You assume slavery is wrong then."

"Yes, I do. Don't you ever question it?" I knew Pa had not rejected slavery. He had written in support of it and had owned a slave.

"I've questioned it, Charley. I know there's much that's unpleasant about it. However, when everything is considered I believe it would be worse to abolish slavery than to continue it."

"How can you say that? Didn't you see the condition of those Negroes back there? Their clothes were about to fall off. There wasn't a smile on any of their faces."

"I saw it, but they would be worse off if they were on their own. They have a harsh master . . ."

"So they would be better off on their own."

"How would they survive? No capital. No education."

"Sounds like most of the farmers in this state."

"Who would compensate the slave owner if they were freed? How would the farmers work their fields or make a profit? You know many of our young men have gone west in the past twenty years."

"So the slaves are nothing but property."

"They are property."

"They are men, Pa!" We had argued this point before, and I knew he wasn't going to change his opinion. There was a blindness in his thinking on this subject. How could an intelligent man fail to see the faulty logic of arguments supporting slavery? And there were so many men who believed these arguments.

"You say the slaves are property," I argued.

"Yes. And owning property is a basic right."

"But you ignore the fact that liberty is a greater right than property, just as life is a more fundamental right than liberty. What man can own property if he has no liberty? Who can have liberty if he is not allowed to live? Therefore the slave's right to liberty exceeds the master's right of property."

"You know most men would not accept your statement that the slave has a right of liberty."

"And what about you?" I asked.

"I'm not sure. But I am concerned that freeing the slaves would lead to a violent revolt."

"Are you saying it's just to jail a man because he might some day commit a crime?"

"A slave is not in jail, Charley."

"I think the slave would disagree with you, Pa."

"And a jail sentence at least has an end to it," added Margaret. "You can't say that for slavery."

"I see I'm outnumbered," Pa bemoaned, then addressing our horse asked, "How about you, Jack? Will you take my side? What, nothing to say? Wise horse. Well, it looks like I'm on my own."

"The problem is you have all too many men on your side," said Margaret. "Just none here in the wagon with you."

"Then I shall have to make my own defense." He paused to consider his argument, but then made a concession. "Honestly, I have no more love of slavery than either of you does. But let me be practical. How is our economy supposed to carry on without the benefit of slave labor?"

I wasn't going to debate that point. "The immorality of slavery is greater than any benefit to the economy, Pa. Our wealth should not be based on stolen goods."

My father had nothing more to say after that. I wasn't conceited enough to think we had won him over. He was just trying to avoid strife. We rode on in silence.

Throughout history there have been ideas which have enjoyed popularity for a time only to be exposed and accepted as immoral in the end. Imperialism, infanticide and slavery belong in this category. How can a society be deluded by such ideas? One answer is that people excuse it on the basis of some other worthy goal. Other times the practice is accepted because "everyone else is doing it." Then there is the Biblical excuse. Men recognize the authority of the Bible and then kidnap that authority to make it serve their own purposes. In those days the slavery proponents referred to Abraham's ownership of slaves or the biblical commands that slaves should obey their masters, and then used these verses to justify the continuation of slavery. In my opinion they excused their tyranny at God's expense.

Pa's stand on the slavery question was bothersome because it reflected on his character. There was a hard-headedness in him when he should have been more open-minded. Once he settled on something he seldom listened to another opinion, even when there was sound reason in it. But he loved his family too much to hold a grudge against us for very long. Soon he had taken up the professor's mantle again and was holding forth on the botany and geology of the Carolina Piedmont.

After several days of travel we were looking for diversion and a reason to spend time away from our bumpy wagon. Late in the morning we spied a large gathering of people in the country outside a town and rode up to investigate.

"What's going on here today?" Pa asked a wizened old man sitting in a wagon.

"What did you say?" shouted the old man.

"What's happening today?" Pa shouted back.

"Gander pull," came the reply.

Margaret groaned as Pa thanked the man in the wagon.

"What?" I asked Margaret. "What's a gander pull?"

"A crude excuse for a social occasion," she shot back.

"Isn't that being a little judgmental?" asked Pa.

"Judgmental? Are we talking about the same activity?"

Pa smiled back at her, and I still wondered what she was upset about. Then she noticed the questioning look on my face.

"Really, Charley, have you never seen a gander pull?"

"Pull what?" I asked, and suddenly both Pa and Margaret burst into laughter. "All right, you two. Stop laughing and tell me what this is really about."

"I think we should stay and see this for Charley's sake," Pa stated after he finally gained control of himself.

"Maybe," Margaret replied. "Perhaps he should see it once just to see how bad it is."

"How bad what is?" I asked in desperation.

My sister and father just looked at each other and laughed again. "You'll see," was their only reply.

We got out of the wagon and found a spot for the horses to graze, then began to tour the grounds of the event. It wasn't long before Pa found a former student and fell into a deep discussion. We left him and wandered on. I could tell that folks had come from miles away for this occasion. The young men and ladies were especially well dressed, and quite a few men were busily grooming their horses. I looked for a racetrack but saw none. Many families were enjoying a meal together in the out of doors, and there were many people selling food and other wares from their wagons. I didn't see any geese, however, and that made me all the more curious.

Pa caught up with us eventually and our little group gathered up some provisions from those selling food and settled down for a welcome meal. Several men campaigning in the local election gave speeches while we ate. There was even a brief sermon and a troubadour who sang a few ballads. But still no geese.

I was about to ask again what all of this had to do with a gander pull when a large man, apparently the master of ceremonies, stepped forward and called the crowd to attention.

"Thank you, one and all, for coming out today," he began. "And isn't it a beautiful day? We've got all the ingredients necessary for a wonderful time . . . good weather, good food, good words, and the gander pull still to come."

There it was again, that mysterious goose reference. I stared at Margaret and Pa but they just smiled back.

"I'd like to recognize one of our visitors," the speaker continued. "All the way from Chapel Hill, noted professor at our state university, the leading geologist in our state and the man who first measured the Black Mountain, Dr. Elisha Mitchell."

Pa stood up and waved as the crowd politely applauded. He usually basked in such moments of recognition, but as he sat back down he was grumbling.

"What did he mean by saying I was the first to measure the mountain?" Pa asked accusingly.

"He was praising your accomplishments," Margaret replied.

"I'm surprised he didn't mention Clingman in the next breath."

It put him in a foul temper that lasted far too long. It might have gone on for hours if not for the merciful timing of the notorious gander pull. As the master of ceremonies explained the rules of the event I saw two men tying a live goose to a tree branch growing horizontally about twelve feet above the ground. The goose was tied to the branch by its feet so that it dangled head-down beneath the branch. The men were mounting their horses and lining up some distance away, and I could see that the goose was positioned at a height almost beyond the reach of the men on horseback.

"As you know," the speaker explained, "the gander's neck has been well greased." Here one of the men tying the bird slapped on another helping of lard for effect. The crowd hollered and laughed. "Now, remember that in order to win this contest, the rider must not only grasp the gander's neck, but also succeed in pulling off the head as he rides by. And riders, be forewarned, sometimes you pull the gander and sometimes the gander pulls you!" Once again the crowd roared.

132

I turned to Pa and Margaret to see them looking at me and trying to judge my reaction.

"What?" I said.

"What do you think of this cruel sport?" Margaret asked.

"I haven't seen anything yet. I've seen worse things before, I guarantee you."

"You may change your mind yet," said Margaret defiantly.

As the contest proceeded I had to admit that Margaret was correct about the cruelty of it. The bird's demise was not quick or painless. Numerous men galloped by unsuccessfully. There were many grabs but just as many slips. One confident looking young man even managed to grasp the neck but was then pulled from his horse. He ended up in a heap on the ground, looking almost as bad as the bird dangling above with its head still attached.

I learned the contest had little to do with the goose but a lot to do with gambling and with the efforts of the riders to impress the young ladies. All of this was washed down with a liberal supply of intoxicating beverages.

All of us, and especially Margaret, were more than ready when the victorious contestant rode away with the gander's head, the prize money, and presumably his admirer's heart. Margaret was immediately on her feet and herding us toward the wagon.

"Now do you see why I groaned?" she asked me as we climbed into the wagon.

"Yes, I do. One gander pull is more than enough for me."

"Of course," Pa added, "you may learn something even at a gander pull."

"Oh, yes. 'Sometimes you pull the gander and sometimes the gander pulls you.'" Margaret tried to mimic the voice of the master of ceremonies.

"And don't take your turn until enough riders have gone by to remove most of the grease," I added.

Margaret and I were laughing about it, but Pa wasn't smiling. "I'm serious," he began. "I found myself sympathizing with that goose more than a little bit. If you're going to stick your neck out in this world, then you'd better expect some people to try and pull it off."

It was a cynical comment that seemed out of place coming from Pa's mouth. He was the everlasting optimist, the eternal humorist, and now he was talking like a man who expected nothing good. Fortunately for all of us, we soon arrived in Salisbury where my sister Ellen and her family lived. The day we spent there did wonders for my father's disposition. We had gone but one day's journey beyond Ellen's when the Brushy Mountains appeared on the horizon. They weren't the Blue Ridge, but Pa's enthusiasm soared at the sight of them.

"My heart's in the Highlands," he sang out, quoting Burns, "my heart is not here; my heart's in the Highlands a-chasing the deer."

"Oh, once you've seen one mountain you've seen them all," Margaret said slyly, trying to raise Pa's ire. It worked.

"You can't be serious!" Pa objected. He stopped the wagon in the middle of the road and stood up from his seat. Suddenly the wagon became a pulpit.

"The variety of the mountains is endless. Give me a lifetime and I could never run out of possibilities for further study. Each one of the hollows you see running up to the ridges is its own little world, with its own variety of flora and minerals. Have I brought my children up in such a way that they don't know such basic things as this?"

He was about to have a fit of apoplexy while Margaret sat serenely, smiling at her success. I had to look down to keep from laughing out loud.

"Each one the same, indeed!" Pa continued. "What about the explorations of Bartram and Michaux? Their journals are full of discoveries of new plants, which they found around every bend in the mountains. Why, I . . ."

Margaret and I could hold it back no longer. Our laughter burst out and drowned Pa's speech. His shock quickly turned to consternation as he recognized the trick Margaret had pulled on him.

"So that's it," he complained as he sat down. "I've raised my children to be comedians." He shook the reins and started the wagon moving without looking back at us. The way he shook his head made me wonder if Margaret had gone too far, but in the next moment I saw his sides were jumping in silent laughter. Soon he was laughing out loud.

A week of travel brought us at last to the town of Black Mountain, a tiny crossroads village nestled in a gap of the Blue Ridge and within view of the peak it was named for. We dropped Margaret off at the home of an acquaintance of Pa's. She would enjoy the comforts of civilization while Pa and I roughed it as bachelors in the North Fork valley.

While we were in town we stopped at the general store to stock up on provisions. Pa and I would be doing most of our own cooking for the next few weeks, and we hadn't brought any perishables with us. As usual my father saw an old friend and got tied up in conversation. This time the topic was the condition of the state roads, another of Pa's interests. I didn't mind the delay because it gave me a chance to look around the store. As I walked the aisles I picked up a saddle and smelled the new leather. In the grocery section I found bins full of onions with their papery skins, new potatoes, salt pork, smoky country hams, and hoops of cheese. There was no fire in the woodstove today. A bearded old man with a hat was leaning back against the stove whittling, and I could smell the pine scent from the chips that lay around him on the floor. Not far away I caught the flowery perfume of the soaps. It provided a welcome relief from the mousy smell that hung around some parts of the store. I walked on past the oils and turpentine until a case of shiny knives caught my eye.

"Excuse me, young man."

I looked up, expecting to see the storeowner, but instead I found a tall man some forty years of age, well dressed in suit and tie and with a neatly trimmed beard. He had a commanding presence about him, of the sort that you find in preachers or politicians.

"Yes, sir," I replied.

"Would you mind telling me your name?" he asked.

"Charles Mitchell," I replied.

"Dr. Mitchell's son?"

"Yes. Do you know my father?"

"Yes, I do. I thought you favored him. Well, it makes me feel rather old to see Dr. Mitchell's youngest so nearly grown."

"I graduated from the University this year."

"Is that a fact? Well, time does fly. Congratulations on your accomplishment. What will you do now?"

"I'm not sure," I answered. "Ma and Pa say I should become a doctor, but I haven't decided yet."

"And how is your mother?"

"She's doing well at the moment. How do you know my parents?"

"I was a student of your father's, as I assume you must have been if you just graduated from the University. I graduated in 1832."

"Was it as hard back then?"

"Hard enough. We had Dr. Caldwell as well as your father."

"How well did you do, if you don't mind my asking?"

"Why should I mind?" the stranger said, smiling. "I finished first."

He had my interest now. I was just about to ask him his name when my father walked up looking ill at ease.

"Hello, Thomas."

"Professor Mitchell," the stranger replied.

Thomas who? I thought. And why did the stranger look so uncomfortable?

"Charley, have you and the Congressman introduced yourselves?"

"I'm afraid I have him at a disadvantage there, Professor. Charles, I'm Thomas Clingman, former student of your father's and currently a Representative in the U.S. Congress."

And challenger to Pa's claim to the highest peak, I said to myself. "Pleased to meet you, sir," I replied, but I didn't sound very convincing.

"You appear to have a fine son, Professor. If you and the University have prepared him half as well as you did me, his prospects should be very bright."

"You're too generous, Thomas. Most of your success has been due to your own intelligence and initiative."

I could see what they were doing. Being noble and polite so they didn't let their true feelings show. The two of them had once shared a deep respect for each other. Now they were only pretending.

As they exchanged pleasantries I took a closer look at Clingman. There was no doubt he was more handsome than my father, in a very rugged and charming way. He looked like a man who paid attention to his appearance. I could see he was the sort of man that would attract a crowd and captivate their attention.

"So, what brings you to the mountains, Professor?"

"You know why I'm here." Pa said it with a temper. The charade was wearing on him. "My son is aware of our disagreement, so let's stop acting like there is no difficulty between us."

"As you wish."

"As for the purpose of our trip, since you and I have been unable to resolve our claims through the papers, I've come here to do it in person."

"Meaning what?"

"Don't worry, Thomas." My father relaxed a bit. "I haven't come here to beat you half to death as Brooks did to Sumner. I'm not going to argue you to death, either. I should know better than to argue with a lawyer. Charley and I are going to make a more accurate determination of the mountain's elevation by running a line of levels to the top."

"Well, that will take a while, won't it? But it won't change the outcome. I tell you, Professor, when you're done you'll be forced to agree that the northern peak is the highest, and that I was there before you."

People in the store were starting to notice the heated discussion between Pa and Clingman. Some stared because they recognized one or the other of the men. Others were busy trying to find out who they were.

"I won't be forced to do anything, Congressman." Pa was red-faced now. "Not by you or your friends in the press. I was on that mountain long before you, so don't try to tell me what is or isn't true about it."

Clingman didn't return Pa's angry words. He looked down at the floor a moment, then said, "I didn't mean to offend you. Good day, Dr. Mitchell." And without looking back he quickly walked out of the store.

My father continued looking at the door where Clingman exited, oblivious to the stares of the onlookers. They soon went back to their shopping, the old man at the stove resumed his whittling, and gradually Pa's anger subsided.

"Let's go, Charley." He turned and walked to the counter to make our purchases. He had just finished paying when I saw the old man standing beside Pa. He reached out and tugged on my father's sleeve.

"Son," the old man said, "ain't you a preacher?"

Pa was surprised by the question. "Yes, I am. Why do you ask?"

"Did you ever preach on loving your neighbor? You know . . . as much as possible, living at peace with all men? Seems to me you could use a little more study on those lines."

I didn't know how Pa would react. I was afraid he would explode at the old man. Instead his shoulders slumped and his hand went up to his eyes. For a minute I thought he would cry, but then he reached out for the old man's hand. As they shook, Pa said, "Your rebuke is justified, sir. Thank you for pointing out the error of a poor preacher."

"It's only what I'd want you to do for me, son. And remember, the Good Lord cares a whole heap more about who you are than about what you amount to."

Pa nodded, then quietly gathered up our purchases and walked out. I shook the old man's hand and followed.

Chapter Thirteen

Measuring

Our eyes were on the mountains as we rode west out of town and turned right into the North Fork valley. The Blue Ridge lay behind us now. The bulk of the Blacks rose up in front of us and kept rising in such a way that the top seemed always just out of sight. The mountain mocked summer. Though an endless variety of greens and yellows blanketed the hills and valleys at its feet, the sleeping giant remained blue, dark, and cold. Below were comfort, life, and warmth. Above, the spine of the range was like the edge of a knife against the sky. The sounds of the valley, whether of water or man or crow, spoke of life. The sound of the peak, though only imagined, was chilly silence. It struck me that such places are a world unto themselves and a place set apart. It was plain to see why many cultures and religions considered the high mountains to be holy.

"Does God live on the mountain?" I asked my father.

"No, God is too great to be limited to any one place," he replied. "But I feel closer to God on the mountain."

"Because it is higher and closer to heaven?" I asked.

"I don't think you can get closer to heaven by feet or even by miles," he said and laughed. "No, I think it's because there are no distractions, nothing but God's creation, which speaks unfailingly about the Creator. I can't help but think he's especially pleased with this part of his creation, and that maybe an extra measure of his spirit is here, but that's speculation and I have no biblical authority for saying so."

He was always clear about the scriptural support for any position he held. However, he had been known to add his own interpretation to scripture if it helped to strengthen his argument.

"Look at all that happened in or on the mountains," he went on, now almost preaching. "Moses received the Ten Commandments and saw God pass by on Mt. Sinai. Later God gave him that glimpse of the Promised Land on Mt. Pisgah before he died. And what about Elijah's contest with the prophets of Baal on Mt. Carmel? Or Jesus' transfiguration?"

"And Satan tempted Jesus by taking him to a very high mountain," I added. That halted his sermon. For a moment I thought he would disagree with me, then he looked down and only spoke again after a long pause.

"Charley, do you think I'm giving in to temptation by coming back here?"

He didn't say it accusingly. He was sincerely questioning his own motives. I couldn't answer him, and told him so. If I looked into my own heart, I saw he and I were dealing with the same problem. On the one hand we wanted to glorify God by accomplishing something great. Behind that veneer of spirituality there was a deep core of personal desire and no small measure of pride.

What a power there is in pride! What an ability to overwhelm reason and blind insight! How easy to rationalize its motivations. How difficult to escape its demands. How common to feel its emotional tug on the heart, and how rare the man who feels that tug yet turns away from it. I know my father felt it. I believe we were there on the Blacks in part because of the pull of pride. Did he give in to it or turn away? He didn't say and I didn't feel at liberty to ask.

Our days fell into a routine of work. We rented a small cabin from Jesse Stepp and did our own cooking, such as it was. Neither Pa nor I would win any awards for the food we fixed. Not long after the sun was up we would be outdoors doing the leveling work, measuring our way slowly up the North Fork valley and towards the peaks of the Blacks. Pa would handle the level while I held the rod and turn by turn we each climbed the mountain one hundred feet at a time. In the evenings we went to bed soon after dark, though not before Pa took time to write. Sometimes the Stepps took pity on us and invited us to dinner. In this uneventful way two weeks passed and we were still only two-thirds of the way to the top of the Black Mountain.

The work wasn't physically hard but it was tedious. There was plenty of time for talk and Pa took full advantage of it. I think he was catching up on all the subjects he had wanted to discuss with me for a long time.

"Charley, are you courting anyone now?"

Another question I dreaded. "No, Pa."

"Why not?"

"No one I'm interested in right now," I answered reluctantly.

"I find that hard to believe. What about the Simmons girl?"

"Sarah Simmons? Pa, you've got to be kidding."

"Not at all. She's a handsome girl."

How did I explain that handsome girls wouldn't give me a second glance or that the very sight of a beautiful girl made my palms sweat and my mouth freeze? I said nothing more and hoped Pa would do the same.

"What are you thinking about military service these days?" he asked, and I was glad for the change of subject.

"I'm still considering it. Lots of my friends are enlisting. Do you think it's a good idea?"

I could tell Pa was choosing his words carefully. "You know I've never served in the military. I'm probably not the best one to advise you. Frankly, the father in me worries about what life in the army means in these uncertain times."

"You mean if secession comes to pass?"

"Exactly. You've never known war in your lifetime, but I remember the last conflict with the British all too well. It was a difficult time even for those who did not fight."

"But if secession comes, I may not have a choice."

"You may be right, but meanwhile I'll hope and pray that day doesn't come."

Pa stared at the ground and I thought he was still brooding about the possibility of war.

"Charley, where do you stand in your relationship to God?"

His question surprised me. I was used to him preaching about God, but I never felt it was aimed directly at me.

"Why are you asking me that now?"

"Because you're with me. I'm afraid I'm much too distracted by my work at home to give you the attention you deserve. Here, my mind is free of those other thoughts, you're right in front of me, and naturally my concern turns to you."

His words made me restless. I couldn't say why. I wanted to talk about something else. "I haven't decided anything yet. There's still plenty of time for that later."

"When?"

"When I'm through with my education and I've decided what I'm going to do with my life. That's what I mean by later."

"What if that later time doesn't come?"

"What do you mean?"

"I mean that no one is guaranteed another day. Not you, not your mother, not me. We live each day by God's grace and mercy. How did James put it? 'Go to now, ye that say, Today or tomorrow we will go into such a city, and continue there a year . . . whereas ye know not what shall be on the morrow. For what is your life? It is even a vapor.'"

That sounded like an exaggeration. I was as solid as the rocks around me. "I think I'm much more than a vapor, Pa. In fact, I think I'm going to be around for many years to come."

"It may seem that way to you as a young man, but from my perspective life is very fleeting."

"How can you say that? You're in excellent health."

"You just don't realize the effects of time. Wait a few years and you'll see. But I'm not talking about my health. I'm talking about the uncertainty of life here on earth, and the certainty of judgment when this life is over."

Judgment. I had heard a lot about it. Not so much from Pa, but from other preachers. It didn't seem possible to me that God, if there was a God, could be that harsh.

"If God is good, then why do I need to worry about judgment?" I asked.

"It's because God is good that there will be judgment. Would you want a judge that let criminals get away with breaking the law?"

"I know what you're saying. I agree that on earth we need judges to uphold the law. But in heaven we need a merciful god."

"So God shouldn't hold people accountable for their actions?" he asked.

I knew his question was meant to trap me. If I said God shouldn't count our sins against us, then my father would answer that God wasn't just. If I agreed that he had to hold each man responsible for his actions, then everyone, including me, would one day face God's judgment.

Pa discerned my difficulty and broke into my thoughts. "I can see you are on the horns of the dilemma. Which will it be, Charley? An unjust God, or an unrighteous Charley very much in need of God's mercy?"

"If there is a God, he must be just or he wouldn't be God."

"Excellent reasoning. Which leaves us with your need, and my need, and everyone else's need for mercy. How can God grant us mercy and still remain just?"

I had no answer.

"By paying the penalty for our crimes himself. Though we are totally depraved and in no way merit it, God in his grace paid the price of our sin by sending his own son to die in our place. God's grace is extended to you, Charley. Can you resist it?"

Pa made it sound so simple and easy, but when I considered the choice he put before me I felt smothered by the prospect of surrendering my own will to that of God. Life seemed open and limitless before me. My university work was completed. I had decisions to make about what I would do and where I would live, but they were my decisions. I knew that committing my life to God meant God should have the final say in those decisions, and I was not ready to give up my authority.

I can't remember where I heard or read it, but it's appropriate. "The heart has reasons which reason does not know." At that moment I was convinced that I knew what I needed better than God. If God had stood right in front of me I'm not sure I would have listened to him. Independence was my goal, and that meant all the decisions would be mine and mine alone. I was very familiar with my father's independent ways, with the self-reliance of most New Englanders, and I wanted that same spirit for myself.

To be as independent as a bird in flight! Yet what bird can fly without the air to beat his wings against? What free-swimming fish can survive without the water? To be like the pioneer making his way through the wilderness. Yet even the pioneer has a mother, a father, a wife. Nevertheless, I clung to independence as though it was my life's blood and the reason for my existence.

Pa interrupted my thoughts. "I struggled with faith in God when I was at Yale, Charley. But my struggle wasn't with God's judgment. No, I was convinced of that. What I couldn't overcome for a long time was the idea that I was totally unworthy of God's grace."

"Why did you feel that way?" I asked, glad to have the focus off myself.

"My upbringing, I suppose. All that Puritan tradition. My father's stern ways with me. But once I understood that grace was totally dependant on God's character, not my own, I welcomed it with open arms. I have no doubt of my salvation, though I still struggle at times with trying to prove myself worthy in the world's eyes."

"Is this argument over the Black Mountains part of that struggle?"

He smiled back at me, but there was sadness in his eyes. "Yes, no doubt it is." Then he jumped up, never one to stay sad for long. "Well, that's enough of seriousness. I wonder how your mother is doing?"

"I'm sure she's missing us."

"No doubt about that." And suddenly he broke into song, bellowing out the lyrics to the empty valley that stretched away for miles below us.

> "Do they miss me at home, do they miss me
> at morning, at noon, or at night?
> And lingers one gloomy shade round them
> that only my presence can light?
> Are joys less invitingly welcome,
> and pleasures less hale than before,
> because one is missed from the circle
> because I am with them no more?"

He wasn't much of a singer, so the deaf hills were exactly the audience he needed. He took a bow and laughed loud and hard as only a man well pleased with himself can do.

* * *

The relationship between a father and son can be like a long walk through the mountains. You start out in the early years in the lowlands where the ground is level and the going is easy. There are streams to play in and the day is young with plenty of time to stop along the way and enjoy each other's company. As time passes you enter the foothills where the elevation increases and the trip becomes more serious. Before long your easy hike has become all work as you reach the steepest part of the climb leading up to the summit. Conversation slows and tempers can flare under the strain of the ascent. When the climbers reach the summit there is an opportunity for unsurpassed fellowship as they rest and enjoy the views from the top, but many a father and son have parted ways before they ever reach the peak.

If fathers could only be experienced guides. Their knowledge of the trail gained from earlier trips would serve their sons well as they avoided dangers and rough sections of trail. They would know when to travel in order to avoid bad weather. They would be sure to walk by the most spectacular vistas and find the best spots for shelter and water. Instead the fathers are often first-time travelers just like their sons, making their way only one step ahead of their child and saying, "this looks something like a trail I was on once" when in fact it is different from any trail they have ever seen before.

It's easy to see this now, but growing up I was blind to it. I thought Pa's guidance was arbitrary and tyrannical. His uncertainties I took as indifference. I thought he was too serious because he wouldn't take time to play, when in fact he was navigating our way around dangers in the trail. His methods seemed so old-fashioned, but he used them because they were the methods he had learned from his guide.

Now that I was older I questioned my guide more and more. Naturally Pa found this hard to accept. He was a teacher, a man of some authority, and he was used to respect. He was the man with all the answers and he usually had the final say. In exerting my own independence of opinion I was doing exactly what I had been trained to do, but the result was unavoidable friction with Pa.

It all came to a climax on the Black Mountain. We had been working long days, making painfully slow process, and both of us were ready for a change of routine.

"Let's go exploring," Pa suddenly suggested.

"Where?" I asked, more than ready to go.

"Across the peaks."

We grabbed some food and water and headed north and upward, out of the Swannanoa Valley and into the high dampness of the Black Mountain. An hour or two of walking brought us to the gap that spanned the short distance between the Blue Ridge to our right and the Black straight ahead. Half an hour more and we were upon Mt. Mitchell itself . . . at least what the locals called Mt. Mitchell. We stood upon its peak and looked down on the rest of the world. Behind us lay the bowl of the Swannanoa Valley framed by the Blue Ridge to the east and the Craggies to the west. Below us to the west lay the headwaters of the Caney River and the valley that descended to the Caney River settlement. Due north the spine of the Black undulated gently but precisely across peak and gap until it crossed the oblong mass of the high peak some miles ahead of us. All the peaks were covered with the straight, narrow, and dark spires of the balsam firs. Only here and there did the greenish-black hue of the forest give way to the gray of tree trunks, where a windbreak occurred, or to the lighter green of a prairie.

I studied the range intently, trying to judge with my own eyes what clue there was to the relative heights of the peaks. But my untrained eyes found no clue. Every peak seemed to have a similar height. Whatever peak we happened to be on seemed to stand taller than all its companions. This was no trick of nature; it was the nature of the mountain itself. The Black was not an ideally shaped peak rising to a single point; it was more like a long roofline with small bumps and sags that had developed over years of weathering.

As I stood in the sunshine observing the mountain the weather suddenly changed. Clouds swept in and blanketed the mountaintop. The range of the mountain was now hidden. What lay even a few hundred feet away could only be imagined.

"This is what we found on our first trip up in '35," Pa yelled above the wind, "and it wasn't much different in '44. The only difference is that it never cleared up while we were on the top, and it was too cool to stay for long."

"I believe that," I said with a shiver. The change in weather confirmed the height of the mountain in a way that no instrument could. The loss of sunlight, the strong sweep of the wind and the dampness of the cloud all testified to our elevation and exposure even in the middle of summer. "So how could you tell where you were?" I asked.

"Once you were on the top of the mountain, you couldn't tell. You made your choice and set your course from a distance. On my first trip I made that choice on Yeates's Knob. You can't see it now, but it's over there across the valley to the west about four miles. The next time I followed my guides and they led me to the high peak."

"But didn't you say that the first time you climbed the mountain you ended up on a peak covered with the balsam fir trees?"

"That's right."

"The high peak is covered with balsam fir trees," I pointed out.

"Yes, but we ended up north of the high peak in '35."

"You don't know that for sure," I insisted.

"Charley, I believe I know more about this matter than you do. I was there, you know."

"And you said the peak you climbed in '44, the one that you called the high peak, was conical in shape and covered with a prairie."

"Yes, what of it?" he asked sharply.

"Pa, that describes this mountain we're on right now to a letter. Now that I'm here I can see it plainly. This peak they've been calling Mitchell's peak for so many years, it looks like the one you said you climbed in '44."

"This is not the part of the mountain I reached that year. It's too far south. Look how far it is to the high peak."

I looked where he was pointing and saw that the clouds had broken and the top of the Black was once again illuminated by sunlight. Three miles beyond my father's outstretched arm lay the oblong peak now known, to my father's chagrin, as Mt. Clingman. I turned my gaze down the western slope of the mountain and into the Caney River valley, mentally counting the ridges and streams that lay before us.

"Pa, do you remember that letter you wrote to Ma when you climbed the mountain in '44?"

"Vaguely. That was so long ago. What about it?"

"Ma read it too me when she received it in New London, and I remember the part where you described your climb up the Black Mountain."

"How could you remember that after so many years?" he asked with surprise in his voice.

"I wanted to be just like you," I told him. "I asked Ma to read that letter to me again and again, and I memorized that part. You said you went . . . up the Caney River, then up one of its branches, over the Pine Mountain ridge, then up another creek, across another ridge and up a third creek. You said you did all that and you still had most of the mountain before you. Do you remember that, Pa?"

"Yes, that sounds correct, but what of it?"

"Look at the ridges in the valley below us," I asked him. "Is that largest ridge coming down from the high peak the Pine Mountain ridge?"

"I believe it is . . ."

"Then look what that means. You crossed that ridge and kept coming this way across two creeks and another ridge before you ever began your final climb up to the top. It makes sense that you could have been this far south before you reached the top."

"Charley, you're mistaken."

"But Pa, look at the terrain . . ."

"You're wrong, I said, and I won't be interrogated on this matter by my own son. You weren't there at the time and you could hardly know what I did or where I went. As for this peak looking like the mountain I first described, it was my description that was in error. You can't expect my memory to be perfect after thirteen years."

He was not being honest, and I withered a little at the realization. But even as my shoulders sank in disappointment my skin flushed and grew hot.

"Why can't you see it?" I shouted. "You're the one who is supposed to be devoted to the truth. Isn't that a necessary part of science?"

"Yes, it is. I want the truth. I believe it is true that I was on the highest peak. That's what I am trying to prove."

"And I say the evidence shows that the mountain you climbed in '44, that you claimed was the highest peak, was this very mountain where we now stand. Pa, I think when you came here the first time and ended up on that balsam covered peak, that you were on the high peak the whole time and just thought you had missed your mark."

He spoke no words but the scowl on his face shouted his rejection of my argument. He took one more look north towards the high peak and the Pine Mountain ridge, then stormed down the trail towards the Swannanoa Valley without looking back at me. I never caught up to him on the walk back to our cabin. It began getting dark and as I hurried I tripped over a root, sprawling forward and cutting my palm on a rock. I wrapped it in a handkerchief and continued on to the cabin. Pa was already inside when I arrived and he didn't look up as I walked through the door. But when he saw me washing my hand in a basin he came over to inspect it.

"Nasty cut," he said.

"Stupid root tripped me."

He doctored it with powder after I finished washing it, and as he dressed it he told me he was sorry for walking away from me.

"You know I've got too much of a temper," he confessed.

"And I was wrong to get angry with you," I offered.

"Then let's not talk about that subject any more. Agreed?"

"That's fine with me," I said.

The rest of the evening was very quiet. When bedtime came I could not sleep because of the pain in my hand. I heard Pa toss and turn for hours as well.

* * *

My father was in a much better mood the next morning. He was already up and cooking when I awoke.

"How's your hand today?" he asked.

"Still sore."

As we ate a meager breakfast of bacon and bread he looked at me and said, "I had the strangest dream last night, and one of the clearest I can remember."

"What do you mean?" I asked. It wasn't like Pa to give much thought to dreams.

"I can remember it so well, all the words and details. I was watching a play, and in the play there was a king. The king said to his subjects, 'We have vanquished all our foes but one. The kingdom is at peace. Let us build up and perfect the kingdom.' So the people went to work, and they had just completed their task when the final enemy, a great dragon, appeared. One by one the dragon defeated the king's warriors until the dragon stood before the king. The dragon said, 'I am death.' The king said, 'Why didn't you tell me? I've been waiting for you.'"

Pa sat there smiling the most pleasant smile while he told me this somber story. I asked him why something so sad made him smile.

"Because it isn't sad. It's reassuring. I don't have to be afraid of death. It's not an enemy. I can trust God to give me the time I need to finish the work he's given me to do. And, because I'm not spending all my time worrying about the future, I can devote all my strength to doing the work at hand."

"Isn't that an awful lot to conclude from a dream?"

"The dream's just a reminder, Charley. These are things I should have already known."

"Seems to me you're thinking too much about death."

"No, not at all. It's living that's on my mind. I've been preoccupied with death before today, I'll admit. But no more." He must have read the puzzlement in my face. "Here's what I mean, Charley. Up until now I've been preoccupied with death insofar as I've been worried about fame or recognition. In other words, I've been afraid that my life would end before I'd made my mark."

"But you have made a mark," I replied. "This mountain is your mark."

"If that's so, then it's a very tenuous mark. The events of the past two years have shown that. But no matter, that's all behind me now."

"What do you mean?" I asked.

"I mean this mountain is not the only thing in life."

"Are we going to stop measuring the mountain?"

"No, of course not. That's what we came here to do and we're going to finish it. I didn't say there was no purpose in measuring the mountain, only that there's more to life than whether or not my name is on this mountain."

I wasn't sure what to make of the change in Pa's attitude. I figured it would all be made clearer by his actions in the coming days. I was right, too, except that it didn't take days to see the result.

He seemed distracted all morning as we worked, ate little for lunch and said less, and as we resumed work after lunch he became more and more frustrated with the leveling. Finally he called me back from my position up ahead of him.

"This leveling is just a waste of time," he said in disgust. "I've only been doing it as a way to put off facing the real problem."

"And what's that?" I asked, already suspecting the answer.

"That I have been mistaken in my judgments about which peak I was on, and when. That I have been wrong in my statements about which peak was highest. That I have only shown myself to be muddled in my efforts to prove myself correct. I have sacrificed what I hold most dear, truth, in order to try and save my own reputation."

My father was not cheered by these confessions. The realization of what he had done, and what he faced, was much too fresh. I wondered if he had the will to say and do what was needed to set things right.

"What now?" I asked.

"I'm going to the Caney River settlement. I want to talk to the men there and get their opinions about what took place in '35 and '44. There's a man named Tom Wilson who lives down there. They say he knows this mountain as well as anyone, and I think he could direct me to my former guides. Whatever they say I will submit as evidence to Clingman and the others. In fact, I'm going to see if Clingman and I can't sit down face to face and sort out the truth of this matter. And if the truth is that he measured the highest peak first, so be it."

"Do you believe that, Pa?"

"Charley, in my heart I don't. But in my mind I'm not so sure."

"When are you leaving?"

"Now."

"Now?"

"Yes, now. The sooner the better."

"But it's already afternoon. You've got a good long walk ahead of you. Maybe twelve miles."

"I may be older than you, Charley, but I'm still strong as a bull. These long legs will carry me quickly. Besides, the sun won't go down until nearly eight tonight, and I won't sleep well until this is behind me."

"But tomorrow is Sunday."

"Yes, and it would do me good to be able to preach tomorrow. The people of Caney River would be pleased by it, too, I believe."

I was caught off guard by Pa's plans. It sounded like too much to do in too short a time. Ma wouldn't be pleased at all if she were here, or if she heard about it later.

"Pa, I don't think you need to be in such a rush. Those men will still be there tomorrow and the next day. And if you don't get to preach tomorrow, there's next Sunday."

"You're worried about your mother, aren't you?" he said, grinning. "Well, let me worry about her. I take full responsibility. Besides, who's the father around here, you or me?"

"If it has to be today . . ."

"It does."

"Then let's get started."

He didn't say anything for a moment. I could tell he had other plans.

"Charley, I would like it very much if you came with me, but your hand is hurt and you won't be able to keep up with me. You've got to reach from one laurel branch to another going down the other side of the mountain, and your hand is going to make that impossible. I'm pressed for time as it is. Besides, we're in desperate need of supplies. We've got nothing left to eat but cornbread and bacon. I'm going to use up two precious days in the Caney River settlement, and I don't want to have to waste more time going into town for supplies when I return. I'm sorry to ask it of you, but I need you to stay behind and do that for me."

There are times when you know exactly what needs to be done and yet are powerless to do it. I didn't continue to argue with my father. Nothing good would have come of it. But I knew it was wrong for him to travel across the high peaks alone.

"You're being stubborn, you know," was all I could tell him.

"Yes, father's prerogative. But I'll be fine. Monday morning ride into town and get what we need for food, then meet me back here at the Mountain House that afternoon. And say hello to Margaret for me. All right?"

"All right. Be careful, Pa."

"I will. See you Monday afternoon." With that he secured his fur cap on his head, turned, and headed up the trail. He stopped after a few yards, looked back at me, waved and smiled and said goodbye.

The power of memory lies in the senses: the smell of the general store you went in as a child, the look of your father's arms swinging as he walked toward you from a distance, the sound of a well known piece of music which brings back to life exactly what you were doing when you heard that music before, the soft feeling of the skin on your lover's back. Just so my memory stirred powerfully as Pa waved, turned, and strode away. The sound of his goodbye and the look of his quick stride brought me back to the years gone by when I would watch as he left on another journey. All at once I could understand my mother's struggles over his being gone. It hurt to see him go. I waited until he was out of sight then headed back down the trail to the Stepp's farm. The sky grew darker and the air cooler as I walked. That night it rained.

Chapter Fourteen

Missing

The poor weather continued on Sunday morning, and I wondered if it was any better in the Caney River valley. Pa would be preaching soon if he could muster a congregation. Mrs. Stepp invited me to have Sunday lunch with her family, and I was happy to accept. She was a wonderful cook, and the bounty of the summer garden added to the feast. She fixed ham and beans as you'd expect, but her biscuits with sourwood honey were a bonus.

As we ate Mr. Stepp kept us laughing with his account of a certain woman and her misadventure at a camp meeting. He went on as though the story was true, but I'll let you pass judgment on it.

"Now this woman, Mrs. Brown, was a proud woman even though she had religious leanings," Mr. Stepp began. "She had been taken in by the latest fashion of wearing bustles, and approached her husband about buying such an article of clothing. Whereupon her husband, being somewhat miserly, said back to her, 'My dear, you know such matters are but vanity and foolishness. And by the by, your natural endowments are such that a bustle is already rendered unnecessary.'"

Here Mr. Stepp paused to see if his story was having the desired effect upon his wife, and indeed it was. She barely managed to hold in her laughter and turned several shades of red in the process.

"Well, Mrs. Brown said nothing more about the bustle, but went back to her preparations for the camp meeting. Her husband eyed the vittles she had prepared with great anticipation. There were pickles, and fruit preserves, and country ham, and a large sausage that looked like it would last them the whole week."

"I'm sure it wasn't as tasty as my sausage," Mrs. Stepp threw in.

"By no means, my dear," assured Mr. Stepp. "Well, the day came for the departure to the camp meeting. Mr. and Mrs. Brown loaded their provisions and rode off. But imagine Mr. Brown's surprise and consternation when, after arriving at the meeting place, he noticed that his wife was wearing a plump bustle that put all the other ladies to shame. He was determined to speak to her about it, but the meeting had already begun and he decided it would have to wait."

"I believe she should have her bustle," proclaimed Mrs. Stepp, and she brandished her fork for effect.

"I'm not saying yes, and I'm not saying no. I'm just telling the story," Mr. Stepp countered. "Now, Charley, you've been to these kind of religious meetings before, haven't you?"

"Yes, sir, though I don't think Pa was too pleased about it."

"Well, you know how excited the people can get, right?"

"Yes, that's a fact."

"Well, this time was no exception. The preacher was a real Bible thumper, and within a short time he had the people real excited. Several of the folks appeared to be moved by the Spirit and began to sing and shout and otherwise carry on. Next thing you know, Mrs. Brown was jumping up and shouting. Why, under different circumstances, you would have sworn she was screaming. Mr. Brown had never known his wife to be so moved at a meeting before. He was somewhat shocked by it, but he didn't want to interfere with the work of the Holy Spirit."

"As well he shouldn't," admonished Mrs. Stepp.

Mr. Stepp ignored his wife's comment. "Several of the ladies came to minister to Mrs. Brown. There was quite a group gathered around her, but they were having no success in calming her down. Suddenly the group jumped back from Mrs. Brown, in terror, and Mr. Brown could hear plainly that she was yelling 'Snake! Snake! There's a snake on me!'"

Mrs. Stepp's humor disappeared entirely as she recoiled in sympathetic horror at Mrs. Brown's plight. "Oh stop, Jesse, stop for goodness sake!"

But there was no stopping the storyteller. "Mrs. Brown had her hand around what she believed to be the snake's neck, and she was crying out for someone to pull the snake off her. It appeared to have wound it's way up her legs and under her dress. The ladies were too terrified to be of any help, and the men were too modest to proceed, so it fell to Mr. Brown to reach up under his wife's dress," and here Mr. Stepp pantomimed the slow, deliberate reach of Mr. Brown's arm, "and grab the wretched serpent."

Mrs. Stepp was nearly in a faint, but her fascination would not allow it. She was, however, speechless. Mr. Stepp took advantage of that fact to complete his tale.

"Imagine the scene. Mrs. Brown screaming in fright as she holds the serpent's neck, too afraid to even look at it. Mr. Brown with his arm up her dress clutching the other end of the snake. A great circle of onlookers at a safe distance. The stunned preacher frozen in the middle of his sermon."

Mr. Stepp paused to let the silence have its full effect. By now we were leaning well over the table to catch his every word.

"Mr. Brown yelled to his wife over her screams and protests, 'Dear, when I yell three, let go of the snake, and I will jerk it away from you.' At this the crowd backed up a little. Mrs. Brown just moaned, 'Oh, Henry, Henry.' Mr. Brown yelled, 'One . . . Two . . . Three,' and gave a great jerk as Mrs. Brown released her end of the vile serpent. The force of Mr. Brown's pull propelled the snake well out towards the crowd, who didn't back up too far to see that what had been wrapped around Mrs. Brown's legs was a great . . . big . . ." And here he paused once more. ". . . sausage."

Our surprise quickly gave way to sidesplitting laughter as we thought about poor Mrs. Brown and her culinary bustle gone crawling. Mr. Stepp just leaned back and smiled.

When she stopped laughing Mrs. Stepp leaned over to me and said fondly, "We sure have enjoyed having you and your father here, Charles."

I assured her the pleasure had been ours. Then she surprised me by asking, "What do you think of your father, Charles?" She recognized the bewildered look on my face and quickly added, "Now son, I have enough experience with my own children to know something about the relationship between a parent and child. I don't believe I'm wrong in saying that there is some difficulty between you and your father. Well, am I right?"

I looked to Mr. Stepp for help, but he had buried his face in his plate. There was no place of escape for me. "Mrs. Stepp, I don't know what you're talking about. And I'd rather not discuss it." I'd unloaded both barrels and there was no more ammunition.

"You're among friends, Charles. Now talk."

I'd missed, and was cornered. "My Pa and I have disagreements like any father and son would," I said in surrender.

"I know that," she said, and continued the interrogation. "What about? Work? Money? Politics? Religion?"

I wanted to say, "What don't we argue about?" Instead I kept quiet.

"All right, Charles, let me ask you my first question again. What do you think of your father?"

"I think he's a great man."

"Why do you say that? Are you just repeating what everyone else says about him?"

She had me. All I could do was hang my head.

"Charles, let me see if I can help you. The father you know is not the great man everyone else knows. Am I right?"

I nodded. She continued.

"He's short with you. He expects too much from you. He's old fashioned. At times his opinions make no sense. At other times he can be just plain hardheaded. And he's often too busy to pay attention to you."

"How did you know?"

"My father was like that. Goodness sakes, I'm married to a man like that."

That brought Mr. Stepp up from his food. "Now Mrs. Stepp, let's not get personal." But his wink showed me he wasn't offended. "And don't you think you're being a little hard on our guest?"

"Perhaps I am, Jesse. Perhaps I am. All right, Charles. Now we know that your father is just like any other father. Let me tell you why your father is not like any other father."

"That's easy," said Mr. Stepp. "Most fathers aren't professors with mountains named after 'em."

"That's true, Jesse, but I think there's more to Dr. Mitchell than that. Charles, would you believe me if I told you that your father would be a great man even if he had never measured the Black Mountains?"

I had to disagree with her. For my whole life it seemed like Pa and Mitchell's Peak had been united, almost one and the same thing in my eyes. To think of him without thinking of the mountain was a very difficult thing. Pa felt the same way, I'm certain.

"Mrs. Stepp, I think my father's measurement of Mitchell's Peak is the very reason most people consider him to be such a great person."

"You're right, Charles, but I want to tell you the real reason he's a great man, so you'll understand him a little better and maybe appreciate him more. You see, your father is a great man because he's a rare man, and he's a rare man because of his character, not because of what he's done."

"Listen to her, Charley. She's telling the truth. I know your Pa has his faults, but I'll take a man like him any day, faults and all. The world is full of men who'll never amount to anything, but your Pa always brings out the best in the men around him."

"What I like about Dr. Mitchell is his curiosity, Charles. He doesn't overlook anything in nature, and he never gets tired of learning about something new."

"Why just the other day, Charley, your Pa and I were out looking at the fish in the Swannanoa, and he turned to me and said, 'Jesse, what do you think I would find if I opened up a trout's stomach and looked inside?' Now, how was I to know what was inside a fish's stomach? Bugs, I said. Lots of bugs. But I don't think he was really asking me what I knew. He was just thinkin' out loud."

"Your father is a very caring man, Charles. Now you, being his son, may tend to see more of the stern side of him . . ."

She was right about that.

". . . but he has never turned his back on those in need. He's not a rich man, but he's provided well for you and still been generous to those around him who were less fortunate. That's what I mean when I say your father is a man of character."

"And don't forget his preachin'," said Mr. Stepp. "You and I both know that what brings him to these parts is the Black Mountain. But I believe that he feels just as strong about preachin' the Gospel as he does about measurin' the mountain. And to tell you the truth, I think most of the folks around here care far less about his mountain climbin' than they do about the fact that he takes the time to preach to them."

It felt like I was the one being preached to. But they were right about Pa, and they had opened my eyes to a side of him I hadn't seen before.

"You're telling me something I needed to hear," I told them. "I have been short with Pa for a while, but when he gets back on Monday I'll try to be more appreciative. And thank you for a wonderful lunch."

"Come back anytime," said Mrs. Stepp. "There's always room at my table for any of the Mitchells."

Later that day I went for a walk along the North Fork and could think of nothing but Pa. I looked up at the hills around me and realized that people have a lot in common with mountains. They have their ups and downs; their hard, rocky areas and their soft, comforting spots; their gloomy days and their bright ones; their dry spells and their showers of love. I had focused on the plain places for too long; now I was ready for a change of scenery. As I walked the sun came out along the North Fork and a plain day turned into a beautiful summer afternoon. But up to the north the clouds were still hiding the peaks of the Blacks.

Monday morning I got up early and rode Jack to the town of Black Mountain, made my purchases at the store and went by to visit Margaret. She was not happy to hear about Pa's trip to the Caney River settlement.

"Charley, couldn't you do anything to stop him?"

"Like what? Tie him up? Even if I could have, it wouldn't have been right."

"What in the world will Ma say when she finds out?"

"That will be between her and Pa," I said hopefully.

"Don't be so sure of that. I think she'll be upset at both of you. You know this is exactly why she agreed to let you come."

"I know that. What would you have done in my place?"

She thought about it and then said, "I would have protested more."

"Right," I laughed. "You could have argued until sundown and he would've still insisted on going."

"Yes, but by then it would have been too late for him to go. There you have it."

She smiled at her solution, and I had to give her credit. "If anyone could have done it, it's you, Margaret."

"Well, I'm never at a loss for words, Charley."

I wasn't about to disagree with her. Besides, it was time for me to be leaving if I was going to get back in time to meet Pa. I said goodbye and rode back towards the North Fork valley. It was after noon before I arrived at the Mountain House. There was no sign of Pa.

"Mrs. Garenflo!" I called out from the saddle.

She popped out of the doorway, smiling and waving. "Hello, Charley. What can I do for you?"

"I'm looking for my father. He said he would meet me here this afternoon. Have you seen him?"

"No, not today. Not since Saturday. You're welcome to come in and wait for him if you like."

"Thank you, but I'll just wait out here. He should be along shortly." So Jack and I waited, but he didn't show up. After an hour of waiting I headed up the trail on foot towards the peaks of the Blacks. There was still no sign of him after covering more than a mile. Discouraged and a little worried I headed back towards the Mountain House before darkness set in and found Mrs. Garenflo waiting beside Jack.

"You didn't see your Pa, Charley?

"No, ma'am. I don't know what to make of him not showing up."

"Well, it could be any of a number of things. He probably got tied up visitin' with all the folks he hasn't seen in so many years. Or maybe someone dragged him off to look at something they found in the dirt."

"That sounds more likely," I said. "He never has turned down an invitation to go see an interesting rock."

"There you have it. I'll tell him you were here waiting for him if he shows up tonight. I bet you'll find him here tomorrow afternoon. Who knows, maybe you and your Pa got confused about which day he was coming back."

That sounded like a good explanation of his absence. I pictured the argument we would have over which day he was supposed to return.

Monday night passed much too slowly, but that's how it is when you can't sleep. I was up early and back at the Mountain House long before noon. There was still no word of Pa, so I headed up the trail in search of him, hoping to meet him on the way. I traveled nearly as far as the high peak before turning back.

That night the darkness began to settle on my spirit blacker than any midnight in the deepest hollow of the hills. Even the counsel of the Stepps failed to encourage me. Everyone had good reasons for not worrying and suggested one more day of waiting. The distance and inaccessibility of the Caney River settlement was the major reason for their decision. For the same reason I found it impossible to think of going on my own. So I waited, sent word to Margaret of Pa's absence, spent one more day fruitlessly wandering the trail beyond the Mountain House, and spent another sleepless night alone. But before I went to bed that night we decided that John Stepp and I would walk to the Caney River settlement the next morning. After three days of waiting I was relieved to be taking action.

Yet no promise of action could take away the loneliness in my heart. Although in the company of concerned friends, I felt cut off. My thoughts climbed up to the high peak where I pictured Pa wandering aimlessly among the balsams, seeking his way in the dark as I sought to reconcile my feelings towards him.

Chapter Fifteen

The Settlement

Half a day later John Stepp and I descended from the high peak and walked towards the settlement through the quiet darkness of the balsam fir forest. The difficulties of the previous days faded from my mind as we entered an ever more verdant deciduous forest. The sights and sounds distracted me from painful memories and revived my hope.

We walked on through dense woods unlike any I had seen back home. Some of the tree trunks were eight feet in diameter, giant poplars dwarfing us, and I thought *these are the real trees.* Those I had seen back home were like Plato's shadows, only incomplete reflections of the reality of trees. A tree is time frozen and preserved. Leaf by leaf and year by year it adds to its storehouse until the day when it falls to the earth and begins to release its treasure of time. Leaves count for seconds, twigs for minutes, branches for years, limbs and trunk for decades or centuries. Sometimes we slow down this release of time by preserving the wood in a piece of furniture, but more often we speed up the process by burning it or turning it into paper. At the rate we are cutting down our forests we shouldn't be surprised that time passes so quickly.

As we walked John pointed out the names and uses of the trees. "Now that there is a sweet gum," he told me. "You can make a fine chewin' gum from the ooze of that tree. Course some folks prefer pine. Over there is a maple. That's the finest wood for whittlin'."

"What about these hickory trees?" I asked.

"So your Pa did teach you a thing or two, didn't he? Hickory is the best wood for burnin'. Makes a real hot fire. Folks who smoke hams use green hickory wood. Nothin' better to use for fashionin' an ax handle, or for fence rails."

"Lots of oaks, of course. What do you do with oak besides build with it?"

"Tan with it. Put the bark in water and use it to tan leather. Most people use oak for their barrel staves."

"Do you remember that song about the old oak, John?"

"I don't know. Sing a little bit and maybe I will."

"Woodman, spare that tree," I sang. "Touch not a single bough! In youth it sheltered me, and I'll protect it now."

"That old familiar tree," John answered, "whose glory and renown, are spread o'er land and sea . . ."

". . . and wouldst thou hew it down?" we sang in unison.

"That's the one," I declared. "Woodman, forbear thy stroke! Cut not its earth-bound ties; oh, spare that aged oak, now towering to the skies!"

"That's all well and good for you outlanders, but around here we depend on the trees for our livelihood, or else we're clearin' them to make room for crops. Necessity don't allow for sentimentality, as my Grandpa used to say."

"I know. It's just that our talk reminded me of that old song. I don't think the trees here on Black Mountain have anything to worry about, do you?"

"Are you kiddin'? Who would ever come all the way up here for wood?"

As we headed down the mountain the variety and vigor of the trees increased. John had a special use for each kind of tree. Sourwood leaves could be brewed to make a tonic. Buckeye wood was the best for cradles. Butternut was used for dying homespun. The fruit of the pawpaw was good for making jelly.

Near the foot of the mountain I heard the loud sound of water.

"We're almost to the Blue Sea Falls," John said eagerly.

"Did the waterfall remind someone of the ocean?" I asked.

"Could be," he replied, "or maybe this was as close to the ocean as they ever got and they fancied this was how the ocean sounded."

Waterfalls give full meaning to the idea of "living water," for the cascades are alive with movement and sound. The sound speaks of ages of time and our own brief course down to the sea. Our time in the life of the waterfall is so brief, and though I might wish to freeze time like a waterfall frozen in winter, I cannot. The irresistible necessity of time pulls me onward to my life's conclusion.

We walked on downstream towards the spot called the Green Ponds where Big Tom lived. Before long we saw his cabin as John had predicted. It wasn't much to look at. Like all the backwoods homes it was made of squared logs joined at the corners. The chimney was constructed of field stones cemented by mud. The roof was covered in oak shakes. A porch had been added in front. It was modest and comfortable looking, but I guessed it had no more than three rooms. There were fishing poles and a loom on the porch, and a small springhouse in the back. It looked like it wasn't closely tended.

The front door was open. We saw a woman cooking inside and said hello to her. She walked over slowly, tying a bonnet on her head as she came. She was small and thin and looked tired.

"What can I do for you?" she asked, wiping her hands on her apron.

"We're lookin' for Big Tom," John answered.

"Gone bear huntin'. Don't know when he'll be back. Could be dark or later. Maybe I could help you."

"Mrs. Wilson," I asked, "you are Mrs. Wilson, aren't you?"

"That's right."

"I'm Charles Mitchell, Dr. Mitchell's son, and this is John Stepp."

"So your Pa is the perfessor who climbs the mountain."

"Yes. And he was headed this way last Saturday to talk with Mr. Wilson. Have you seen him?"

She didn't answer immediately. I began to think she didn't understand me. Then she said, "Son, I ain't seen your Pa."

My stomach suddenly felt queasy.

"Mrs. Wilson," asked John, "have you heard of anyone who has talked with Dr. Mitchell?"

"Not a soul, and believe me I would've heard of news of a visitor in the settlement."

I had to sit down. As I turned to do so I saw a tall thin man with a rifle walking up. He had sandy hair, a long beard, and piercing blue eyes.

"Hello, Big Tom," said John as he stepped forward to shake Tom's hand.

"Why, it's John Stepp isn't it? Jesse's boy?"

"That's right. And this," he said as he pointed to me, "is Professor Mitchell's son, Charley."

I stood up and walked weakly to where the two men stood. Big Tom grasped my hand before I could reach out for his.

"Pleased to know you, Charley. Folks around here sure think a lot of your Pa. How is he?"

I saw Mrs. Wilson begin to gesture at her husband, trying to stop him from saying anything more. John saw it, too, and brought the matter to its conclusion.

"Tom, the Professor is missing. He left the Mountain House last Saturday heading here to see you. He didn't come back on Monday like he said he would. We've come lookin' for him, hopin' he was here and maybe just laid up in some way."

"He ain't been around here at all. I've been out in the hills a good bit the past few days, no luck with my huntin', but I believe I'd have seen him if he'd been this way. I ain't heard nobody say they've seen him, either."

My head was spinning and I collapsed down on the porch. I was holding back tears with all my effort, but they were just boiling up stronger inside me. When Mrs. Wilson put her arm around my shoulder the sobs burst out loud and tears poured out against her dress where I had buried my face. Then just as quickly as they came they were gone. I took some hard, deep breaths that were mostly strangled sobs and dried my face as best I could with my hands.

"Mr. Wilson," I said without getting up, "I want you to help me find my father."

"Now, son, what makes you think I can find him?"

"You're the best tracker around. John swears to it."

"I appreciate your compliment. But let me be honest, Mr. Mitchell. Your Pa is dead."

"Tom Wilson!" the tracker's wife shouted in surprise. "What kind of Christian comment is that to make to a poor boy who's already in distress?"

"It's the truth, Niagara. There's no charity in telling a lie. John here says the Professor has gone missin' since Saturday. Now it's Thursday afternoon. John and the Professor's son have covered the trail between here and the Stepp's. Ain't that right, John?"

"Yes, sir."

"And no sign of the Professor?"

"None."

"Well, Niagara, there you have it. The man is missing for five days. No sign of him on the trail. Somethin' happened to him and then some varmint probably carried him off. Sorry Mr. Mitchell, but that's just the way I see it."

Strange as it seemed at the time, I appreciated Big Tom's honesty. I had been dodging the truth for days. Now that it was here, part of me welcomed it. But another part was not ready to let go of all hope.

"Mr. Wilson, I know there's a lot of truth in what you told me. It's hard, but I needed to hear it."

"Son, I'm just an old bear myself. I ain't got the sensitive feelings a person should have for an occasion like this. I meant what I said, but I'm sorry I had to say it."

"Mr. Wilson, I still want you to look for my Pa."

He paused and then replied slowly, "I thought you might."

"Whether he's dead or alive, we've got to find him. If by any chance he's out there still breathing but too injured to get up and walk, we've got to get to him. If there are animals that would hurt him, we've got to find him before they do. And if you're right, and it is too late, then we've still got to find his body to give him a proper burial."

"You're right of course, son." He smiled and squeezed my shoulder with his big hand. "I'll do it."

And for the first time in days, I smiled as well.

* * *

It was too late to think of returning to the North Fork valley, so John and I spent the night in the Caney River settlement. We found ourselves invited to a wedding in what seemed like the oddest conjunction of circumstance. The time of my grief was also a time of joy for an unknown couple, strangers to me but representative of all those whose lives carried on oblivious to my loss.

Weddings in the settlement took place at a home instead of a church. After the ceremony there was a big meal and a dance. All the furniture was moved out of the house and the floor was covered with bran and sawdust. Soon the room was noisy with fiddling, stomping feet, and the cheers of the wedding party. I didn't feel like dancing. It just didn't seem right to enjoy any pleasure at a time like this.

John was dancing like he was born for it. Strange that he could be smiling and looking so lively now. He was usually so serious. I decided that it all had to do with his priorities. When business was the priority he allowed no thought of pleasure to intrude. Now I saw that he was equally devoted to pleasure when that was the priority.

I didn't begrudge John or the other revelers their hour of merriment. How could they know the loss I was feeling? In my self-pity I actually appreciated the festivities for making me feel more miserable.

"Excuse me, I couldn't help but notice you was by yourself."

I looked up to see a girl standing beside me in a red and green linsey-woolsey dress. She looked younger than me, but not by much. Her dark hair was pulled back. Her face was light in complexion and a little sunburned. She seemed friendly and her face was appealing.

"Hello," I said, standing up. "How do you do? My name is Charles, or Charley, Mitchell."

"Pleased to meet you, Charles, or Charley."

"Just call me Charley."

"Good. I like that better. You Professor Mitchell's son?"

"Yes, that's right. And what's your name?"

"I'm sorry. I must have left my manners at home tonight. My name is Mary . . . Mary Riddle."

We shook hands awkwardly. I'm not sure which of us was more nervous, but my hands were sweating more.

"Mr. Mitchell . . . Charley . . . we're all awful sorry about your Pa. I never knew him, but I've always heard folks talk highly of him."

"I appreciate your kindness, Mary, but I haven't given up on Pa, and I hope you and the others won't, either. I know what you've heard . . ."

"Didn't Big Tom say . . ."

"Yes, he said my Pa's probably dead. I'm not saying anything against him . . . he's an experienced mountain man and he may be right, but until we find my Pa I've got to give him every chance, even if that chance is a very small one."

"Let's go outside and talk where it isn't so loud," she said.

Outside the cabin it was quieter, though the sounds of the fiddling and dancing still hung in the air. A whip-poor-will was whistling nearby. The stars were out in full, but the silhouette of the mountains blackened great swaths of the sky.

"Sit down, Charley." I sat beside her on the porch steps. People wandered in and out of the cabin as we talked, mostly groups of young men with a jug of corn liquor, taking some refreshment before returning to the dance. They would look at us as they walked by, trying to identify the stranger with Mary Riddle.

"I can tell by the way you talk that you've had a lot of schoolin', Charley. I like the way you talk. But sometimes schoolin' ain't worth much if you ain't learned the right things . . ."

She was struggling for the words, trying not to offend me.

". . . and I don't know how much good your book learnin' does when it comes to findin' your way in these hills. When I saw you sittin' by yourself inside, I felt right sorry for you because you looked so out of place."

She made me smile in spite of myself. "Do I look that bad?"

"Charley, you look awful sad and blue. That's only natural. I'd be the same if I'd lost my Pa" and then she added quickly, "or if he was missin'."

"Thanks for your sympathy. And I appreciate your advice. You may be right about my book learning, Mary. Some of it is pretty worthless."

"Aw, there I go again, forgettin' all my manners. I don't mean to say your learnin' is worthless. I just mean that you don't have that much learnin' in the mountain ways. If you did, Charley, I think you might understand better why Big Tom said what he did."

"All right, why don't you teach me," I said.

"Right now?" she protested.

"Yes. I'm ready to learn. I need to learn."

"But these things take a lifetime to learn. And I'm not a teacher. I'm not even your elder."

"Mary, you might be the best teacher I've ever had. You certainly have my attention."

"I'm talkin' about life and death, Charley. Are you ready for that kind of talk?"

"Believe it or not, my Pa was trying to talk to me about that very thing the last day I saw him."

She looked at me, weighing my disposition and her willingness to discuss such serious matters. "All right, Mr. Mitchell, I just might not have a chance to see you again, so I'm going to speak freely. The trouble with most folks is they live their life like they've got all the time in the world, when in fact each day might be their last. You might think I'm too young to have such a hard view of life, but I've seen plenty of hardship and death in my life already. Have you experienced such things?"

"I had a baby brother that died when I was only four. I don't remember a whole lot about him. I know it was a sad time."

"Death is always sad. But I'm not sayin' it's always bad. Dyin' is part of livin'. My granddaddy always said that the sad things in life make you appreciate the good things all the more. I don't give up on life because I've gone without things I wanted or lost people I loved. I cherish the things I've got even more. It's like when a fire goes through the forest, and afterwards, when a few flowers come up a bloomin' yellow or red against the burned black woods, you can't help but see them and ache over them because their beauty stands out so much."

The passion in her voice and the spark in her eyes as she spoke were spellbinding.

"What are you trying to tell me?" I asked her.

"I want you to understand that there's more to life than what you can see and touch. You need to know that there is life beyond this life, and death isn't the terrible thing that you think it is. Understand that, Charley, and you'll be able to understand and accept what Big Tom said."

"How do you know what I believe or understand?"

"By lookin' in your face. There's a sadness on you that isn't brand new. It's been growin' there for some time." She paused as if expecting me to respond.

"You may be right," I said almost under my breath.

"Why are you sad, Charley?"

I looked at her and thought, who is this person that is asking me to share my private thoughts, and why am I so willing to consider doing it? I stood up and walked away a few steps, not sure if I should stay or go.

Turning back to her, I said, "Mary, I . . ."

She waited, watching me but saying nothing.

"I don't know how to begin, or if I should."

She smiled, but was silent still.

"I'm sad sometimes for reasons I don't understand," I said as I sat back down beside her. "I'm sad because it troubles me that I don't know what I want to do with my life. It bothers me that I feel like my father is never satisfied with what I am doing. I'm sad because I feel alone. It's not that I feel this way all the time . . ."

"Just enough that it takes away the joy of the good times."

"That's right."

"Charley, every thing you've told me speaks to me of the emptiness of your life. You feel lonely because someone is missing from your life. You feel lost because you need someone to show you the way. There's only one who can help you, and it ain't any man or woman. It ain't your father and it ain't your mother or any other person."

"I know what you're going to say," I interrupted. "It's God I need. I've heard that all my life. Well, I'm not so sure I want to run to God with every problem I have. I believe if I can handle my problems myself I'll be a better man for it, a stronger man."

She looked down a moment, then said slowly, "Sometimes we all need someone to show us the way."

"Yeah? Well how about blazing a trail where no one has ever been? How about making your own way? Don't you think that's important?"

She smiled at me and said, "I admire a man who has the courage to go where others haven't been, but it's a fool who tries to follow a trail and ignores the blazes."

My face turned red with the sting of her words, for they were true. I looked at Mary in my embarrassment and wondered.

"How did you get to be so wise?" I asked.

"Oh, I'm not wise. Now my granddaddy, he's wise. Just about everything I know I learned from him, and I think everything he learned is either from the Bible, his own experience, or from the signs and sayin's."

"What are the signs and sayings?"

"Don't they teach you anything in that school of yours?" she scolded. I rolled my eyes but she kept talking. "I'm sorry. I didn't mean that. I'm sure you've been to a very fine school. It's just that, around here, a body can hardly make it without payin' attention to the signs and sayin's. For instance, there are the signs about the weather."

"Sure. We learn about those. Red sky in the morning, sailor take warning. That sort of thing."

"Children know that sort of thing, Charley. I'm talkin' about things like the signs you get from a fire burnin' in the hearth. When it makes a cryin' sound you know it's goin' to rain. Or when it sounds like a man walkin', you can be sure company's a comin' to visit. And if it makes a soft crunchin' sort of sound like a man steppin' in snow, then you can tell that a good snowfall is on the way."

"I never heard any of that before. Tell me some more," I said.

"Well, when the chickens all gather on the high ground, that means you're in for a good, hard rain. If you see a circle round the moon, you know it's either gonna rain or snow. And then there's the animal signs."

"What do they tell you?"

"The thicker the coat on a bear or squirrel or rabbit, the harder the winter you can expect. Same goes for the number of spiders you find in your house. More means a worse winter. Course a large crop of chestnuts or acorns means the same thing."

"Do you believe all these signs, Mary?"

"Sure I do. I've seen them proven time and again. Here's another one. If an owl is hootin' and won't let you sleep, just put an iron in the fire and he'll quit. Works every time."

Just then another visitor rode up to the cabin, this one on a white horse. I watched in puzzlement as Mary wet her right index finger, drew it across the palm of her other hand, and then stamped her right fist into the palm of her left hand. She gave a very satisfied smile and looked proudly at me.

"What in the world was that for?" I asked in amazement.

"When I count a hundred white horses, then I'll find my husband to be."

"And how many have you counted?" I asked with some concern.

"Oh, don't you worry, Charley. I've got a long ways to go yet."

That relieved me, but I told Mary that most of what she had to say sounded like superstition.

"I know," she replied. "That's what most outlanders think. But not everything that's true can be seen or touched or understood. The things I've told you have been passed down from generation to generation, even carried across the sea when our ancestors first came to this country. Why do you think they hung onto these sayin's?"

"I don't know," I admitted.

"Because they found them to hold true in their own experience. It gave them the comfort of havin' a wise friend there with them, tellin' what to do, though that wise friend might have been dead a hundred years or lived in another country."

The darkness of the valley closed in around us and would have swallowed us except for the lights of a few fireflies and the lamp glow coming through a window of the cabin. I felt how the isolation of this place drew the people closer together and caused them to depend more upon one another, just as they depended on the signs. For my part, I thought of the stern independence of my own ancestors, and I wondered who was better off.

"Charley, it's gettin' late. I'm gonna get my granddaddy and head on home. I've enjoyed talkin' with you. I hope I didn't upset you with the things I said."

"No, Mary, I appreciate everything you told me. You taught me a lot. Hopefully I won't look so out of place the next time you see me."

"I hope I do see you again." She sounded like she meant it.

"John Stepp and I are going to be leaving early in the morning, Mary. Big Tom says he's going to recruit some of the men from the settlement to help him look for Pa, but John and I have got to get back to the Swannanoa side and ask the Buncombe County men to join the search. So maybe I should say goodbye."

"Perhaps it is goodbye, and if so, God bless you, Charley."

"Goodbye, Mary."

We shook hands and she walked inside the cabin. Before long she was back with her grandfather and I watched the two of them walk slowly away by the light of a pine knot torch. Her grandfather talked to Mary as they walked, but her face turned back towards me.

I sat on the porch and brooded over the contrast between the two worlds surrounding me. There was the world of life and light and happiness that filled up the cabin and came streaming out through the windows in lamplight and fiddle music and footsteps on the bran-covered floor. There was also the world of darkness and solemn quietness that brooded all around the cabin and seemed ready to overwhelm it. The darkness spread out in every direction and up to the sky. Only here and there was it interrupted by starlight, fireflies, or the glow of the soon-coming moon still hidden behind the towering silhouette of the Blacks. I felt drawn to the deepness of the dark. There was a comfort and familiarity in it. As members of the wedding party headed home in small groups to the various parts of the Caney River valley, their voices echoing and their lanterns flickering until they disappeared, I realized why the emptiness of the darkness drew me. It threw nothing back at me . . . no expectations or requirements . . . only faint starlight and a katydid chorus. It was a blank tablet, an empty stage, waiting to be filled with whatever ideas I wanted to put into it. It did not criticize or judge. It listened.

Tom and Niagara Wilson were gracious to provide lodging for us that night. Their hospitality made up for any comforts they lacked, and we weren't the only ones who took advantage of their kindness. A cadre of Tom's neighbors and hunting companions showed up to share in the warmth of Tom's fire. I basked in the warmth of the fellowship and soaked in the sounds of the men laughing at their jokes and tall tales. The small space helped to emphasize the feeling of closeness and security. It amplified the merriness of the voices. It concentrated the smells of the food and drink. All the essence of life seemed distilled into that small space.

I carry the memory of that night with me. I open it like a bottle and take a deep draught on days when life grows too stale and gray. I hold it up like Mary's flowers against the blackened woods and I remember that life goes on even amidst its trials. As I fell asleep in Tom's cabin later that night the men still talked and laughed and my dreams were full of firelight.

* * *

Mary was waiting for me when I came out of Big Tom's cabin the next morning. She was a pleasing sight on what looked to be a dreary day.

"Good mornin'," she said, and offered me something in her hand.

"What this?" I asked.

"A goin' away gift. Somethin' to remember me by."

I looked at what she handed me and saw it was a hand-made woolen cap.

"Thank you, but you shouldn't have . . ."

"Now don't go tryin' to return my gift, Charley. It ain't proper."

"All right, Mary. It's a beautiful cap." I tried it on. "Fits perfectly."

She made some adjustments to the cap then stepped back to admire her handiwork. "Looks handsome if I say so myself." Then she paused as if she was trying to make up her mind about something. "Charley, it's altogether improper of me to say it, but you may not be around for a while, so . . ."

"Go ahead," I prodded.

"If you were going to be around, I wouldn't mind it if you courted me."

Her comment caught me by surprise. "But what about your hundred white horses?" I asked, only half joking.

"Oh, I'm further along than I let on. I'd have my hundred before we got through courtin'."

She was serious. I looked at her and the thought of courting her was very appealing. I longed to be close to someone. The grief I was feeling for Pa made the desire even stronger. But I knew without thinking that this was not the time, and the emotion I was feeling was more loneliness than love.

"Mary, the way you've cared for me is a far greater gift than this hat. You're wise beyond your years and I want to thank you for being so kind . . ."

"But you don't love me."

"Courting you would be a real pleasure, but no, I don't love you. You were right about me having an emptiness inside, and I think that has to be fixed before I can love anyone that way."

"Then I think my talk with you last night was worthwhile. You're a wise person, Charley, if you can learn from others and not depend on yourself alone."

"Charley, let's get started." It was John calling from the cabin.

"I've got to be going," I told Mary. "I don't know when I'll be back. Thank you again . . ."

"Goodbye, Charley." With that Mary kissed me on the cheek and quickly turned and ran away.

As I watched her go John walked up beside me and asked, "What was that all about?"

"Seems I'm always watching people walk away. Let's go, John."

"Suit yourself. Are you sure you're ready for the trip back?"

"My feet aren't nearly as heavy as my heart. I'm ready."

We walked uphill now, climbing away from the settlement and back towards the high peak. John sang as we climbed, the old song "Annie Laurie," but for my sake he changed the words a little.

"Her brow is like the snow drift,

her throat is like the swan.

Her face it is the fairest that e'er the sun shone on,

that e'er the sun shone on, and dark blue are her eyes,

and for bonnie Mary Riddle I'd lay me down and die."

"Very funny, John. You're just jealous because you didn't get a wool cap."

"Or a kiss on the cheek," he added.

"Take my advice and leave the singing to others." But he kept on, looking back every few steps to make sure I was properly annoyed.

"Like dew on the ground lying is the fall of her fairy feet;

and like winds in summer sighing,

her voice is low and sweet,

her voice is low and sweet,

and she's all the world to me,

and for bonnie Mary Riddle I'd lay me down and die."

Funny, I thought to myself, as we came down to the settlement my hopes were high. Now we were climbing back up and my hopes were all but gone.

Chapter Sixteen

The Search

As we came out of the balsams into the clearing of the Mountain House, Jesse Stepp and a dozen other men were waiting for us. Their faces were hopeful and expectant, but that changed as soon as they saw our disappointment.

"Well, what's the word, boys?" asked Mr. Stepp.

"Nothin' good," muttered John. "No trace of him along the trail and no one in the settlement had seen or heard of him. There's no doubt he's missin', and Big Tom Wilson was pretty well convinced he's suffered a terrible mishap." He looked at me to see how I reacted to his report.

"John, you might as well come out and say it. Big Tom thinks my Pa is dead, Mr. Stepp."

Mr. Stepp didn't speak but bent over with his hands on his knees and hung his head. Another man who looked familiar stepped forward and put his hand on my shoulder.

"Mr. Mitchell, I'm very sorry to hear about this misfortune. My name is Zeb Vance . . ."

"Yes, you were a student of my father's. I knew I had seen you before."

"That's right. I was at the University back in '52. In the short time I was there I developed the deepest respect for your father. He is truly one of the great men of this state, and of the nation."

Zeb Vance was one of those uncommon men gifted with the combination of appealing looks and the skillful use of language. Though only 27 years old at the moment, he was destined to become North Carolina's governor within five years.

"How do you happen to be here, Zeb?"

"Purely by happenstance. It's Charles, isn't it?" He had the politician's memory as well. "Well, Charles, I'm working as a lawyer in Asheville, but I love to get out and explore these hills. With the amenities of the Mountain House so close at hand, I find it hard not to slip out of my office and make my way here. You can be sure that your father had no small part in my appreciation of the mountains."

He meant it as a compliment, but it only served as a painful reminder of Pa's absence.

"I'm sorry, Charles. My fond recollections are no solace to you at a time like this." He looked at me earnestly for a moment then turned to the other men and spoke with conviction. "Gentlemen, you know that the situation before us is grim and the prospects of a suitable outcome are small. You also need no reminder of the inestimable value of Dr. Mitchell to all the people of this state, and to our community in particular. We have with us his only son, who serves as a tangible representative of all the Mitchell family. Can we look at him and not be moved to action? Considering all Dr. Mitchell has given us, is there anything we would not do to aid him, even to the point of searching out every crag and hollow between here and Burnsville?"

Cries of "that's right, Zeb" and "let's get started" rang out from the circle of men around Vance. Only John remained silent, his chin cupped against his palm. He understood, as I did, the tremendous difficulties facing those who would search for Pa.

Vance must have picked up on our thoughts, for he resumed his speech in a quiet and somber tone. "Let none of us doubt the situation. Dr. Mitchell has been missing for six days. The terrain we will be searching is among the most rugged imaginable. The chance that the beloved professor can be found alive is remote, but . . ." and here Vance paused, "while there is hope we will dare to hope. My commitment is to do all I can do. Would you want anything less done for you?"

This time there were no loud shouts, only a soft chorus of no's and the silent shaking of heads. Vance had grasped the only inspiring tidbit of truth in the sad reality of Pa's disappearance, that his fellow men owed it to him to offer every possibility of rescue until there was no possibility remaining, and he had served that tidbit with the skill of a master chef. Even John in all his practicality agreed with Vance's request.

In the next few minutes plans were made and orders were given in the fashion of a military campaign. Runners were sent through the North Fork Valley to recruit more soldiers for the search. A request was made and granted for the Mountain House to be taken over for use as a headquarters and barracks. Mrs. Garenflo made the decision willingly on behalf of the owner, Mr. Patton. Captains were appointed, and in addition to Vance and Jesse Stepp included brothers Fred and Eldridge Burnett. The Burnetts were hunters with years of experience in the wilderness surrounding the Black Mountains. A few men went out for a preliminary reconnaissance but were unable to search for long because of darkness. About 20 men soon settled into the Mountain House and their number grew as the night passed.

In the Caney River settlement of Yancey County, a smaller group of men planned for the search. Knowing Big Tom, I imagined his group would operate more like a hunting party than an organized military campaign. He wouldn't approach the search with the high idealism of Vance but with the pragmatism of a seasoned mountain man. I had no less faith in his efforts. On the contrary, because of his reputation, experience, and honesty I felt he was as likely to succeed as any man.

Lying in the Mountain House that night, I saw that the search for Pa had moved beyond me. The floor around me was covered by men who now shared in that search. Hour by hour their numbers grew as more stumbled in to find a spot to sleep. This was no longer my search and I no longer carried the burden alone. From now on others would make the decisions: Vance, Tom Wilson, Jesse Stepp and the Burnetts. I felt like a man putting down a heavy pack after an all day hike. At last I slept.

When I woke up Saturday morning and stepped out of the cabin it was quiet, cold and foggy. We were in the clouds. Later I heard Vance say that it only got up to 44 degrees on the peak that day. The weather was so bad that people complained the mountain was conspiring against us. The gloomy skies seemed fitting to me. I didn't think much about whether there was a purpose behind it.

It had been a week since Pa left me to cross the Blacks alone. Today was the Fourth of July, supposedly a day of celebration. Back home in Chapel Hill there would be picnics and a parade. Speeches would be made, with high spirits and grateful hearts, about the sacrifices of our forefathers and the value of our independence. But here on both sides of the Blacks men with sad hearts would undertake an effort that had little chance of success.

The area we would search covered thirty-two square miles. It stretched north from the Mountain House to the high peak of the

Black Mountain and several miles beyond. From the mountaintops it fell down to the west three or four miles and three thousand feet in elevation. The peaks formed the eastern boundary of our search and the Caney River marked the western border. Three branches of the Caney River divided the western flank of the mountain range roughly into thirds. Heading from south to north they were Beech Nursery Creek, Sugar Camp Creek, and Cat-tail Creek. Steep ridges stood to the north and south of each creek, with Tom Wilson's cabin located near the mouth of Sugar Camp Creek. Beyond Cat-tail Creek the Caney River continued flowing north towards Burnsville.

This accounting of miles and elevations only begins to tell you what the terrain was like. The mountain's surface tilted at an eighteen-degree angle over a rocky uneven ground. Dense forests and laurel hells covered the mountainsides. The only trails were the one along the crest of the range, the new trail from the high peak to Tom Wilson's, and scattered animal trails such as those made by the bears. Like men standing around the rim of a deep lake or ocean, we tried to look into the depths and could only see the surface.

On Saturday the Buncombe men filed north along the peaks and waded down the western flank of the range to differing depths. Burnett and some of his men made it down Beech Nursery Creek, the first branch of the Caney, and spent the night camped there. Others including Vance and myself ended up back at the Mountain House. Still another group met Wilson and the Yancey County men near the high peak. Wilson's group of seven hunters had come out of the valley and searched up the north side of the peak without finding any sign of Pa. Wilson's group and the Buncombe men they encountered retreated to Wilson's cabin to spend the night and plot the next day's strategy.

Back at the Mountain House John Stepp sought me out to hear my news.

"Where did you search today, Charley?"

"Along the mountainside below your father's cabin," I told him. John's father had recently built a primitive cabin for excursionists in the gap just before the high peak. "There wasn't any trace of a man having been there."

"Sounds like my day," John replied wearily. "Course there were plenty of false alarms. I don't know how many times someone shouted out that they'd found a sign. Everyone would weave their way over to the spot, argue about it for a while, and then try to follow it only to find it led nowhere. I tell you the truth, Charley, it was discouragin'."

He didn't have to elaborate. I knew exactly what he was talking about.

"Only thing I can't figure," he continued, "is where in the world your Pa could be. I mean, think of all the men who were out there today, coverin' all the ground where he was likely to have gone. God forbid it, Charley, but if your Pa is dead or seriously injured then he's not goin' anywhere and he should just be just lyin' there waitin' on us. Sorry to be so heartless but that's the way I see it. On the other hand, and this is what keeps me hopin', maybe he's not dead but somehow senseless and wanderin' around in a kind of stupor. Maybe that's why we can't find him. Maybe he's even wandered so far in the past week that he's completely away from where we're searchin'." He waited for an answer and then blurted out, "Well, what do you think?"

"I don't know," I answered weakly. I was afraid to hope. John's theory seemed to be well thought out, but then I remembered the tangle of rhododendron hells and the huge territory we were trying to cover and I wondered out loud, "Who can say what's likely in a place like this?"

"You're right, Charley. We'll just have to keep on lookin'. That's the word from my Pa and Vance anyway. Whatcha readin'?"

I told him it was a letter from my sister, Margaret, who was still in the town of Black Mountain.

"How's she holdin' up?"

"Surprisingly well. She spends most of the letter trying to encourage me. That's just like her, thinking about me instead of herself. She's also worried about Ma."

"But your Ma couldn't of heard yet, could she?"

"No, I'm sure she hasn't received our letter yet. Margaret is just worrying in advance."

"Anything else in the letter?"

"Margaret says she doesn't blame me for letting Pa go alone. She says, 'We all know how determined Pa is and how little he listens to us when we try to change his mind. I'm sure any arguments you made were to no avail.' She's right about that."

"Of course she's right," agreed John. "I've only a spent a little time with your Pa but I can vouch that he's got a stubborn streak in him. That can be a good thing when you're up against it, but it can also make you ignore good advice."

There was plenty of advice being dispensed on Saturday evening after our first full day of searching. It seemed everyone had an opinion about where to search next and what had likely happened to Pa. What we lacked were any real answers and any sign of where he had gone.

* * *

Sunday began badly. It was foggy and rainy like the day before, which everyone took as a sign that we were in for another disappointing day. Once again the men in the Mountain House fanned out across the Blacks following the trail to the high peak. Those staying at Tom Wilson's in the Caney River valley split into two groups. The Yancey men followed the Beech Nursery Creek upstream towards the high peak, while the Buncombe searchers headed up a prong that led west of the Caney River. It led them out of the valley and back to the Mountain House. It was about three in the afternoon when the majority of the search party made it back to the cabin. They were cold, wet, and hungry.

"What have we got to eat?" the men asked. I told them that the cabin had already been emptied of food. Some of them hadn't eaten since the day before, and the prospect of fasting longer didn't sit well with them. Zeb Vance was standing nearby and heard their grumbling.

"All right, what's the trouble?" he asked.

"No food!" was the frustrated reply.

Vance considered the possibilities and then eyed a heifer that a North Fork farmer had set loose to find summer pasture on the mountainside.

"There's your food," he said, pointing out the cow to the hungry men.

"But what will the owner think?" one of them asked.

"We'll explain it to him later. Right now we need food so you don't starve. Now, who's got a gun?"

A man named Ephraim Glass stepped forward with his rifle and put down the heifer. The hungry men quickly butchered the cow. Then, to my amazement, they began to eat strips of the meat raw. Vance was just as shocked by the sight. He immediately arranged for a party of men to go into town for provisions of food and drink. Drink in this case meant corn liquor, or "extract of corn" as the locals called it. That was ironic because Pa had always been a vocal supporter of temperance.

It was dark when the men returned with food. We could see them coming for miles, our hunger adding to the anticipation, as their torches crept up the hillside toward us. It reminded me of a religious ceremony with pagans approaching the high place to offer a sacrifice. As the torch bearers came into the clearing around the cabin I could plainly see their illuminated faces. These were not pagans, but men like me. Walking into the clearing two abreast they no longer looked like men bringing a sacrifice, but instead like a funeral procession coming for my father.

Who said you cannot mourn someone before they die? That man is a fool, or has never experienced the sadness that comes from watching a loved one die slowly. He has never sat out the long days waiting for the letter or visit which tells him the news that his loved one has been taken away. I don't know if mourning in advance reduces the mourning we must do, but we do grow used to our losses in rehearsing them.

"Come on, Tom. Tell us about bear huntin'." I turned to see a group of Yancey County men gathered around a nearby fire. Every face was turned to the lanky figure of Big Tom Wilson. He stood out as the focal point of the circle even as he stooped by the fire. Tom smiled at the request to talk about bear hunting. He knew that every man and boy in the mountains loved to hear about bears.

"What's to tell, fellas. You all been bear huntin' before, haven't you?"

"You just don't want to give away no secrets. Is that it, Tom?"

Tom's reputation as a master tracker was widely known. The men weren't looking for secrets as much as a good story.

"There's only one secret I know about bear huntin'," said Tom.

"What's that?" they all asked.

183

"Don't hunt alone."

"Tell us somethin' we don't know," laughed one of the men.

"Don't laugh," said another. "I heard William Austin went after a bear by himself just last week. Lost two dogs, had two others torn up bad, and never even laid eyes on the bear."

"Exactly my point," added Tom. "Any fool knows one man can't keep ahead of a bear, not unless you're huntin' with traps."

"Let's don't talk about traps. Tell us about your most memorable hunt, Tom." All the men urged Tom on.

"You know you don't have to prod me to get me talkin'. My most memorable hunt you say." Tom thought back upon all the bears he had pursued from the time he had gone on his first hunt as a boy. He remembered the men he had gone with, some of them no longer living. He saw the places he had hunted and knew that houses and fields now stood where there used to be only woods. He mentally fingered and handled the various rifles he had used through the years. "All right, boys, let me tell you about my most memorable hunt."

"Was it your first hunt?"

"No, it weren't that one."

"Was it when you shot your biggest bear?"

"No, though that was quite a hunt, too. No, this hunt was memorable for other reasons." The mountain men settled in for the story, and Tom wet his throat with a sip of corn liquor. "It was an October day. You know the kind. Startin' off cool but quickly warmin' up to that perfect temperature that keeps you from sweatin' when you work. The air was so fresh and clear you could smell coffee from the next county."

"Forget the coffee. Tell us about the bear, Tom."

"Patience, man. I'll get there. Let's see. I was 17 at the time. My pa had promised to take me huntin', so the two of us plus one of my brothers and two of Pa's friends headed out that mornin'."

"Where did you hunt?"

"We were headed up Raven Fork towards Black Knob. We had seen some good bear sign there. The neighbor men and my brother were the drivers. My Pa and I took out ahead of the others up Raven Fork and took our stand along the ridge north of Black Knob. I remember how tiring it was just to get to the ridge. Didn't seem to bother Pa none. Once we were there we waited. It was awful quiet at first, then we began to hear the bayin' of the hounds."

"What kind of dogs did you have?"

"I don't remember for sure. They was good dogs. Pa never had nothin' but good dogs. He always preferred a dog that was part hound and part cur. Said they had the trackin' ability of a hound and the natural ferociousness of a cur."

There was general agreement among all the men on that point, washed down with a generous portion from the jug that was making its way around the circle.

"We must have been on top of that ridge for an hour or two," continued Tom. "The sound of the dogs was gettin' closer all the time. Only you could tell the bear wasn't comin' straight up the mountain. Sometimes the sound would wander to our right hand, and then back to the left, but always gettin' closer. That bear was either mighty fast or mighty smart, cause you could tell from the hounds that they were trackin' and not fightin' the bear. And there were no shots either, so my brother and the men below us were havin' a time keepin' up."

"Must not have been a very fat bear," observed one of the listeners.

"You're right about that," agreed Tom. "This bear was much too quick to be real fat. I think that was a pretty dry year and the pickin's had not been too good for the bears. Bad for the bear, I guess, but good for the hunt. Well, anyway, the minutes ticked by and now the sound of the dogs was gettin' real close. My pa leaned over to me and said, "Tommy, you take the left and I'll take the right. There's a clearin' on my side and I 'spect the bear will come through it. But if it doesn't, you be ready on your side. And remember," he said, "give yourself plenty of time to take a second shot in case your first one misses." Well, I headed towards the left just as he said. We were probably about a hundred feet apart. At first I could still see Pa. Then the unexpected happened."

Everyone knew what was coming, but we still leaned forward in anticipation.

"The bear came my way," said Tom with a big grin. "Only she didn't come right at me."

"So it was a she-bear," exclaimed an older man with excitement in his voice.

Tom confirmed it was. "I couldn't see her yet, but the sound of the dogs told me the bear was goin' further to my left. I followed the sounds for thirty, fifty, a hundred feet, and then I saw it."

"Saw what," moaned an exasperated mountaineer. "Come on, Tom, tell us!"

"It was a bear track in the laurel. I knew for certain that the bear would be comin' right up that tunnel, so I took my position in the mouth of the track and waited. Sure enough, the sounds were comin' right at me now. I felt the sweat on my neck, though I wasn't the least bit overheated. I could feel the dampness of the air in the bear track, and then I heard it . . . the pantin' of the bear as she lumbered up the track. I knelt down in the tunnel and steadied my rifle against my shoulder. My heart was poundin' in my ears like the tick-tock of a great big clock. The pantin' of the she-bear sounded like a saw rippin' through soft wood. And then I saw her."

"How big was she?" The question burst out from half a dozen men.

"The biggest I'd ever faced up til then, though not the biggest since. She was somewhat gaunt, like you reckoned, but she was chargin' up that track like she had only just started to run. I took aim on her at a hundred feet, but my shot either missed or had no effect. The bear kept comin', and I had been knocked down by the kick of my rifle."

"And how did you get out of that fix?" I asked.

"Well, Charley, I thought I wouldn't. That she-bear was within 50 feet of me and I was still fumblin' with my powder horn. I was prayin' for forgiveness and tryin' to load my rifle all at the same time, with my hands tremblin' like an old woman with the palsy. I was tryin' to imagine how I could wrestle that bear, when all of a sudden I heard a loud explosion right behind my head."

"Your Pa!" shouted the excited old man.

"Yes, my Pa, God bless his soul. His shot dropped that she-bear dead in her tracks, with the foam from her mouth blowin' right into my lap. My ears rang for a week, but that didn't matter to me."

"What did your Pa have to say?" I asked.

"He just said, 'Remember when you hunt, Tommy, the most important thing is lookin' out for the other men you're huntin' with.' He wasn't angry or upset. He was as calm when he said it as I am now. But I'll never forget what he said."

They say Big Tom could talk up one side of the mountain and down the other, and I don't doubt it. The cheerfulness of his voice was a welcome antidote to my disappointment. I curled up in a blanket under the stars and fell asleep to the tune of another of Big Tom's tales.

* * *

Monday dawned brighter, and after two full days of fruitless work many felt this would be the day that made the difference. Perhaps because of the improved weather, and perhaps because of superstition about the charm of the third try, hopes were higher that morning. There were also twice as many men present to help us search. I counted at least a hundred. But the day got off to a difficult start. The Burnett brothers reported that they had seen convincing signs near the westward prong of the Caney River. Big Tom disagreed with the plans to search there.

Eldridge Burnett made his case first.

"Listen here, Tom. Fred and I saw some bent twigs in the undergrowth down there yesterday. It got dark on us before we could pursue it, and I'm convinced that's where we should look today."

"It don't make no sense," Tom argued back.

"Why not?" asked Fred Burnett.

"What would he be doing so far from the trail to the peak or my house? Why would he be heading west, away from the direction of my house? And if he was there why didn't any of you see him yesterday?" Tom stuffed a pipe in his mouth and waited for the rebuttal.

"I can give you plenty of reasons," Eldridge Burnett snapped back. Tom just waved his pipe inviting Burnett's response. "He could have been lost. It might have gotten dark on him. Maybe he was trying to double back to the Mountain House without goin' all the way to your place. And as for not seein' him, the same could be said for every other part of this mountain, Tom."

"You don't give him no credit at all," commented Big Tom.

Zeb Vance then stepped into the discussion. "Gentlemen, both of you have made fine points. The fact is that either one of you may be correct, but we need to marshal our resources and make the most of the many men who are here today. If I may make my contribution to the debate, then let me point out that we have repeatedly searched the trail to the high peak over the past few days. Why not follow the Burnetts' lead and explore this less searched area?"

"I agree completely," said Fred Burnett, and his brother seconded him.

Big Tom puffed away on his pipe, then stated without emotion that he would abide by the wishes of the majority. He and the Yancey men would help search the west prong area. And they did. We all did. The west prong saw more human footsteps that day than it had seen in a hundred years or more. But as the sun fell behind the Black Mountains that evening the result was the same as the previous days. We returned to the Mountain House with empty hands.

Back at the Mountain House the men were quiet and discouraged. As I walked around the camp I heard little more than "Sorry, Charley" from the tired searchers. Then I noticed the captains standing together and talking. Jesse Stepp saw me and invited me to join the group.

"How are you holding up, son?" he asked.

I told him I was tired.

"Yes, we all are. Look, Charley, we've been talking among ourselves and with some of the men. We think it's time to stop searchin'."

Mr. Stepp said nothing more. I looked from him to Vance to the Burnetts and Tom Wilson. Some looked back at me with sorrow in their eyes. Others looked at the ground or away. No one spoke.

"I'm not ready to quit," I blurted out.

"Course you're not. I understand." Mr. Stepp was trying to calm me. "If it were my Pa I wouldn't want to quit either, but look at the facts. We've searched three solid days with up to a hundred men. We've looked in all the likely places and have followed every lead. What more can we do?"

"We can keep looking until we find him," I pleaded.

Fred Burnett spoke up. "Son, these men are tired. Don't forget they've got farms and families to tend. I'm sure we could find Dr.

Mitchell eventually, but what if that takes another week or two? These men don't have that kind of time, and neither do I."

Vance spoke next. "Charles, there's general agreement that the buzzards should notice the body and point out its location in the next few days. We're only stopping the search temporarily. We'll resume it with a good chance of success in a few days."

"Zeb, waiting for the buzzards to find Pa is the last thing I want. What happened to your desire to do everything that could be done?"

"My desire is no less, but I believe we've done everything within reason."

I looked around at the captains. Everyone had spoken except Tom Wilson. Tom always had something to say, and in this case he was my last hope.

"Well, Tom, what about you?"

"Charley, these gentlemen are tellin' you the truth . . ."

My hopes sank.

". . . but I'm not ready to quit yet."

And just as quickly they sprang back to life. The group exploded in protests and questions of "why not, Tom?" Wilson just chewed on his pipe and waited for them all to quiet down.

"I love to bear hunt," he continued, "and I hate nothin' worse than to lose a bear I'm trackin'. The way I see it, quittin' now is like givin' up on that bear while he's still in the woods. I told you yesterday we needed to scout the area around the high peak again, and I still believe that. If Mr. Mitchell wants to continue searchin', then I for one will keep at it."

The others objected, but with Tom standing firm it wasn't long before their pride led them to relent and continue the search.

"I'd like to put one condition on my decision," Eldridge Burnett requested.

"What is it?" asked Big Tom.

"If you search the peak tomorrow and find no sign, no trail to follow, then we call off this bear hunt."

"Agreed," Tom answered without hesitation.

"Charley?" Jesse Stepp wanted my opinion as well.

"Agreed," I replied reluctantly.

Big Tom wasted no time. "I'd best be on the move," he said. "I want to get an early start tomorrow, so I'll spend tonight on the peak.

Some of the Yancey boys and I will stay at your cabin there if it's all right, Jesse."

"That's fine, Tom."

"Then good huntin' tomorrow. If we find anything we'll send you a signal by horn or gun."

Tom loped off to find his neighbors. I wanted to go with him, but I had the sense to know that I would only slow him down. He was the last hope for finding Pa, and I didn't want to interfere.

Chapter Seventeen

Discovery

Tuesday morning Tom Wilson was up and hunting before I saw the light of day. Four other Yancey men were with him, including Adoniram Allen, the son of Pa's guide on the first climb up the Black Mountain. They began by scouring the peak for signs once more, but finding none they began a slow descent down the north side of the mountain. They had gone no more than a quarter mile when Allen called out.

"Tom, come here!"

Tom and the others hurried across the slope to find Adoniram kneeling over a patch of moss.

"What have you found?" asked Tom.

"Looks like a print in the moss. Take a look for yourself and tell me what you think."

Everyone agreed the depression in the moss was a footprint of some kind, but did it belong to a man or a bear?

"It's a man's footprint," said Tom, and no one disagreed. They waited for the explanation they knew would follow.

"A bear would stick to the rocks and the ridges where he's harder to track and follow. Only a man would wander through this wide-open space and through the moss where his steps would be so easy to see. Had to be a man."

Everyone agreed with Tom's reasoning. The group moved forward carefully, away from the peak and further down the slope. Another twenty steps brought them to a rotting tree trunk lying on the ground across their path.

"Wait," said Tom. "Let's take a look at this. Somethin' knocked this trunk over, and not long ago by the look of it. Now a bear would have just gone around it, but a man, especially a tired man, might have stopped to lean against it and rest. A little pressure on the rotten trunk and over it goes."

Adoniram spotted something more. "There's a print on either side of the trunk, Tom."

"You're right. Why, look at the prints close and you can see the depression at the toe end on the near side of the trunk. The heel end is more sunken on the far side. Just what you'd expect if a man took a step across a fallen log. Fellas, this is the track of a man without a doubt."

The trackers could hardly restrain themselves now, but they slowed their advance down the mountain so that they missed nothing. Two hundred yards more brought them to a clearing in the balsam forest. From it they could easily see Tom's farm, located six miles away in the valley below them. Here they found another footprint. The men studied it exhaustively as other men might examine a rare coin or jewel. Not everyone was convinced it belonged to a man, but once again Tom settled the question.

"What bear paw ever had tacks in it?" he asked, and then showed them the faint but clear indentions of the tacks from a shoe heel. The five trackers quickly held a conference in the clearing.

"What do we do next?" asked Adoniram Allen.

"We keep searchin'," argued his brother, James. "This has got to be Mitchell's track."

"It's Mitchell's track all right," agreed Benton Austin.

"Tom?" asked Adoniram.

Tom was lost in thought, looking down from the clearing towards his farm in the valley below. "Sorry, fellas, I was just tryin' to put myself in Mitchell's shoes and figure what he was thinkin' when he stood here. He had to know he was off the trail. He would've seen my farm, that's for certain, and I believe he thought he could make a quicker journey down the mountain by following the line of sight to my farm."

"What do you think we should do, Tom?" asked James Allen.

"We've got to head back to the peak, fellas. This news is too important not to tell the others."

"We could fire off a rifle shot and let them know to come this way," suggested Bryson McMahan.

"And bring a hundred men swarming down through here? No, they'd only ruin any chance we got of followin' this trail. Let's head on back and talk to the rest of the fellas on the peak. Then we'll come back with just a small group of men. Besides, I want to take another look up above and see if we can figure out where Mitchell lost his way."

Back at Stepp's cabin Big Tom and his men found other searchers from both Yancey and Buncombe counties. Tom and Adoniram recounted their steps and the signs they had found. Everyone knew this was the most promising lead they had found all week, and they quickly organized a somewhat larger search party. McMahan and Austin had to return home, but several Buncombe men took their places. Before they returned to the search, Big Tom stopped to take another look at the place where Pa seemed to have lost his way.

"Fellas, if you stand right here where the trail to my farm takes a sharp left turn, what do you see?"

Adoniram Allen had the sharpest eye and saw it first. "I see a faint trail, probably just a bear track or horse trail, but it's headin' in the general direction where we found the signs."

"That's just what I see," agreed Tom.

"So you think he mistook this bear track for the trail to the valley?" asked Calvin Patton.

"He might have," said Tom. "The new trail does cut sharply away to the left here, and he might've missed it. Or he might have taken this faint trail on purpose."

"Why on purpose?" asked James Allen. "That don't make no sense at all. That'd just be askin' for trouble."

"Maybe so," said Tom, "but maybe he thought it would be quicker on account of bein' shorter, and maybe he just wanted to retrace his steps from before."

"Meanin' what?" asked a Mr. Burgin.

"Meanin' that Mitchell came up this way," answered Adoniram Allen, "when he first climbed the mountain with my Pa back in '35."

"That's right," said Tom. "Maybe he wanted to follow that trail again to prove to himself that this was the peak he climbed in '35."

The party of seven searchers didn't wait any longer to ponder Pa's motives. They descended along the faint trail and their earlier track until they reached the clearing with the view of Tom's farm. It was dinner time by then, and the group sat down to eat and consider what might lie ahead. Tom, with the hunt ever on his mind, didn't bother to sit down but wandered around the clearing eating slices of salt pork. Soon he was striding back and forth across the clearing with his eyes on the ground.

"Tom, what are you doin'?" asked Calvin Patton.

"There's footprints here going back and forth in the clearing. I reckon the Professor was tryin' to get a better view over the trees to see the valley below."

Tom's impatience cut dinner short and forced the men to resume the search. The party continued their descent towards the valley, dropping fifteen hundred feet in elevation as they followed the signs and neared a creek. They could hear the water though it was still hidden by the trees.

"Does anyone know where we are?" asked Calvin Patton.

"Not exactly, and I'll bet no man has walked here before us," replied Adoniram Allen.

"Except for the man we're tracking," corrected Tom Wilson. "I reckon we're headin' towards a branch of the Sugar Camp Creek."

"How are you followin' the trail, Tom?" asked Mr. Burgin. "I don't see any signs."

"It's the leaves on the laurels. See how the leaf is bent back here so that the pale underneath is showin'? The Professor bent that back as he brushed by it." Tom stopped and pointed to something on the ground. "Now look here."

"I see it," said James Allen. "There's a whole area here where all the leaves have been brushed away down to the bare dirt."

"What happened?" asked Mr. Burgin.

"Mitchell lost his balance here," explained Tom, "fell to the ground, then slid down towards the creek. I'll bet it was dark by the time he got here. That's what gave him such a hard time with his footin'."

Now they were at the creek and the trail disappeared.

"I see what he did," Tom announced as he waded into the water. "He decided to follow the creek. In the dark that was easier than forcin' his way through the laurels."

"That explains why his trail disappeared," said Adoniram.

"Exactly. Only it didn't disappear completely. Look in that raft of sticks and such downstream. You can see some of it's fresh. Mitchell must have knocked some of it loose as he made his way into the creek."

"He probably decided the creek was his best path down the mountain," said James Allen.

Tom agreed with him. "Especially in the dark."

The searchers felt they must be getting closer to their goal, though none of them knew what to expect. They were nearly two miles below the mountaintop and at least halfway to the valley floor. The end of their search might lie around each bend they rounded, but what would they find? The group split in two and took opposite sides of the creek. As they followed it downstream they watched for any sign that Pa had left the waterway, and listened for any human voice. They heard no sound except the water, and it was growing much louder.

"Waterfall ahead!" shouted Adoniram Allen.

"Boys, I'm afraid of what we're goin' to find," warned Tom.

Now they were at the top of the falls. The full course of the stream crashed down forty feet into a deep pool, but it was interrupted by the trunk of an upended balsam that stretched from the apex of the falls to the pool below.

"Look here, fellas," Tom shouted over the cascade. He was standing on a shelf of rock running above the falls and to the right. Several of the trackers gathered around Wilson and saw what he had discovered: bare rock where a great swath of moss had been stripped away, and above it all a branch of laurel broken clean off.

"This is it, boys. We'll find . . ."

"Tom!" came the shout from Adoniram Allen. "It's the Professor!"

The men ran and slid to the base of the falls where Allen was standing. He pointed into the pool. There, six feet underwater and held down by a submerged branch, the body of my father floated face down and lifeless. Some of the searchers sank down in despair while others stood in reverent respect. Everyone was quiet until Big Tom spoke.

"I see plainly what happened, fellas. The professor came to the top of the falls in the dark, traveling more by sound than sight. He made his way to the right along the shelving rock, but the rock itself dimmed the sound of the creek and made it seem farther away than it was. He cut back to the left to follow the creek, but he turned too soon and fell over the ledge to his death."

"Grabbing for the branch and scraping away the moss as he fell," added James Allen.

"I found this floatin' on the edge of the pool," said Adoniram Allen, holding up Pa's fur cap. "I saw this, then I saw his body."

The search party stood around the pool and looked through the glassy water at a body so well preserved by the icy stream that it seemed my father had only just fallen in and might rise up at any moment. Common sense and the body's unnatural stillness told them that this would not happen . No one wanted to remove the body. All of them felt defeated by what they found rather than heartened at the success of their search. It was small consolation when Big Tom reminded them that it would have made no difference if they had found Pa days earlier. He had been dead within moments of falling into the pool.

"What do you reckon killed him?" someone asked.

"Maybe he hit his head on the rocks," one suggested.

"Maybe he broke his neck," said another.

"Either way," said James Allen, "he wouldn't have been breathin' when he went into that water."

Then Tom spoke up. "Fellas, don't you reckon we ought to say a prayer for the Professor?"

"Let me do it," said Calvin Patton. As the waterfall whispered in the background, seven men stood still with bowed heads around the pool. "Dear Lord, we come before you now with sad hearts to ask you to remember our brother, Elisha Mitchell. Lord, in your mercy we ask you to forgive his sins and receive him into your eternal care. We thank you for the good he did while he was here on Earth, and we ask you to bless and comfort his family in their time of great loss. Lord, may we be humbled by what we see here today and remember that each one of us must one day give an account of his life. In Jesus' name we pray, Amen."

"Amen," came the unison reply, and once again only the waterfall spoke.

At that moment I was miles away with Zeb Vance, searching along the headwaters of the Beech Nursery Creek. Another frustrating and fruitless day suddenly changed when we heard a series of rifle shots from some distance away and to the north, followed by horns and more shots from the area of the peak. It was news, and from the repetition of the shots it sounded like big news. My heart pounded at the possibility that Pa had been found, and that soon I would know his fate. I turned to Vance to see his reaction.

"Sounds like the shots came from near the peak, Charley. I'd suggest we head that way and see what we can find out."

It took hours to hike up from the Caney River valley to the high peak. By the time we arrived at Stepp's cabin it was dark. There we learned about the discovery of Pa's trail and how Tom Wilson had followed it down the mountain. When the shots were fired a group of men had gone down the mountain in the direction of the sound, but they hadn't returned.

"What do you men think it means?" asked Vance.

"I don't like to speculate," one of the mountaineers replied, "but if'n he was alive, I think they would have come back with him by now."

No one knew anything more. The hours dragged by and at some point I fell asleep. When I woke up it was about one in the morning, and Jesse Stepp was leaning over me. By the light of lanterns I could see a number of other men gathered in the tiny cabin. Vance was there, and John Stepp, and others I did not know by name. No one was smiling.

"I'm sorry, Charley," Mr. Stepp began.

I ran out of the cabin and into the night. The moon was full, lighting the peak as bright as twilight. The air was cold and dry and it cleared my head to breathe it in. As I stood there breathing deep and long John Stepp walked up and looked me in the face.

"Charley, you better watch that heavy breathin'. You look mighty pale. You're goin' to make yourself pass out if you're not careful."

I didn't tell him the idea appealed to me. Instead I slowed down my breathing and told him the moon made me look pale.

"Right," he said skeptically. "Tell yourself what you like, but I know how hard this is for you."

"How do you know?" I demanded. "When did you ever lose your father?"

"And when are you going to start being thankful for having had such a father?" he yelled back. Then he turned away and said over his shoulder, "I'm sorry, Charley. I take it back. I had no right to say that."

But he did have the right. Shocked as I was to hear him say it, I knew it was the truth.

"How do I learn to be thankful?" I asked him.

"You can start by remembering the things your father gave you, like a good education and a good name, a good mother I reckon, and a nice home. Am I right?"

"Yes," I answered. We were not rich, but in comparison to the mountain people we were very wealthy.

"How about food and clothes? Did you have plenty of those?"

"Yes."

"Did he beat you?"

"No."

"Did he take you to church and make sure you knew about God?"

"Yes."

"So why wouldn't you be thankful?"

Why wouldn't I indeed? How could I mourn my father's loss if I wasn't thankful for him?

"It's sad that you've got to lose someone before you can appreciate them," John added.

He was right, but I didn't have the courage to say so. "John, all I can say is thanks for being honest with me. I'm getting cold, and I'd like to hear more from the men at the cabin, so let's go back."

Inside the cabin I heard how Pa's trail had been followed to the falls, how the cold water had preserved his body, and how the men had left him where they found him until the coroner could examine the body. There were other details and plans, but I was in too much shock to comprehend much of what was said. The night dragged on slowly as the wind blew outside and men talked in low voices inside. Some smoked and some snored. What sleep I found was separated by long stretches of restless tossing. Before daylight I got up for good and wondered outside to find a small group of men sitting around a carefully tended fire.

"Have a seat, Charley," invited a stranger. "I'm not surprised you couldn't sleep."

"How about you?" I asked.

"Oh, I'm used to bein' up early. Besides, that crowded cabin ain't much for gettin' a good night's rest. I'm sorry about your Pa."

"Thank you," I replied quietly.

Everyone was quiet. There were no words that were fitting for a time like this, when fatigue and disappointment numbed the mind and tightened the throat. All eyes were fixed on the fire; it hurt too much to look into another man's face. Only the crackling and popping of the flames interrupted the silence. Just when I felt that I couldn't take the heavy quietness any longer, one of the men began to sing. He sang softly but well, and with a voice full of tenderness.

"Tell me the tales that to me were so dear,
long, long ago, long, long ago.
Sing me the songs I delighted to hear,
long, long ago, long ago.
Now you are come all my grief is removed.
Let me forget that so long you have roved.
Let me believe that you love as you loved,
long, long ago, long ago."

As he sang the sun broke over the horizon and brought no comfort. Its sharp light cut me with the certainty that this day dawned without my father. The day we came to the mountain seemed long ago indeed, and my grief would not be removed.

I ran from the sunrise and down through the darkness of the balsam fir forest on the opposite side of the mountain. I was running from reality and running for release. The mist mixed with my tears and covered my face and blurred my eyes. I ran without seeing and without wanting to see. I ran until I fell, and face down on the ground I lay and cried and wished to die. When I finally looked up I saw that I had fallen only feet from the edge of a cliff. In my sorrow and stumbling I had almost taken my life.

I sat up and looked out over the cliff in time to see a vulture circling closer. It headed straight towards me and landed awkwardly in the top of a dead tree not ten feet away. "It's small for a buzzard," I thought. "Must be young to show such a lack of fear." The vulture eyed me curiously and I yelled at it, "Go find your meal somewhere else." I wasn't dead. Despite the pain and fear and loss, I wanted to live. I left the buzzard and ran back to the cabin, searching through all the faces until I found John Stepp.

"John," I said, "I want to go see where they found Pa."

"All right. I'll go with you."

It wasn't hard to find the way now. The scores of people that had been down to the waterfall had left a visible track. Even my untrained eye could follow it, and a steady stream of men coming up from below let us know that we were on the right trail.

"I wonder what he was thinking when he walked past here?" I asked.

"Your Pa? Well, you can be sure he wasn't thinking about a waterfall. I imagine he was trying to figure out the quickest way down the mountain."

"I guess there's mercy in that."

"No doubt about it," assured John. "When it's my time, let it be just like that. No worryin' ahead of time. No long, drawn out sufferin'. Let me do my job right up to the end. Let me die doin' my job if I can't die in my sleep."

"Well, he didn't die doing his job, but I know Pa felt his work here was just as important."

"Course it was," replied John.

"But his work isn't finished. He wouldn't have felt good about that."

John stopped walking and stuck his hands in his pockets. He looked out over the range of mountains and then looked back at me.

"Charley, these mountains are big. Your father could have spent another twenty years working here and still not have learned everything there is to know about them. I think history will look back with favor on what he did."

Just then my eye caught a glint of light from something shiny on the ground. I walked over and bent down to find the source of the reflection.

"What is it?" John asked.

"A knife. Pa's knife. Must have fallen from his pocket as he walked past here."

"So you got your proof. Is it any consolation?"

"It's a little late for my purposes, but it belonged to Pa, and right now I'm thankful to have anything of his."

I saw John smile at my remark.

"I'm learning," I said. He just kept smiling.

We hadn't descended another quarter mile before we heard a commotion down below. Voices rang out giving commands and shouting encouragement. We heard heavy breathing and grunting, as if men were straining against some great weight. John and I quickened our descent and soon saw Big Tom Wilson.

Tom waved at us, but then quickly looked down at the ground as he leaned against a tree with his hands on his knees. I didn't know if he was exhausted or despairing.

"Tom, are you all right?" John asked as we walked up.

"I'm fine, just out of breath. I reckon that's what you've come to see." He pointed down the hill. Through the balsams we saw a large white canvas, tied at each end to a long pole and drooping down under a heavy load, with men in front and back straining to carry it up the slope.

"I guess you heard what we found," Tom stated.

I couldn't speak. The physical evidence of Pa's death, even shrouded, was too real to accept. John had to answer for me.

"We heard," he answered. "We made it to the peak at dark. Some of the men woke us up during the night and told us you'd found him."

"We waited til the coroner got here this mornin' before we took your Pa's body out of the water," Tom explained. "Thought that was the best way to preserve him, the water bein' so cold."

"Mr. Wilson . . ." I tried to speak but the words were painful in my throat. "Tell me what happened."

"Charley, it looked to me like it was dark before he ever got to the falls. Only God knows why. Did he spend too much time explorin' the peak? Was there a storm that trapped him up there til it was late? I don't know."

"What was he doing here in the first place?"

"Hard to say. Might've missed the cleared trail up top. Might've come this way on purpose to try and save time. But I'm sure of this much, by the time he made it down here it was dark or nearly so. We found his trail goin' into the creek, then followin' the creek, then leadin' around a ledge at the top of the falls. He slipped or turned too quickly at the top of the falls and fell into a pool at the bottom."

"Why didn't he just climb out of the pool?" asked John.

"Must've hit his head when he fell. Never came to before he drowned. I'm sorry it had to be this way, Charley."

By now the other men, perhaps ten in all, were coming up to give me their condolences. They wanted to know if I wanted to see the body, but I said no. I wanted to remember Pa the way he had been.

There was nothing more that could be said. The men took up their burden again and resumed the climb. They struggled with every step to carry my father's body up the mountain. Their faces were red with the strain and their sweat dropped steadily onto the white shroud. They grunted and slipped and every few feet a new man would grab one end of the pole to relieve his exhausted neighbor. I stood above the struggling men in awe at what I saw. They worked as if it were a fight for life, as though their effort could somehow overcome death.

"Why, John? Why do they do it?"

"You mean why do they work so hard for someone they hardly knew?"

"Yes. Do you understand it?"

"I think I know how they feel. It's their way of showin' respect."

"Because of his fame?" I asked.

"Partly that. Partly because it's the nature of these men to help anyone in need. And the Yancey men don't want to be outdone by the Buncombe men, or vice versa. But I think there's more to it than that."

"There must be," I said as I watched my father's body being hoisted step by step up the tree-covered slope.

"They respect him because of what he did," John continued. "They know how hard it was to climb the mountain twenty years ago. They respect him for using them as guides. They're thankful for the recognition he brought to this area. They respect him because he showed them respect."

I looked at the scores of men on the mountainside and was struck by how much things had changed in twenty years. Pa had come here the first time with only two other men. Now there were fifty or more around the peak. He came to a tree-covered summit with no human imprint. Now the peak was cleared and a crude cabin had been built there. In the past Pa had struggled to reach the peak; now others struggled for him.

It was two miles from the falls to the peak and it took hours to bring Pa's body to the top. By the time we reached the peak the men were beyond exhaustion. I was sure they would rest before taking any other action, yet no sooner had we arrived than a major argument erupted. Some of the Buncombe men had brought a casket to the peak and were ready to carry the body to Asheville for burial.

"That's crazy," shouted one of the Yancey men. All his fellows agreed with him. "The Professor should be buried here on the peak. That's the only thing that would be right and fittin'."

"He's a Presbyterian minister and should be buried in the Presbyterian cemetery in Asheville," retorted a Buncombe man.

We were standing in Yancey County, and that fueled the argument. It went back and forth until Zeb Vance stepped in. "There's merit in what both sides have said. I myself would like to see Dr. Mitchell buried here on the peak which he first measured, but the fact of the matter is that his family has requested that he be buried in Asheville."

That was news to me, but Vance went on to explain that Margaret had been in touch with him and made the request. I hadn't given any thought to where Pa should be buried, and there was no way to overrule Margaret even if I wanted to.

Things moved quickly. Pa's body was placed in the casket and the Buncombe men started with it on the long trip to Asheville. The mountain men began to drift away to their farms and families. I sat and watched the men go, some heading south to the Swannanoa Valley and the others heading west to the Caney River settlement. Soon I found myself alone on the peak, sitting among the rocks on a grassy prairie.

I looked at the rocks and wished Pa had only studied rocks and left mountains alone. Rocks are predictable. What man ever lost his way on a rock? You can get your hand around a rock. Who ever handled a mountain?

Once I erred and called rocks dull. Once was enough for that mistake, for it led to my indoctrination in the science of rocks at the school of Professor Mitchell. Then I had spurned the knowledge. Now I regretted my ignorance.

"Charley!" In my mind I could hear my father's professorial voice as I looked out over the mountaintop stones sitting like students in an outdoor classroom. "Pay attention," his voice said. "The science of mineralogy is a key that unlocks the treasures of the earth's interior. Learn the language of the rocks and learn the secrets of the world." I looked across the prairie at the stone-faced students but heard no words. It wasn't that they spoke a foreign language; they weren't speaking at all. These rocks were keeping their secrets. For once I wanted to know the stone speech that I might ask them what had happened to my father. I longed for an interpreter but there was none. In vain I searched through memory for a clue to the code.

"Let us begin with the primitive rocks," intoned Professor Mitchell. "And before you say it, Charley, these are not ignorant or simple rocks. These rocks are primitive in the sense of being primary. That is, they were formed first, and so are the oldest. What are these primitive rocks, class?"

My stony fellow-students said nothing, so I answered. "The crystalline rocks. Granite, gneiss, mica slate."

"Where are they found?"

Again I spoke to break the silence. "New England, the Adirondacks, and the Piedmont lying at the foot of the Alleghany Mountains and the Blue Ridge."

"Thank you, Charley. Now let us move on to the Secondary rocks, also called the *flöetz* or stratified rocks because they are laid down in layers. As you would expect, these were formed later than the primitive rocks. What types of rocks are these, and where are they found?"

"Sedimentary rocks which are found beyond the Alleghanies. Sandstone, gypsum, limestone."

"Very good. Now, imagine if you will, the line of contact between the primary and secondary rocks. The rocks in this formation are folded and transformed. Where would you draw this line of transition, and what are these transitional rocks?"

"The line of transition runs through the Alleghany and Blue Ridge Mountains."

"Correct. Finally, we come to our youngest rocks. Formerly called the alluvial rocks, they are now referred to as tertiary rocks in our scheme of primary, secondary, and tertiary. What does alluvial refer to, Charley?"

"To the way these rocks developed from sediments that were washed downstream from higher elevations and deposited, as at the mouth of a river."

"Yes, and where do we find these alluvial rocks?"

"In the coastal plain."

The voices of my past faded for the moment as I focused on the terrain surrounding me. The ultimate point of the transition zone rose up beneath me, elevating me to a viewpoint both physical and metaphysical. This land of perpendicular ridges drew my eyes heavenward one moment and down to the depths in the next. The rocks beneath . . . argillite and flinty slate, Gray-Wacke and breccia and conglomerate . . . were proof of the tremendous forces that had churned and heaved the ridges. But there was no answer to the question of whether these forces were a happenstance event or an effort of God's will. Perhaps these forces were still at work and impacting all those who entered upon this land of transformation.

"Charles, your mind is wondering again. What are you thinking about?"

"I'm sorry. I was wondering about the origin of the forces that created the transitional zone, and if they are still active."

"Excellent question. Class, let's review the theories of formation of the earth as we know it. In the last fifty years we have seen the conclusion of the great debate between those men who believe all rocks were deposited from a worldwide ocean, and those who believe that heat from beneath the surface caused molten rock to cover and change the earth. What are these two groups, students?"

I strained to hear any answer from my classmates. The rocks were reticent, and I responded for them, "The Neptunists, from Neptune the god of the sea, and the Plutonists, from Pluto the god of the Underworld."

"Exactly. We now know that the Plutonists were correct. But that is not the end of the story. Another equally important argument is undecided. Do the changes that occur in our earth occur in a uniform manner, or do they occur in great catastrophes such as the Biblical flood? Tell the class what you know about the men who have proposed both sides of this argument, Charley."

The names came spilling out of my mind, names any one of which might have served as an interpreter between the rocks and me. Cuvier and Agassiz who argued for the cataclysms of geology that led to drastic changes of climate and topography and massive extinction of species. Hutton who described the world as a great machine which continuously and imperceptibly ground down and rebuilt the surface of the earth, a process so uniform that he said he could find "no vestige of a beginning, no prospect of an end." Lyell, who championed Hutton's uniformitarianism and applied it in reverse to the present world to explain all that had preceded it.

"Dr. Mitchell," I asked, "whom do you believe is correct?"

He thought long before answering. "I wish I could speak from experience, but even at my somewhat advanced age . . . speaking in human terms you understand . . . I must profess my ambivalence. I don't discount the effects of Noah's flood and other catastrophes, but I think these events are so remote and infrequent that their significance pales beside that of Lyell's uniformitarianism. As I look upon the world, I see one day following another with only the slightest changes, and so it must have been for ages."

And then I heard it, the slightest sound, the cool stony voice of the rocks speaking to me and whispering, "the unconformity."

"What does that mean?" I asked the rocks anxiously. "What is the unconformity?"

The professor answered. "Class, tell Charley about Hutton's unconformity."

From the shelves of my memory a book fell down and opened to an engraving of the Scottish countryside. The earth had been exposed by a stream, and there for all to see was the unconformity: a deep layer of strata that had been turned on edge so that its layers ran vertically like fence posts, and above it a newer layer of horizontal strata. Hutton had seen it and realized its implications for the formation of the earth's surface. The deep layer of strata, once lying flat along a sea floor, had been raised and tilted, eroded, and then sunk again to the depths of the sea. A new layer of strata had been laid down upon the ancient tilted layer. Then the entire assemblage had been raised above the sea again, where in the passage of time it had been cut open by a stream. Finally, its surface had been covered by vegetation and roads built by men. I saw the engraving in my mind's eye, and wondered.

Then the rocks spoke plainly. "Men walk about upon the earth and are blinded by the similarity of one day to another. In their brief passage through life they do not see enough of eternity to understand the tremendous changes that happen over time, or the cataclysmic changes that sometimes happen in a moment. Look upon the unconformity and learn that life is full of change and the unexpected."

And I saw my father walking across the peaks, and I heard him saying to himself, "These mountains are as they have been for ages, and as they will be for ages to come. And I myself am the same man who has traveled these peaks before, and what changes I have seen in my life are little compared to what remains the same."

And I understood what the rocks had tried to teach me. My father had come to the peak expecting it to be as it had always been, thinking that he was as he had always been, and had run into the unexpected, the unknown and unplanned for, the unconformity of life, and he had not survived it.

I stood up in the prairie and looked down on the dark and uniform balsam forest surrounding the peak. Earlier I thought of it as a deep lake that frustrated my efforts to see inside. Now I thought of the deepness of time and understood that men live and walk on the edge of time just as we walk about on the edge of the forest. Eternity spreads out around us like the wilderness around the high peak. We know it is there. We see it. But it remains unexplored and unknown. A few men manage to penetrate it, but only with great effort and sometimes at great risk.

I breathed deeply and plunged my mind into the dark woods of eternity past. Where did it start? Was it a few thousand, a few million, or a few billion years ago? Did that matter? I could see that eternity was independent of my measurement of earthly time. If I looked in the other direction and tried to see the reemergence of eternity beyond the end of earthly time, I saw it shining there as new and untarnished as ever. I looked at my own life and saw it looming large, overshadowing all else from the viewpoint of earthly time, yet in the span of eternity it was a mere spark. The weight of eternity pressed down on me and threatened to extinguish that spark. In pride I fought against the weight but felt I could not win. I was drowning in the deep lake of eternity.

"Mr. Mitchell." Tom Wilson was shaking my shoulder. "Mr. Mitchell, I've come to say goodbye."

Big Tom stood before me, pulling me back from eternity. He had a peaceful look, the look of a man who knows he is in the right place and doing what he was meant to do. I slowly stood to shake his hand.

"Thank you for your help, Mr. Wilson. Thank you for sticking with the search to the end. I'm not sure we would have ever found Pa without your help."

"T'were nothin'. Anybody would've done it, and I'm pleased to have been of service. Besides, sometimes we all need someone to show us the way."

The words hit me like cold water.

"What did you say, Tom?"

"I said, sometimes we all need someone to show us the way."

As the scales began to fall from my eyes, I suddenly saw what I had always been looking for. I saw Big Tom, showing me the way to my father that I could not find by myself. I saw Mary Riddle teaching me the wisdom of the signs and the need to learn from other people. I saw Ma caring for me as a child when I could not feed or clothe myself. I saw my father trying to teach me the words of life when I was lost and destined for Hell.

I saw eternity, but it no longer threatened to swallow me. It was the home of God, and he held out his hand to show me a way that I could never find without him. I saw that if I but put my hand in his, the way through eternity would be clear, and open, and limitless.

It was a fork in the road. To the left ran a solitary road where men and women traveled alone and tried to make their own way. To the right passed another path with room for walking side by side, hand in hand, sometimes leading and sometimes being led. On the right path I saw time and again how people were snatched from defeat and pulled back from despair by the hand of another. On the left there were men and women who sank in the mire with no one to pull them out or who took a wrong turn and wondered blindly down the wrong trail until they . . . until they fell as Pa had fallen.

I saw with thanks that the two roads did not separate forever but were woven back and forth and in and out of each other. The road builder had been merciful in his design. There were many chances for rescue, if the traveler would only lay down his burden of pride and take up the light hand of the road builder. I saw and understood that I was never meant to find my way through life or eternity alone.

I thanked Tom again as he walked away on the trail back to the Caney River. It was easy to tell the choices he had made and where his future lay. Now it was time for me to make my choices.

Chapter Eighteen

Mt. Mitchell

Thousands of feet above the Black Mountains moist air cools and condenses, air which the bulk of the Blacks forced upwards and which now the laws of nature constrain to condense into rain. Inevitably the drops are pulled to earth where they combine with other drops in a relentless march to the lowest elevation. So the rain on the high peak falls from tree to grass to ground, from puddle to rivulet to creek, and over the falls to the pool where my father's body was found.

If you concluded that Elisha Mitchell's death was as inevitable as the rain, you would be wrong. I've thought about it over the years and I'm convinced that his death resulted from the choices he made and not from any unbreakable law of nature.

I praise God for the privilege of making choices. It's a big part of what separates us from the rest of creation and gives us the "image" of God. Our choices can be good or bad but they're ours and we get to make them. We also get to live with the consequences.

My father made the choice to explore the Blacks and it led to accomplishment and a measure of fame. Years later he chose to refute Clingman's challenge to his claims about the Blacks. He chose to cross the mountain alone on his final day, to proceed though delayed by storm and God alone knows what else, to press on despite the limitations of age and darkness. In other words he decided to take the risk. Some people are good at taking risks, but no one does it perfectly.

You may argue that personality, pride, or the pressure of his peers influenced Pa. Certainly they did. This was the stream he swam in, but like any other man he could choose to be swept along by the current or to swim against it. As often as not he made his own current. On his last day he forced himself into a precarious position where the weight of accumulated errors caught up with him and pulled him down.

The greatest error of all was the thought that he could do it alone. Before the action was the idea. Before he set out across the peaks alone there was the conceit that he, by himself, was able to face whatever obstacles he might encounter. Oh, the harshness and finality of his test! Would that he had the opportunity to learn from his mistake and take the test again. Yet I am forced to wonder how many times he *had* taken this test before.

A year after his death my father's body was carried up the mountain one final time, this time to be reburied there. The Yancey men had been right in their inclinations after all. It is a burial place unlike any other. When the wind blows as it often does, and clouds cover the mountaintop, it seems the most lonesome spot in the world, a scene well suited to match our grief. Yet on a sunny day when the green hills expand beyond the horizon and the blue sky crowns the vault of heaven it becomes a majestic setting worthy of a king. Don't look for a king's tomb, however. All you'll find is a simple cairn of rocks growing slowly as pilgrims add their own piece of the Black Mountain to the pile.

I said in the beginning that my father was redeemed, and he was, in both an earthly and a spiritual sense. It's true that he lost his life, but he was not lost from the eternity of God's love. And though he lost his life, in the end Pa regained the mountain. I believe he was there on the high peak in 1835, but wise men have argued otherwise and who am I to say they are wrong? In the end the people decided with their hearts more than their heads that Mitchell should be the name of the high peak, and so it stands. It's a name that's fittin'.

The End

Afterword

The sympathy for Elisha Mitchell that poured out across North Carolina following his death ensured that the high peak would be named for him. His wife lived another twenty years.

Charley studied medicine, enlisted in the Third NC Artillery as an assistant surgeon, and died during the Civil War. Thomas Clingman served as a Brigadier General in the CSA and continued to explore the mountains. The highest peak in the Great Smokies was named for him, as well as the Black Mountain peak originally called Mt. Mitchell.

Logging of the Black Mountains beginning in 1912 severely damaged the peak, but it also led to an outcry that resulted in the establishment of Mt. Mitchell State Park in 1915. About 300,000 tourists visit the park each year. The trees grew back, but are declining once again due to a combination of acid rain and infestation with the balsam wooly aphid.

Bibliography

Battle, Kemp P. *History of the University of North Carolina, 1789-1912. Two Volume Set*. Raleigh, N.C.: Printed for the author by Edwards & Broughton Printing Company. 1907.

Battle, Kemp P. *Diary of a Geological Tour by Dr. Elisha Mitchell in 1827 and 1828 with Introduction and Notes, Published as James Sprunt Historical Monograph No. 6*. Chapel Hill, NC: University of North Carolina, 1905.

Beeson, D.R. *In the Spirit of Adventure, a 1915 Mount Mitchell Hiking Journal*. Seymour, TN: Panther Press, 1995.

Chamberlain, Hope Summerell. *Old Days in Chapel Hill: Being the Life and Letters of Cornelia Phillips Spencer*. Chapel Hill: University of North Carolina Press, 1926.

Chamberlain, Hope Summerell. *Life Story of Elisha Mitchell*. North Carolina Collection, Library of the University of NC at Chapel Hill, 1945.

Clingman, Thomas L. "Topography of Black Mountain." *Tenth Annual Report of the Smithsonian Institution* (1856), 299-305.

Clingman, Thomas L. *Measurements of the Black Mountain*. Washington, DC. 1856.

Dugger, Shepard M. *The Balsam Groves of the Grandfather Mountain. A Tale of the Western North Carolina Mountains*. Shepard M. Dugger, 1892.

Gould, Stephen Jay. *Time's Arrow, Time's Cycle*. Cambridge, MA: Harvard University Press, 1987.

Jeffrey, Thomas E. "The Clingman-Mitchell Controversy." *The North Carolina Historical Review*, LXX, No. 3 (1993), 241-265; and No. 4 (1993), 401-429.

Kephart, Horace. *Our Southern Highlanders: A Narrative of Adventure in the Southern Appalachians and a Study of Life Among the Mountaineers*. New York: The Macmillan Company, 1936

McVaugh, Rogers. *Chapel Hill and Elisha Mitchell, the Botanist*. Botanical Garden Foundation; January 1996.

Mitchell, Elisha. *Black Mountain: Professor Mitchell's Reply to Mr. Clingman*. North Carolina, 1856.

Mitchell, Elisha. *The Elements of Geology*. North Carolina, 1842.

Mitchell, Elisha. "The Mountains of Carolina." *The Raleigh Register*, 3 Nov. 1835.

Mitchell, Elisha. *Papers, 1816-1905*. Manuscripts Department, Library of the University of NC at Chapel Hill, Southern Historical Collection.

Otey, James H., and David L. Swain. *A Memoir of the Rev. Elisha Mitchell, D.D.* Chapel Hill, NC: J.M. Henderson, 1858.

Parris, John. *Mountain Bred*. Asheville, NC: Citizen-Times Publishing Co, 1967.

Parris, John. *These Storied Mountains*. Asheville, NC: Citizen-Times Publishing Co., 1972.

Parris, John. *Roaming the Mountains*. Asheville, NC: Citizen-Times Publishing Co., 1955.

Parris, John. *My Mountains, My People*. Asheville, NC: Citizen-Times Publishing Co. 1957.

Schwarzkopf, S. Kent. *A History of Mt. Mitchell and the Black Mountains. Exploration, Development, and Preservation*. Raleigh:. North Carolina Division of Archives, 1994.

Sheppard, Muriel Earley. *Cabins in the Laurel*. Chapel Hill, NC: University of North Carolina Press, 1946.

Sondley, F. A. *A History of Buncombe County, North Carolina. 2 vols*. Asheville: Advocate Printing Co., 1930.

Warner, Charles Dudley. *On Horseback: A Tour In Virginia, North Carolina, And Tennessee With Notes Of Travel In Mexico And California*. Boston and New York: Houghton Mifflin And Company, 1889.

Vance, Zebulon B. "The Search for Professor Mitchell's Body." *The Asheville Spectator*, July 1857.

Vickers, James, Thomas Scism, and Dixon Qualls. *Chapel Hill: An Illustrated History*. Barclay Pub, May 1985.

Webb, Charles A. *Mount Mitchell and Dr. Elisha Mitchell*. Asheville: Asheville Citizen-Times Co., 1946.

Zeigler, Wilbur G., and Ben S. Grosscup. *Heart of the Alleghanies; or, Western North Carolina; Comprising its Topography, History, Resources, People, Narratives, Incidents, and Pictures of Travel, Adventures in Hunting and Fishing, and Legends of its Wildernesses*. Zeigler, Wilbur G., and Ben S. Grosscup. Raleigh, NC: Alfred Williams; Cleveland, OH: William Williams, 1883.

About the Author

Robert Dellinger was born in Charlotte, NC in 1956. He grew up in North Carolina and began hiking the Blue Ridge and Great Smoky Mountains as a teenager. He graduated from North Carolina State University and received his MD from the University of North Carolina at Chapel Hill. He is married to Wanda and has two nearly grown children. He practices family medicine in Thomasville, NC. You may contact the author at CalebsPress@aol.com.

How to Order *Mitchell's Peak*

Email: CalebsPress@aol.com

Website: www.CalebsPress.com

Write: Caleb's Press
421 Seminole Ct.
High Point, NC 27265

Fax: 1-888-726-9304

Send: $15.95 plus $3.00 shipping and handling

Name _____

Address _____

City, State, Zip _____

Phone number (____)_____

Please send me ____ copies of Mitchell's Peak.

I have enclosed $15.95 plus $3.00 shipping and handling
for each book.

ATTENTION CORPORATIONS, UNIVERSITIES, COLLEGES,
AND PROFESSIONAL ORGANIZATIONS: Quantity discounts
are available on bulk purchases of this book for educational, gift purposes, or as premiums. For information, please contact Caleb's Press,
421 Seminole Ct., High Point, NC 27265.